# DIANASAURUS REX

# DIANASAURUS REX

## SHELDON GLEISSER

Hydra
Publications

ISBN: 978-1-948374-21-7

Hydra Publications

Goshen, Kentucky 40026

www.hydrapublications.com

*To Ann and Arnold Gleisser, who loved a good yarn.*

# PROLOGUE

From the diary of Diana Dunphy:

    Dear Diary:

    When I found you in the markdown bin at Staples and brought you up to the sales guy, he wrinkled his nose. "You don't want to do a blog?" he asked.

I shook my head.

He raised his eyebrows, ringing me up. "I thought all you kids wanted to do was blogs these days. We can't even *give* diaries away anymore."

Sales guy didn't know Mom would never let me do a blog even if I wanted to do one, which I don't. The point of a blog is for other people to read it, right?

That's why blogs aren't for me. Too much I have to say is a secret.

And too much I have to say would sound completely crazy. No way I want someone else reading it. I know you can set your blog to private and all that, but if you haven't figured out that nothing's really private anymore, you should. I know this guy

Billy Scrumholtz,(we call him Scum, 'cause he's kinda scummy) he's in my English Lit class? He somehow hacked Selena Gomez. Got her personal phone number and E-mail and spread it all around school and everywhere else. She changed it all up pretty quick, but if that's what happens to Selena Gomez, what kind of protection is there for an ordinary sixteen year-old girl living in Columbus, Ohio, right?

Ordinary, that's a good one. Could an ordinary girl pick out specific scents, some of them from miles away, just by sticking out her tongue?

Lizards smell things by sticking out their tongues, I bet you didn't know that.

Does the skin of an ordinary girl seem like anybody else's when you touch it, but if you shot her, and I mean picked up a gun, aimed, and fired, from like, two feet away, all you would do is knock her down? As in, the bullet would bounce right off of her?

Would an ordinary girl be able to get right back up again after being shot? I'm not saying it wouldn't hurt, I'm just saying I'd get right back up.

Could an ordinary girl not only outrun a car, could she lift it up and turn it over?

I know what you're thinking, diary, you're thinking, 'This chick is nuts, she's read too many comic books,' but stick with me.

I happened to weigh myself on the day before "the incident," as my Mom calls it, and I was ninety-four pounds. After "the incident," I mean once I'd slept for two days and had the strangest dreams you could possibly think of, I weighed one hundred sixteen pounds, and it wasn't from fat, either. I got real used to my friends saying, "Hey, you been working out?" and "What gym are you going to?" My best friend Patrice just wrinkled her nose and said, "You're a buff chick now? I hate you."

I wasn't trying to show off, I swear, but when I put on the clothes I had before? They still fit, but they were a lot tighter. My Mom, I thought she was going to have a cow when she saw. We went straight out and bought all new, lots baggier clothes.

I'd never been a buff chick before, but I didn't become one by going to the gym. I mean I've started to do some weight training now, but I can't really go to a regular gym anymore, not and get a real workout. What I do is...well, let's just say it involves the local junkyard and a lot of wrecked cars.

Okay, Diary, here it is ...did you know that the DNA of a person is, like ninety-eight per cent the same as the DNA of a chimp? It's true. Somewhere, in that two per cent, we lost all that body hair, (well, most of us) we got lots better posture, and instead of mainly eating bananas, we started eating all *kinds* of stuff. Know what else we got? Music (from Mozart to Taylor Swift), not to mention the atomic bomb, Hostess Twinkies, water skiing, Stridex medicated pads, NASCAR, YouTube, weed whackers, and The Constitution.

All of that stuff came out of that teeny, tiny little two per cent of our DNA that makes us different from chimps.

Kinda makes you think, doesn't it?

Diary, I did not mean that as a joke, but it does seem a little funny, saying 'kinda makes you think,' because that's exactly what that little bit of DNA does! It makes you think! And that's why we're people and we can do all this stuff, and they're chimps and they spend most of their time screaming, flinging their poo, picking lice off each other, and swinging through the trees.

So here's what's going on, Diary: my DNA, my DNA which is just a little bit different from most people's DNA the way most people's DNA is different from chimp DNA? Mom says it makes my bones, muscles and tendons all way different. "Heavy duty," is what she calls them. See, my Mom is this big-time scientist, professor, PhD, whatever, so I'm used to seeing her look at things and frown, but when my DNA test came back from the lab she sent it to? Well, I've never seen her frown like she did when she looked at those test results. "It's impossible to manipulate the DNA of a mature organism," Mom said, and then she hugged me. I was going to say, 'Mom, you know me, I watch Cartoon Network and still have a Teddy Bear, I'm not a mature organism,' but she started to cry, so for once I kept my mouth shut, and she whispered, right into my ear, "I'm so glad you're all right."

Well, I felt fine, I looked good, and I could do stuff I couldn't do before (okay, stuff no one could do before) but there are things about the way I am now that aren't so pleasant, so her saying I was 'all right' might have been pushing it.

Because it gets lonely, Diary. It gets really lonely sometimes, being as different from other people as other people are from chimps. My Mom has me seeing a therapist, but she always says, 'only talk to her about what happened to your father, don't talk about *anything* else!' And I guess that's the way to go. I mean, what am I supposed to do, tell Dr. Siddons all this stuff about what I can do? And when she laughs, or says I'm crazy, prove I'm right by crushing her Sigmund Freud coffee mug in my bare hands? What good would *that* do?

I can talk to Mom about it, sure, and I know she tries, but there's no way she can really get it.

That leaves you, Diary.

And as much as Mom wouldn't like me writing stuff down, (she's afraid if anybody finds out they'll drag me away and stick me in a lab somewhere) who can you really talk to about being...

...a species of one...?

# INCIDENT

"Learn from me, if not by my precepts, at least by my example, how dangerous is the acquirement of knowledge, and how much happier that man is who believes his native town to be the world, than he who aspires to become greater than his nature will allow."

-Mary Shelley, *Frankenstein*

# CHAPTER ONE

*Instant death*, Rita Dunphy thought. *It would all explode. Or was that implode?*

Carefully moving the welding torch down the seam between two titanium plates, Rita told herself to calm down. There wasn't going to be any explosion because she would get this right, she always got it right, she was an experienced welder, all the tests had been positive, everything was going to work just fine.

Rita thought about her daughter Diana, sixteen going on thirty. Would she be there for the test?

Because if she, Rita, didn't get the seam exactly right it would mean instant death for everyone in the room, including her daughter.

But if she did screw it up, and the chamber did explode during the test, would it be possible that those in attendance would be vaporized so quickly there would be no pain?

*Okay*, Rita told herself, moving the torch down the seam, *such thinking isn't useful. What's useful is to keep your mind on the task. Weld the seam...*

There would be no trace, not of any of them, if she got it wrong. Nothing left of Rita, or Diana's father (her ex-husband Aaron) or of Diana.

The entire Dunphy family blinked away with the creation of one loose quantum singularity.

Instant death...

*Weld the seam*, Rita told herself, *it had all been tested already, dozens of times. The math worked. The scale models worked. Everything worked.*

*Relax...*

Next the building would explode.

*Weld the seam*, Rita thought.

Then, if Rita's calculations were correct, the structure would quickly implode, sucking air and debris into what would amount to a tiny, briefly existing wormhole. In the resulting reverse blast wave, every building in Columbus, Ohio's north side would be rendered structurally unsound at best. At worst, those buildings would, well...

An implosion would turn the buildings so brittle that all you would have to do to cause their collapse would be to take a deep breath and blow on them.

*Weld the seam*, Rita thought, *all you can do is weld the seam!*

Turning off the torch, Rita examined her work. The titanium plates were now perfectly melded.

Eighteen feet off the ground on a scissors-jack, Rita, in her late thirties, had the build of a gracefully aging dancer, not that anyone could tell in her baggy welding jumpsuit. She moved to the next set of titanium plates, joining them together on the surface of what her ex-husband had dubbed 'The Tachyon Chamber,' a tube half the length of a football field. Three city buses could have been driven through The Tachyon Chamber side-by-side with room to spare.

Rita's mask, and the crackle of the welding torch, prevented her from hearing the entrance of her ex-husband Aaron, leading a small group of men and women into the room and past the scissors-jack.

* * *

Aaron Dunphy was tall and rangy, his dark hair combed back over a high forehead. In his teaching days, he inspired the occasional coed crush, if the young ladies were partial to lean, bookish, bespectacled men with features just shy of handsome, but it wasn't some May-December dalliance that had broken up his marriage to Rita.

What broke up their marriage was the Tachyon Chamber, whose skin Rita was putting the finishing touches on, the functions of which Aaron was busily answering questions about. He walked to the front of the huge tube, entourage trailing behind.

Craig Farkus, in his late forties, hardhat on, his gravy-stained tie sticking out over a modest paunch, asked, "How do we make sure it ends up outside, and underground?"

"Compensate for the Earth's rotation times the amount of days we're going back, and then figure in the distance auditorium two is from the pump."

Scribbling furiously on a clipboard, Craig said, "So by 'day,' you mean a twenty four hour unit of measure..."

"One earth rotation," said Aaron.

"Times the amount of..."

"Payload, yes!"

Craig stopped scribbling and looked up at Aaron. "This

would be a lot easier if I could get a copy of the software," he said hopefully.

"We've talked about this Craig," Aaron said before pointing outside. "Go!"

"I'm gone," said Craig, heading for the door and signaling for his people to follow. When the last of Craig's people had left, Aaron had only Zachary Guillermin to contend with.

"I have to admit, Aaron," said Guillermin, "I'm impressed."

Aaron responded with a smile just this side of sincere.

Always impeccably dressed, Guillermin looked like he'd been called up from central casting to play 'Head of Fortune 500 Company.' Lean, square jawed, with just a touch of grey at his temples, Aaron supposed Guillermin could have been an actor, but had somehow wound up here. "Always happy to impress you, Zachary," Aaron said.

"How long have we known each other?" Guillermin asked.

Aaron thought it over. "We started trying to put Crock Pot together about eight years ago, so...?"

"Sounds about right."

Aaron nodded.

Of course Guillermin had said no all those years ago, but at least he hadn't scoffed and laughed the way most had. Instead, Zachary had kept a watchful distance, although his contributions to the project never amounted to more than paying for the occasional lunch. Every now and then he dropped by the makeshift lab that in their marriage's better days Aaron and Rita had put together in their garage. Guillermin would look over one of their shoulders as they soldered something together, or smile and nod when Aaron spoke about Tachyon bursts and particle interactions.

But whenever Aaron hit Guillermin up for money, the answer was always the same polite "no."

"Then why are you here?" Aaron finally asked while Rita rolled her eyes and found an excuse to go back into the house.

"Just interested in theoretical physics," Guillermin would say, or "just wanted to see the latest developments," or "just wondering how you two geniuses were doing," all with the same odd, neutral expression, a strange, pursed smile that didn't reach his eyes, as if he were perhaps happy, or perhaps not that happy to be there.

When the funding came through at Gotelle Institute, Auditorium two of which Crock Pot now occupied, Guillermin's visits became less occasional and more regular.

"Of course he's interested now," Rita said one day after another lunch Guillermin paid for at Columbus' newest upscale restaurant, "someone *else* has not only expressed interest, but put up the money. This is not an innovative guy."

Rita's words came back to Aaron. He regarded Guillermin for a moment. "Is that why you're impressed now, Zachary," he asked, "because someone else has expressed an interest? Put up the money?"

Trying to laugh it off, Guillermin said, "Aaron, really..."

"This would have meant a lot more eight years ago, when I came to you hat in hand," Aaron said.

"You know what they say," Guillermin responded, "only the amateurs stay mad."

"Who said I was mad?"

"Who indeed? I invest or I don't invest. It was nothing personal."

"Just business, right."

"Of course," Guillermin said, walking toward the Tachyon Chamber.

*How do I get rid of this guy*, Aaron thought. He found himself looking up at his ex-wife as she joined more titanium plates together.

"Don't look at an active welding torch unless you have eye protection," Rita would have said had she seen him watching her, and she'd have done it in the bored tone of a third grade teacher admonishing a particularly thick student.

Aaron looked away from the welding torch, trying to hew to the task at hand.

"And this thing... it will really do what you say it will do?" Guillermin asked, gesturing toward the huge chamber.

"Well," Aaron answered, "the numbers are all there. The prototypes have all worked flawlessly."

"But this is the first one built to scale?"

"Yes. And size has been compensated for."

Guillermin gave him an uncertain look.

Aaron returned a look of confidence. "Of course, we won't really know until..."

"The big test, sure," Guillermin finished for him. "So is it or is it not too late to get in on the game?"

Not quite knowing what to make of the question, Aaron looked incredulously at Guillermin. "The 'Game?'" he asked.

"Yes," Guillermin said, taking a checkbook out of the inner pocket of his suit jacket.

"By 'The Game,' you mean Crock Pot?"

Guillermin laughed. "Sorry," he said, "I've just always loved that name."

Now Aaron found himself losing patience. "Put your checkbook away, Zachary," he said, "I couldn't get you in now even if I wanted to."

"So you don't want to?"

"It's out of my hands. You know how these things work. Gotelle put up all of the money, they want all of the return."

"That can be smoothed over," Guillermin said. He had produced a pen from somewhere and was now flipping through the checkbook. *How had he found that pen without me seeing it,* Aaron thought? *Was this guy not just rich and good-looking, but some damn sleight-of-hand artist?*

Out of patience, Aaron walked toward Guillermin and took him by the arm. "Zachary, please," he said, "I just don't have time for this now, we're less than eighteen hours away."

Looking at the hand on his arm, Guillermin shrugged free, but let Aaron walk him to the exit. At the door, he looked to Aaron as if trying to decide how patient to be. "All right, Aaron," he said, "you know what you want."

"Zachary," Aaron said, "good to see you."

With a bit of a smile, and a bit of a nod, Guillermin was out.

Aaron closed the door behind him and put his back against it.

Shoulders slumping, Aaron thought perhaps he might be free, for maybe the next two minutes, from questioning techies, opportunistic hangers-on, and... ex-wives?

Carefully keeping his eyes off of the welding torch, Aaron walked to just below the scissors-jack and called, "Rita?"

The scratchy whine of the torch continued down the seam.

Waving his hands over his head, Aaron yelled again, "Rita?"

The welding torch didn't deviate from its path.

Aaron found a piece of paper on the ground. Wadding it up into a ball, he threw it at Rita, scoring a direct hit at her shoulder.

The anonymous welder's mask turned in his direction. The torch's light extinguished. The scratchy whine was gone.

Rita lifted the mask, and Aaron thought, *how can she still look so great, even with all that sweaty hair matted to her face?*

"Did you talk to her?" Aaron asked.

"I mentioned it," said Rita.

"And--?"

"She made a noise."

"A noise?"

Rita nodded in response.

"What kind of noise?" Aaron asked.

Rita shrugged.

"Was it a good noise or a bad noise?" Aaron prodded.

"It was... a teen-aged girl noise," Rita said.

Letting out a sigh, Aaron took off his glasses, putting his thumb and forefinger to the bridge of his nose. "Rita," he said, in a caricature of patience, "will she be here or not?"

"Well," Rita said, "there's this new invention, the phone?" She held her hands out, indicating the size of a smart phone. "A small device, about yea big? You might even own one already. You could perhaps use such a device to communicate with your daughter yourself."

Aaron looked away, shaking his head. He gave himself a three count, like their long-ago and little listened-to marriage counselor had advised. Then he looked back up at Rita. "You're living with her. She's right there, is there some reason you can't talk to her?"

Rita nodded, leaning on the railing of the scissors-jack. "So let me get this straight," she said, "a man about to re-write most of the laws of physics, who is about to change the balance of power in the Middle East, and, oh, by the way, re-shape the world economy, is incapable of picking up a phone and speaking to his teen-age daughter?"

Aaron looked up at his ex-wife. "You know what it's like when Diana and I talk," he said.

"It might not seem like it, Aaron, but she wants to hear from you."

"No, she doesn't," Aaron said. He began walking away, dismissing Rita with a wave of his hand, "but you wouldn't know anything about it."

"What's that supposed to mean?" Rita called.

"Come on, Rita," he said, turning back to her as he walked, "it's easy for you."

"Oh? Why is it easy for me?"

"You're the one she likes," Aaron said.

\* \* \*

Rita watched Aaron walk into his office and close the door.

*Impossible man,* she thought. *I'm so glad I divorced him!*

She flipped the welding mask back down, then said out loud, "Glad I divorced you!" where it was muffled, indistinct, and unlikely to cause a fight.

She turned the torch back on.

*When this Crock Pot test is over,* Rita thought, *when this is all done and in Gotelle's hands, and I can just kick back with my percentage, I will start dating again.* She looked forward to it, to the idea of it, men picking her up and taking her places. Places for which she would have to dress up in order to go. They would pick her up in suits and bring her flowers and never be sarcastic or short with her. And she would wear earrings and heels and the guys would see her and wish, just wish...

*Yes,* she thought, following the seam with the torch, *those would be good days, spent with men who were trying to impress me. There had to be lots of nice, good looking, age-appropriate geniuses out there in Columbus, Ohio, right?*

*R-i-i-ght,* Rita thought, finishing the seal, wondering if Diana would want to move with her to Portland, or Seattle, or maybe Silicon Valley.

\* \* \*

Aaron sat in his cramped office.

*The computer was supposed to lead us toward a paper-less society*, he thought contemptuously, *why do I now have more paper than ever?* Paper fairly poured out of every conceivable space in his office, stuffed into files, stacked into piles, bound together in reports, results, and conjectures, how had he let the place get this way?

Along the walls were framed posters for the first Back to the Future movie, along with the first two Terminators, gag gifts from their marriage's better days. Rita had even managed to find a vintage poster from the first George Pal version of The Time Machine starring Rod Taylor. "How did you find this?" he had asked Rita, laughing, "And how much did you spend to get it?"

She had shaken her finger at him, a smile on that perfect, pretty face. "Never ask the price of a gift," she had said.

He hoped she hadn't become embroiled in some eBay bidding war.

Frowning, Aaron began to stack the papers strewn across his desk into some measure of order until he found it, the best present *ever*—a scale model of Rod Taylor's time machine that you could hold in your hand, like the one the Time Traveler shows his friends in the movie.

Aaron had supposed perhaps such models existed, but Rita, unable to find one, had simply rolled up her sleeves and *made* it out of bits of scrap metal and wire coat hangers of varying thickness. "I made the chair," Diana had told him.

At that point his daughter had been, what, eight years old? Or was she ten? He couldn't remember, although he definitely remembered her little smiling face as he put his index finger on the tiny upholstered cushion. "It feels very comfortable," he'd said, and she returned a huge, gap-toothed smile. His little girl had positively beamed at him. Laughing, he had lifted her into the air.

How had it happened that calling the fourteen year-old version of that little girl was something he had so come to dread?

Was it all those years on Crock Pot, sacrificing everything to the project? Was the divorce from his wife, her mother, just an extra, added bonus irritant, more fuel for his daughter's contempt?

Aaron picked up his phone, looking for a moment at its dark, blank face. Sighing, he got to contacts and hit the button for 'Dunphy, Diana.'

# CHAPTER TWO

"No. Sorry. Can't. Impossible!" Diana Dunphy said into her phone.

She was lying across her bed, head hanging over the side, legs fully extended and braced against the wall.

Diana was thin, some of her less charitable classmates might even say bony, but she had inherited her mother's expressive grey eyes and dishwater blonde hair, which she kept long and in a ponytail. Her mouth was set in a fuller-lipped version of her father's pensive frown.

On the phone, there was a pause, and then her father said, "Diana, what have I always told you about that word?"

"What word?" she asked.

"You know what word."

"What? I did *not* swear."

"I'm not talking about swearing, it's worse than swearing."

Diana closed her eyes, unable to believe it. "Oh, my God," she said, "you mean 'impossible?' *That's* still the word you're so upset about?"

"Yes. And do you remember why?"

"Dad, I'm not eight years old anymore."

"Do you remember why?" he repeated deliberately.

Diana sighed. "Because it's inaccurate," she said.

"Right," her father said, "because while many things are improbable..."

"Nothing is impossible!" Diana finished. "I remember, okay?" She found herself looking at the trophies on her wall: one for Outstanding Dramatic Performer last year, another for Ballet, and yet another for Karate, both this year. Frowning, Diana wondered if her father's drilled-in antipathy toward the word 'impossible,' however cornball, had helped her to win those trophies, especially the one for Dramatic Performance. She had been up against Candy Siler, who everyone so thought would win for her female version of the Stage Manager in *Our Town*.

But Diana had somehow beaten Candy in the role of Emily in the same play. She went out of her way to meet up with Candy later. "You were so good," Diana had said, "don't pay any attention to it, it was just a stupid award, it doesn't really mean anything," Diana had been sincere, but the damage had been done. Neither Candy nor any of Candy's friends had ever spoken to Diana again.

And Diana had to admit that Candy was great in the part, the main reason she hadn't even thought about the award. Such a win was way too much to hope for against that kind of competition.

Diana had considered it, okay, *impossible* to beat Candy Siler but had done it anyway. Perhaps her father had been on to something after all.

"I sure should remember not to use the word 'impossible,' " Diana said, "you made me put a quarter into the 'impossible' jar every time I said it."

There was a small, self-satisfied pause on the other end of the line. Diana could just see him sitting there, a little smile on his face. "But a quarter in the jar every time you said it taught you to think without limits, right?" her father asked.

"It taught me my Dad was trying to get rich off of his eight year-old daughter! What did you do with all those quarters?"

"Show up tomorrow night, and you'll find out!"

"No, Dad, I told you, I have other commitments."

"You're fourteen years old...

"Sixteen! God, you don't even know how old I am!"

"The point is, you're a teenager! What possible 'other commitments' can you have?"

"That's nice, coming from you," Diana said, rolling over onto her stomach. "What about all the school plays and dance recitals *you* missed?"

"Let me show you why I missed all those plays and recitals, this will revolutionize everything!" He sounded almost like some little boy. Diana tried to stay distant and uncaring, but it was harder now, with him so excited. "Not everyone can go to this, you know," her father said, "it's really just supposed to be for investors, but because I'm your father..."

"And Mom's my mother," Diana finished.

"You can be right there, on a historic date, a date people will remember along with the day Alexander Graham Bell made the first phone call!"

"Nobody remembers that," she said.

"March tenth, eighteen seventy-six, or the day IBM introduced the first commercial scientific computer!"

"Nobody remembers that either," Diana sighed.

"April seventh, nineteen fifty-three, or the day Edward Teller tested the first atomic bomb!"

She thought about that one for a moment before saying, "Okay, some people might remember that, but I don't."

"July sixteenth, nineteen forty-five, the point is, you'll be a witness to history!"

"God, you sound like you're narrating something. You been watching the National Geographic Channel again?"

"How did you get to be so sarcastic? I'm not sarcastic. Your mother isn't..."

"Hello? have you met my Mom? Rita Dunphy, about five five, thin, long blonde hair, pretty?"

Her father was quiet for a while.

The silence stretched so long, Diana started to think maybe they'd lost the connection. She was about to say 'hello' again when he spoke slowly and sadly. "Diana, please be there tomorrow night," he said.

Was that a little quaver in his voice?

"I know I haven't been the best father, you might not think I know that, but I do," he went on, "I should have been around more, I know that, and I would have been, except...there are things that are bigger than you and I."

Diana heard him take a breath.

"I know that's a terrible thing to say to your child, I know that," he said, "I just...after the demonstration is over, you'll understand what kept me away. I'm asking you, please, to do this, okay? I need you there. I need you to see it. None of it will be worth anything if you're not there."

She wanted to say something to him, but she had no idea what.

"Please?" he asked.

Diana hung her head over the side of her bed, staring at the floor. Resigned, she started tapping the phone against her temple, thinking how most people had to choose between this thing or that thing, but not get both. So you could eat ice cream every day, but you'd gain ten pounds pretty quick. You could watch a movie every night instead of doing your homework, but your grades would suffer. You could ignore your child and work on your big project for your whole, entire life, but pretty soon your daughter would forget all about you.

Everyone had to make choices like that except for her father. *In the end*, Diana thought, *Aaron Dunphy always got everything he wanted*.

# CHAPTER THREE

"I knew you'd just do whatever he wanted you to do," Rhonda Bolling said.

*She's using it*, Diana thought as she circled Rhonda, *using something I told her in private. She's trying to make me angry, because anger can be a tell.*

*Well, if you think I'm giving you any tells, honey*, Diana thought, *you can think again.*

She, Diana, had to calm down, not show Rhonda anything. Because right now, Rhonda really wasn't her friend, but simply her opponent...

Diana had paired off with Rhonda in Karate class like they usually did; not just because Rhonda was one of her best friends but because Rhonda was far and away the best fighter. Taller, stronger, and, okay, more beautiful than any of the other girls, Rhonda's 'Property of McAuliffe High School Athletics Department' T-shirt was stretched tight across her chest, tied at the midriff over toned abs. Diana's mother would never let her wear gym shorts as short and as tight as Rhonda's. Diana knew she was too skinny, knew that her clothes just seemed to hang on her, she could never have gotten away with dressing the way Rhonda did.

There were all sorts of reasons to hate Rhonda Bolling; she was gorgeous and knew it, flaunted it in fact, and she loved having it front and center in the faces of the other girls. When she walked down the hall boys watched and wanted, but she just flounced haughtily past while having Chuck Leadingham, the best looking and most popular boy in the school, trail along behind her as if he were some puppy.

*Yes*, Diana thought, *there were lots of reasons to hate Rhonda, but for some reason I don't.*

Rhonda had taken a liking to Diana since she transferred in last year from a school in some European country where her father was a doctor and her mother worked for some internet security company. Somewhere, secretly, Diana liked that this girl, who had been everywhere, had singled her out as someone to talk to, someone to study with, someone to *be* with.

The fact that Rhonda was the only girl capable of giving Diana a real fight was an extra added bonus.

Diana and Rhonda continued to circle one another, each looking for an opening.

Rhonda kept her eyes moving up and down Diana's body, checking for the telltale movement that would signal a non-protected chest, shoulders, neck, or head.

Diana kept her eyes mainly on Rhonda's face, looking for her tell.

From months of observing Rhonda beating all of her class-mates, and from months of sparring with her, Diana had figured out that Rhonda's eyebrows arched, just for an instant, before she would lunge in for the attack. Diana hadn't seen the arch yet, so maybe....

*Maybe I can get her to do it*, Diana thought, *maybe I can get her to arch those eyebrows...* the trick would be to not make it so deliberate that Rhonda would notice. She didn't want Rhonda to be able to *tell* that Diana knew her tell...

Diana moved her right forearm away from her torso, just a little bit, as though she were making some adjustment before an attack.

Rhonda arched her eyebrows.

Diana, trying to keep her expression neutral, parried left, ducking under Rhonda's rush, then stood up and turned, flipping Rhonda over so she landed with a satisfying *thwack*, her back flat against the wrestling mat.

A small cheer went up from the other girls. Diana looked around, putting her hands up, then bounced triumphantly up and down.

It took Rhonda a moment to open her eyes and look up at Diana. She shook her head with a bit of a smile. "Relax, all you haters," Rhonda said, "I taught her everything she knows."

"It's true," Diana said, extending her hand to Rhonda, "everything I know about lying on a mat and looking up at someone who just kicked my ass I learned from Rhonda Bolling."

That got a big laugh. Rhonda gave Diana a warning look, then took the offered hand, pulling herself back up and taking another defensive stance. "Okay, self-defense Barbie," said Rhonda, "let's see you do that again."

\* \* \*

Diana, her locker open, was just buttoning her blouse.

Rhonda, already in a T-shirt with "Flirt" emblazoned across the chest, stood up, turning to Diana. Rhonda held a hot pink T-shirt in front of her "Flirt" shirt, "You Wish" written across the new one in bold black. "Isn't that cute?" Rhonda asked.

Diana nodded. She supposed it would be a cute thing to wear if you looked like—and were built like—Rhonda, but how many girls were?

"I don't know," Diana said, "isn't it a little...brag-ish?"

"Yeah," Rhonda said as if it were obvious, "that's the point, hello?"

"I don't know," Diana said, "I don't like bragging."

"Oh, yeah, little Miss 'look at me, I flipped Rhonda over' out there."

"That's...different."

"What's 'different' about it?"

"I don't know," Diana said, trying to figure out what, indeed, was different about it. "It just is."

Rhonda laughed, sticking the "You Wish" T-shirt into her locker and slamming it shut. "You just think you can't wear something like that, but you totally could."

Diana shook her head.

"Don't kid yourself," Rhonda said, "you're the second-best looking girl in this school."

Diana gave Rhonda a wry smile and shook her head.

"I am totally serious," Rhonda said. "I am totally getting you a 'You Wish' shirt like that one."

"Well, I won't wear it."

"You will."

"I will not!"

"You totally will!"

"Yeah, right. You coming with me to this thing tonight or not?"

Diana saw Rhonda's expression change, as if she were

suddenly smelling something terrible. Since Rhonda was looking past Diana, it could only mean one thing...

Diana turned around, and directly into Patrice Heath, Diana's other best friend. Patrice, drinking a soda and unable to stop moving, spilled it all over Diana's shirt.

"Oooh," Rhonda said, "way to go there, Bride of Winnie the Pooh."

Patrice's bright blue eyes quickly widened in embarrassment. "Oh, Diana!" Patrice said. "I'm so sorry!"

"I'll forgive you," Diana said, holding the now sopping-wet shirt away from herself, "as long as you don't let..." Diana turned back to Rhonda. "That Bride of Winnie-the-Pooh comment get to you!" Looking from Rhonda to Patrice, Diana said, "you know how much I wish my two best friends didn't blanking hate each other so much?"

"I don't hate her," Rhonda said, indicating Patrice, "I just think she should know this is the locker room! It's not the cafeteria!" Rhonda narrowed her eyes, studying Patrice. "Although I suppose for her every room in the school is the cafeteria."

"Rhonda..." Diana said, in a warning tone.

"She's not supposed to have food in here!"

Patrice clicked her tongue and crossed her arms. "Rhonda," she began, "you're such a..."

Rhonda stepped toward Patrice, clicking her tongue back. "What, Patrice?" she asked. "What am I?"

"Other than the football team pass-around pack? Not much."

Diana saw Rhonda's features darken, but at least the eyebrows hadn't arched, not yet anyway. She stepped between her two friends, holding her arms out, separating them. "Relax, you two, this is no big deal, okay?"

Patrice and Rhonda looked at each other across the gulf

Diana provided. Finally, Rhonda shook her head and turned away.

"I really am sorry, Diana," Patrice said.

"Like I said, no biggie." Diana looked down at the soda stain, then at Rhonda, who finally turned back around after Patrice walked away. "Uh...Rhonda?" Diana said, "Would you mind wearing your new shirt today? Maybe I can wear the one you're wearing?"

"You?" Rhonda said skeptically. "Wearing a 'Flirt' shirt?"

"You just said I should be wearing a 'You Wish' shirt."

"That's different."

"What's so different about it?"

"For one thing, you never flirt with anybody. Except maybe Artie Urlin!"

"Ew, he wishes!"

"Here's what else he wishes," Rhonda said, holding up a finger, "first, propose to Diana Dunphy, she says yes!" Rhonda held up another finger. "Second, Captain Kirk performs the ceremony, his nerdy friends hold up crossed phasers for you two to walk under." Rhonda held up a third finger. "Third, Diana Duphy has a bunch of my freckled, ginger nerd babies. Eek!"

Diana held her hand out in a 'give me the T-shirt' gesture.

Rhonda sighed. "You're lucky I have a soft spot," she said, lifting the 'Flirt' shirt over her head, "for girls who are future wives of Artie Urlin!"

The flung 'Flirt' shirt hit Diana in the face.

The truth was, Diana couldn't wait to get rid of the 'Flirt' shirt.

Devon McCarey, in her black leather jacket and super-short skirt, pointed at her and laughed as Diana headed down the hall to her locker.

Opening her locker, Diana rifled through it, thinking she had left some kind of a T-shirt in there, she knew she had...

A telltale bit of dark blue cloth was peeking out from under her history text. Diana grabbed it and pulled. It was a Students Against Drunk Driving' T-shirt that had been in there since the group's first meeting. When had that been, anyway, April?

Grabbing the SADD shirt, Diana sprinted for the girl's bathroom.

\* \* \*

Outside McAuliffe High, Rhonda approached a dented, late model Volkswagen Jetta. She shook her head, wondering how it was possible to smoke so much pot that you couldn't see into a car's interior.

She opened the door, and the white smoke wafted out.

Long faced, red-haired Artie Urlin sat in the driver's seat. He looked up at Rhonda, eyes narrowed, joint still in his mouth.

"Are you crazy?" Rhonda asked, dropping her American accent, a British one taking over as she waved the smoke away, "they're going to smell it on your clothing."

"I have been higher than the Hindenburg Blimp every day I've been in that God forsaken school," Artie Urlin said in a German accent, "and they haven't found out yet."

"Well, you had better make sure today isn't the day that somebody does find out."

"Don't worry, it's Hanussen Blend."

"What blend?"

"Hanussen blend, from Germany, very expensive. Bred and cross-bred so that there isn't any smell on your hair or clothes."

"Pull the other one."

Artie held the joint out to her. Rhonda hesitated for a moment, then took it.

He watched her puff in a lungful, taking in her short, tight skirt and dark hose. "This entire gig has been bullshit," Artie said. "The only thing I like about it is seeing you every day looking like the teen-age slut."

Rhonda locked eyes with Artie. Holding her breath, she bent down toward his face. Artie opened his mouth and Rhonda shot-gunned him.

Closing his mouth, Artie looked up at her, wanting to keep her breath in his lungs for as long as he could. "Why wasn't your phone on?" Rhonda asked.

Still holding his breath, Artie shrugged.

"We're very close," Rhonda said, "it's happening tonight. I called and texted but neither went through. You want to be out of here?"

Artie nodded.

"You want to be rich?"

He nodded again.

"Then get yourself ready. You're on in ten."

As she walked off, he let the breath slowly out of his mouth. Once his lungs were clear, he yelled, "Hey!"

She stopped, turning to him.

"You look amazing both walking toward a man *and* walking away from him."

Rhonda grinned. Turning around, she made sure there was more of a wiggle to her hips. She heard Artie's laugh almost all the way back to the front door of McAuliffe High.

## CHAPTER FOUR

"Flirt" shirt on the sink, Diana finished tucking the end of 'Students Against Drunk Driving' into her jeans.

"Outa the way, Double D," Frannie Lightfoot said, elbowing Diana out of the way so she could do her make-up in the mirror. Captain of the girls' basketball team, Frannie was tall, beautiful, and plenty nasty. A spill of long dark hair ran down her back. It had to be tied in a ponytail in order for Frannie to play.

"There's plenty of room without you pushing me out of the way," said Diana. "And stop calling me Double D."

Lipstick half done, Frannie looked innocently at Diana. "But what's wrong with calling you Double D? Aren't those your initials?"

Diana gave Frannie a 'don't piss me off' look.

"What's with the look?" Frannie asked, then rolled her lips together. "You're lucky your middle name isn't Dorothy, you'd be triple D." She smirked at Diana again. "Or, let's say your name was Emily Edmunds, you'd be Double E."

Approaching the taller girl, Diana said, "You aren't going to call me that."

"Oh," Frannie said, backing away, "I get it, now I get why you're offended. 'Cause you're barely a B cup and here I am calling you Double D! I'm so insensitive!"

"Excuse me!" Patrice called, bustling into the bathroom. She knocked Frannie out of the way so she could check her own make-up. Frannie stumbled, then recovered her balance.

"Oh, that's great," Frannie said, "the *real* Double D is here. That why you two hang out all the time? She makes up for your," Frannie pointed to Diana, "lack of chest, and she makes the future lap dancer look smaller?"

Patrice frowned, applying her eyeliner. "I've never met a girl as obsessed with boobs as you are," she said. "I mean we don't mind, it's cool, we're very tolerant here at McAuliffe High. You should come to a meeting. Of the Gay/Straight alliance."

Diana smirked, shaking her head.

"It's this Wednesday at three-thirty, Frannie. Maybe you'll meet somebody."

"Is that where you two met?" Frannie asked.

Diana put her arm around Patrice, kissing her on the cheek. "Yeah," Diana said, "but we're still trying to figure out which one's gay and which one's straight."

"And trying to make an alliance," said Patrice, right eye mainly finished.

"Losers," Frannie said, and stalked out of the bathroom.

"Wednesday, three-thirty, remember!" Patrice called, before turning to Diana. "Think she'll be there?"

"You see Rhonda?" Diana asked.

"No," Patrice said, "can't you tell? I'm still in a good mood!"

"You two..."

Done with her eyes now, Patrice looked at Diana. "Not *us* two, *you* two!"

"What do you mean, 'us two?' "

"You! And Ms. Euro trash, I didn't get it when you started hanging out, and now I don't get it even more."

"What's to get?"

"I don't know, she's so...she's just so..."

"Cosmopolitan?"

"More like B-word Monthly."

"She's not *that* bad."

"She's not that bad to *you*. And you seem to be the only one she's not bad to."

"That's not true, she's..." Diana frowned, thinking about it.

"Uh-huh, girlfriend? See?"

"I'm sure there's...somebody else she likes..."

"Chuck Leadingham," Patrice said in a sing-song voice, "but who doesn't like Chuck Leadingham? And, if you notice, she only seems to like him half the time."

Opening her mouth to respond, Diana could only frown.

Patrice pointed at her. "See? Food for thought from Auntie Patrice. Now come on," she said, "today we're getting a lecture from Cochrane on..." Patrice lowered her voice, then looked around. "Teen pregnancy!" she whispered, before grabbing Diana by the arm and hauling her out of the girls' bathroom.

As they joined the hallway traffic, Diana said, "Hang on a minute," and stopped at her locker. She threw the 'Flirt' shirt inside, slammed the door, and spun the dial. Then she and Patrice walked on to Ms. Cochrane's class.

\* \* \*

"Where's my 'Flirt' shirt?" Rhonda asked, after Diana had paid for their lunches.

The bad news about Rhonda was that she was the ultimate mooch; the good news was, she never ate much. Today, all she had on her plate were three of the 'fresh carrots,' although, Diana thought, *you'd have to expand your definition of the word 'fresh' for the term to be accurate.*

"Your 'Flirt' shirt's in my locker, I had to get to class," Diana said.

"You should have kept it on," Rhonda said as they headed to their usual table near the cafeteria's windows.

"It's not really me," Diana said. Rhonda made a show of looking straight ahead when they passed table where Chuck Leadingham sat with his friends Guy and Monroe.

Chuck, teen-idol handsome, had a gaze that bored into Rhonda. She just pointedly smirked.

"So," Diana said, "you and Chuck: is this a broken-up period, or a non-broken-up period?"

"It's a 'be quiet and get to the table' period," Rhonda answered.

Rhonda had made sure she was sitting with her back to Chuck, but Diana could still see him, straddling the chair, staring at the back of Rhonda's head with a mixture of defiance and hurt. Diana looked at Rhonda, then back at Chuck, and understood; Rhonda was beautiful and sassy and always dressed with, well, a flair that other girls didn't have. But she treated Chuck, one of the most popular boys in school, pretty much like dirt. Rhonda was with him when she wanted to be and not with him when she didn't, and how did you *do* that and get away with it?

*If I had a guy like Chuck Leadingham looking at me the way he looked at Rhonda,* Diana thought, *looking at me the nice way, not the way he was looking at her now, I'd have just about everything I wanted. But maybe the reason it was the way it was between the two of them was that things pretty much came easy to Chuck, and he wasn't used to wanting something--or someone--that he couldn't have.*

Diana sighed, watching Artie Urlin pay for his lunch and then look around the cafeteria as if trying to find someone, the someone in question probably being her. "Oh, no," Diana said, "you-know-who. On his way."

"Your future husband?" Rhonda asked. Just ignore him."

"Right," Diana said as she watched Artie approach, "like trying to ignore some big, huge zit that's right between your eyebrows."

Artie stopped at the table, holding his cafeteria tray out in front of him as if expecting to be invited to sit down. "Hi, Diana!" he said, all trace of German accent gone.

"Hi, Artie," Diana replied, "I was just talking about you."

As soon as Artie Urlin had found out Diana's Mom and Dad were Aaron and Rita Dunphy, all he wanted to do was hang around Diana and talk about all the boring science stuff. It bored her when her Dad talked to her about it, so what was she supposed to say to Artie?

Artie had messed up hair and a sprinkling of freckles across his nose. He wore frameless glasses and his face was a little too long. *He might be cute if he dressed better and did something with his hair* Diana thought, *but why do that, why care about the way you look when all you did all day was obsess about physics and look for people to bother?*

"I heard a rumor," Artie said. "Some big test at Gotelle? Your Mom and Dad?"

Diana shook her head. "How'd you find out about that? God, there must be some geek-only version of Facebook or something." She found herself looking from Artie to Chuck, thinking, *if only I had Chuck's attention instead of Artie's...*

"Don't you think it would be a great time for me to meet your Dad?" Artie asked.

"Hey, Artie," interjected Rhonda, "pushy much?"

Artie ignored her, keeping his focus on Diana, his voice taking on a whiny quality. "You're always saying sometime, how about this, tonight? Please? I'd love to see what they're testing over there!" He leaned in toward Diana. "I talked to a guy once who said Gotelle was working on a *Death Ray!*"

"What guy? Was it Mr. Eich?"

"No!" Artie said a bit too quickly.

Diana gave Artie an 'Oh, please' look.

"Okay, yes," Artie said, "but Mr. Eich knows things."

"Artie," Diana sighed, "last year Mr. Eich forgot his meds and almost jumped off the roof with wings that he made out of patio furniture strapped to his arms."

"That was so cool!" Artie said excitedly. "He told us all about that! He was trying to re-create Leonardo DaVinci's heavier than air..."

Diana waved him quiet. "Artie, listen to me: there isn't anybody testing any Death Rays at Gotelle. Just a lot of boring labs and people in cubicles with pictures of The Big Bang Theory or The Orville cast hung up on their walls."

"So you *have* been there!"

"As a matter of fact," Rhonda said, "she's going tonight!"

Diana's eyes widened. She gave Rhonda an 'if looks could kill' stare, but her friend just smiled at her. "I'm coming, Artie," Rhonda said, "why don't you come too?"

Diana returned the fakest smile she could muster. *Thanks a bunch*, the smile said, *you rhymes-with-witch.*

# CHAPTER FIVE

A large panel truck was parked outside Rhonda Bolling's house. Painted on the outside, in huge red letters, was the logo "Hager's Meats."

Inside, Bette Nordgrem, originally from Sweden, who had perfected a flawless Midwestern American accent as Rhonda's mother, was busily packing her shoes into a large box. She had made sure that keeping the shoes was part of the deal; after almost a year she had accumulated quite the collection.

From where she stood Bette could hear Neo Landry in the garage. The Frenchman--who had also pulled off the year-long feat with his own flawless accent--was humming happily. The humming was accompanied by odd metallic clanks. Bette grinned. Neo, she knew, had made a deal similar to that of her shoe deal, meaning he kept the hand and power tools.

As the man and woman who stood in for her parents busily packed their items into boxes, Rhonda was seated on the floor of her former bedroom. The room had been stripped to the bare walls; no furniture, clothing, not so much as a spare orphan sock remained inside. Rhonda was stuffing cash into envelopes, one labeled "Mommy," the other, "Daddy."

Bette, now taping up a box, smiled when Rhonda opened the door to her room. Bette was tall, pretty, and in her early forties. Rhonda always thought the woman certainly could have passed for her mother. Neo, now walking in from the garage, was tall, rugged looking, wearing a down vest. He held out his arms when he saw her, bellowing, "Sweet daughter, give daddy a kiss!"

"Neo," Rhonda said, in her native British accent, "even though you're only standing in for my father, that's still rather creepy." Rhonda handed him the "Daddy" envelope.

"She's far too young for you, even if she is...what?" Bette asked.

"Twenty-four." Rhonda said with a smile.

"She got the job because she is so young looking." Neo said, dropping his own accent in favor of his native French one, "But no matter how young they look, as long as they are over eighteen, they are fair game." He shrugged. "I am only a man." He peeked into the envelope, quickly fanning the money.

Handing the envelope marked "Mommy" to Bette, Rhonda said, "A pleasure working with you."

When Bette looked inside the envelope, her eyes widened. "This is more than we..."

"I know, love," said Rhonda, "but we believe in rewarding good work. And tonight is the big night. You will both be out of here by nine p.m.?"

"We will be out of here by eight p.m.," Neo said.

"That's good," Rhonda nodded, "please see to it."

Neo couldn't help returning a predatory grin. Bette rushed over for an embrace. "If I ever had a daughter...." she said.

"But you don't," Rhonda countered, holding her at arm's

length, and I'm not your daughter, so what do you say we get on with it?"

Bette hesitated, then nodded.

"All right then," Rhonda said before walking out to the garage. Her weather-beaten, slightly dented 2002 Volkswagen Cabriolet awaited. She took the top down and headed off to Diana Dunphy's house.

* * * * * *

Rhonda picked up a still fuming Diana, who sat, arms crossed, in the front passenger seat, saying nothing most of the way to Artie Urlin's house.

"Oh, stop it," Rhonda finally said, back now to her mid-Ohio twang.

"I can't believe you invited him," Diana answered.

"You know you're in love with him, stop trying to deny it. Think of me as...Cupid! I'm just trying to speed up the process for you, I know you're shy."

"Not funny, Rhonda."

"Oh, come on," Rhonda said as they drove up to a modest, middle class ranch-style house, "give the little nerd-ball a thrill!"

Artie was already seated on the front porch stoop, his backpack on. As soon as he saw Diana and Rhonda, he ran to the Cabriolet with wild abandon.

Diana looked at him and tried not to smile. *Of course,* Diana thought, *this is Artie's version of going to a rock concert.*

"Hi, Rhonda, hi, Diana," Artie said, getting into the back seat. He fumbled around in his backpack long enough to bring out a copy of the book *Photons, Tachyons, and Imaginary Mass* by Aaron Dunphy.

It had been a long time since Diana had seen that book.

Never a huge seller, except with science professors and geeks, *like there's a difference*, Diana thought. Her Dad had written it back when he and Mom were not only still together, but still loved each other.

Turning over the aged hardcover, Diana saw the picture of her father on the back. She could see why her mother had fallen in love with him. He wasn't just a thoughtful, sensitive genius, he looked good on the book jacket photo, and how many times did those things go together?

Diana re-read the dedication, 'To Rita, my everything.'

"Do you think your Dad would sign it for me?" he asked.

"Where'd you get this, Artie? Neil DeGrasse Tyson have a garage sale?"

"Actually, Mr. Eich had an extra copy, and I had a set of Star Trek blueprints he liked. When I told him about those blue-prints, his eyes just lit up, and..."

"Thanks for sharing," Diana said, "nothing more thrilling than stories of free trade among the geeks."

Diana flipped back through to the dedication, looking once more at the words. "To Rita, my everything," she read aloud, then said, "Amazing."

"Divorce sucks," said Rhonda.

"How did he get from dedicating a book to her to barely being able to be in the same room with her?" Diana asked.

"Marriage sucks, too," said Rhonda.

"So you think he'll sign it?" Artie asked.

"It's great having you here, Artie," Diana said. "A little glimpse into what life must be like if you were the daughter of a rock star."

"Rock star?" Artie considered for a moment. "You know, I never thought about it that way, but your Dad *is* a rock star of physics!"

Diana rolled her eyes.

"Oh, cool," Artie said, "here's something: what if your dad had been a geologist? Then he really would be a rock star, get it?"

There was silence in the car.

"'Cause geologists study rocks?" Artie prompted.

"Sure, Artie, he'll sign it for you," Diana said.

When she had called her father and told him she'd be there with a couple of friends, Diana thought he might have been doing some little victory dance, he sounded so happy. Well, as happy as Aaron Dunphy could sound, anyway. "Really? You're really coming?" he had asked.

"Me and two of my friends, okay?"

"Sure, sure, just tell me their names for security."

*Security, right*, Diana thought, *like anybody cares enough about whatever you're doing for it to need armed guards.*

They drove to the security gate, and Rhonda rolled down the window. Diana leaned over and said, "Hi, I'm Diana Dunphy. I'm here for the demonstration. And plus I've got two friends with me. Rhonda Bolling and Artie Urlin."

The guard looked down to a clipboard and frowned. He flipped through a couple of pages, nodded, and waved them through. Getting out of Rhonda's car, they all had to suddenly shield their eyes from a bright light. When the light dialed down, they saw a video camera set up with a small crew, plus a guy in a hard hat next to what looked like a small oil derrick.

"What's going on there?" Diana asked.

Rhonda and Artie exchanged a look, but when Diana turned their way, they were back in character, Artie excited, Rhonda bored with it all. "They discover oil here or something?" Diana asked, laughing.

When they got to the door, there was another security

check, and then when they got to the door of the demonstration area, there was yet another.

"Rhonda Bolling and Artie Urlin?" asked a blonde security guard. She was tall and kind of pretty, her hair bobbed short. She leaned back in her chair and studied Artie and Rhonda up and down. There was a look on the guard's face, Diana thought, as if she were smelling something really bad.

Aaron walked by in a dark blue suit, looking very serious. "It's okay, Bethany," he said, "they're with me. This is my daughter and her two friends—"

"Hello, sir," Artie said, "it's such an honor, *such* an honor to meet you, I can't believe it!"

"Thank you, thank you," Aaron replied then turned to Diana. "C'mon, I've got seats for you." He motioned them forward, heading to the front of the auditorium, where three chairs had tape across them along with a "Reserved" sign. Aaron took off the tape and said, "Sit, sit!" then started walking up the stairs to the stage.

Diana watched her father stop, as if he were remembering something. When he came back, he kissed his daughter on the cheek.

"Shut up," Diana said, watching Aaron walk back up to the stage.

"I didn't say anything." Rhonda responded.

"You are *so* lucky!" said Artie.

"Would you like Diana to get her father back here?" Rhonda asked. "Maybe she can get him to kiss you on the cheek? Or is tongue action the only thing that will satisfy?"

Diana saw her mother walk out from behind some huge curtains. She also wore a lab coat over a dark blue outfit. Mom motioned dad toward her and whispered something in his ear. Her father nodded urgently and walked backstage.

When mom saw Diana, she gave her a big smile, and waved. Diana waved back. Then mom was back to all business, pushing her glasses up her nose and following her ex-husband.

The auditorium doors were shut. Descending from the ceiling was a large projection screen, rumbling to a stop as Aaron walked out from behind the curtains.

"Hello," he said into a microphone at a podium to the left of the screen, "I'm Dr. Aaron Dunphy, and this is the first demonstration of what we call 'Operation Crock

Pot..' " He looked around the room. "Now I know what you're asking yourselves, you're asking, 'what the heck is Operation Crock Pot?' "

A picture of a gas station sign appeared behind Aaron on the big screen. It said, 'Unleaded regular, $4.35 per gallon.'

"Operation Crock Pot," Aaron went on, "aims to solve two problems at once. The first problem is oil scarcity, which has driven prices at the pumps far past the point where our economy can easily absorb them. We are, in the end, a petroleum based market, and despite our best efforts, a petroleum based market we remain.

"The second of these problems—" a picture of a trash dump appeared behind him— "is solid waste disposal. Columbus, Ohio, alone produces three hundred thousand tons of organic waste each day, and we're an average sized city. Imagine how many tons this country produces in total when you add in New York, Los Angeles, San Francisco, Chicago, and then," he raised his index finger, "then think about the solid waste production of the entire world."

Rhonda was obviously bored. Artie's could have been listening to Moses at Mount Sinai.

A picture of a dinosaur in a jungle appeared behind Aaron. "It takes one hundred ninety-six thousand tons of prehistoric plant and animal life to produce one gallon of gas," he said, and then a picture of the Earth appeared. "This planet, is in essence, a huge slow cooker, a crock pot, if you will, for making oil. We call oil a fossil fuel because organic material, dead animals and plants, died and were covered with sediment. This material rots, compacting itself. After millions of years...oil! We are addicted to oil. And our nation's dependence on countries that don't like us very much causes all sorts of problems, one of which is the constant threat of terrorism."

Aaron paused for a moment, moving his gaze around the room. "But what if we could take the millions of tons of organic waste we produce each day and place it in this crock pot of ours? What if we could take organic waste produced today and stick it back in this country, sixty-five million years ago, and let it, in essence, cook? Let it become oil?"

There was a murmur in the audience.

Diana had to admit she thought it was crazy, too. How were you going to take trash produced today and stick it in the ground sixty-five million years ago?

"I give you," Aron said, "Operation Crock Pot," and he moved away from the podium, gesturing to a curtain behind him. Someone—probably Diana's mother—opened the curtain to reveal a big, tall, long tube made out of what appeared to be steel.

Someone behind Diana whispered, "You think he actually pulled this off?" That person was violently shushed amid some soft laughter.

But Diana knew her dad. If he said he could do something...

The tube behind her father was about thirty feet long and was certainly large enough to walk around in. There was a window in a door at the front of the tube with one of those huge spin dials on it like you'd see in a submarine. Through that window, Diana could see all kinds of stuff just packed in there. What was it?

"In this reinforced tube," her father said as if in answer, "is one day's organic waste from the city of Columbus. Coffee grounds, grapefruit peelings, apple cores, what have you. There is even, and I apologize in advance to any pet lovers there may be in the audience-some dead dogs and cats."

Her mother came out with silver framed, red-tinted goggles around her neck. She had a box of them that she started passing out to the crowd. Everyone in the audience put them on while Aaron went to a laptop on a podium and started tapping buttons on the keyboard.

A low hum filled the room.

Aaron put on his own goggles. "I advise you not to look directly at the light that comes from the window in the tube," he said, "even with your goggles on."

The hum got louder, accelerating up to a low whine, then a high whine, and then the tube shook. The brightest light Diana had ever seen lanced out the small window.

The light filled the auditorium.

Diana looked away, expecting to feel heat, but instead it felt cold, colder than a person could imagine, and then, with an eerie suddenness, everything was right back to normal.

The light was gone, and there was no more electronic whine.

The only thing that had changed was the tube, now empty.

Without knowing what she was doing, Diana stood up, removing her goggles. *Holy shit,* she thought, silently mouthing the words.

On the screen behind Aaron, a live video of the guy Diana had seen outside by the oil derrick appeared. "Hey!" Diana said, turning to Rhonda, "that's what we saw coming in here..."

Rhonda shrugged, rolling her eyes until Diana turned back to her father.

"This is Craig Farkas, one of the Gottelle Memorial Institute's geological engineers," Aaron said. "We calculated, factoring in the earth's rotation, where this trash would land. Now, everyone knows there is no oil on Gottelle property, right? Am I right?" He looked around the room, prompting a buzz of affirmation. Aaron put on a hands-free headset and asked, "How's it going out there, Craig?"

"Just great, Dr. Dunphy," Craig said on the screen while a jet of shiny black oil spurted out of the derrick. He stuck his hand in it, then showed his hand to the camera.

Artie reached into his backpack, Rhonda, into her purse.

Taking off the hands-free head-set, Aaron said, "I show you the way to energy independence, I show you a way out of Middle Eastern entanglements, I show you..."

Then it was as if someone had turned on a jack-hammer to break concrete while simultaneously drilling Diana's teeth. She put her hands over her ears, eyes shut tight, trying to get away from the noise.

She could see people screaming, running for the exits. She looked back to her father, where bits of wood and plastic burst off the podium in front of him.

Diana saw her father grimace, then sink from view.

*My God*, Diana thought, *it's...someone's shooting! That's what--*

She turned, hands still over her ears. *Rhonda and Artie, had they made it to the--?*

Artie stood behind her, machine gun in hand and ear protectors on, a terrible, self-satisfied grin on his face.

*No*, Diana thought, *no, this can't be*—until Bethany, the blonde guard from outside, appeared in the doorway, taking careful aim with her revolver.

Then it was Rhonda, with her own ear protectors and machine gun, who was firing.

Diana screamed over the nightmarish noise, seeing the machine gun's muzzle flash rather than hearing it as the security guard was blown back into the hallway.

*The time for shock is over*, Diana thought, as she tackled the girl who used to be her friend. Rhonda hit the ground face-first. Diana grabbed the gun, and in their struggle over it, managed to wrestle the weapon to just below Rhonda's neck.

Diana pulled back, Rhonda clawing at her hands. *Wish I could hear you gasping for breath, you bi--*

And then something hard hit her in the side of the head, and Diana fell on top of her opponent.

Diana was conscious of something wet running down her head, but then she was rolled away. She just sprawled there on the floor, looking up at the ceiling. *This is a surprise*, she thought, oddly calm, staring up at the beams and lights.

*Terrorists? Artie and Rhonda? I mean, seriously?*

*How did I end up with friends who were terrorists, and was my Dad okay?* Diana thought, looking over to him.

He was collapsed behind the podium, but where was her mother?

Diana looked up at Rhonda and Artie. They had their guns trained on her. "Oh my God, who are you guys?" she asked, unable to hear her own question. Then she caught the butt of Artie's machine gun in her face, and everything went dark.

# CHAPTER SIX

"Get the thumb drive in there!"

"That will copy the software, not the process. Think how much more it would be worth if something was in there while the chamber was powering up."

"You're not seriously thinking what I think you're thinking, are you?

"Why not? Isn't this whole thing about better uses for trash? If the thumb drive is in while the chamber sends something back, we'll have everything about this Crock Pot we could possibly need."

"C'mon, then, get her up, get her under the other arm. Teach her to tackle me, the little Bint!"

Diana was barely conscious of somebody getting her under one arm while somebody else lifting her under the other. They got her up off the ground, and she could see the auditorium, see everyone who hadn't run out into the hall, all dead, either slumped over in their chairs or sprawled out on the floor.

Now they were dragging her up to the stage, up the stairs. They had gotten her to the front of the big metal tube.

The big, metal tube that had the trash in it.

The trash that had all disappeared.

The trash that had sat in the ground for sixty-five million years. The trash that had compacted upon itself and become the oil that her father had shown everyone.

Diana started to struggle weakly. Rhonda kept her up while Artie worked the spin-dial, opening the door in the big metal tube.

She saw the interior of the tube, smooth and gleaming, with no trace, not so much as the odor of the trash that had been inside.

"No..." Diana said, still unable to hear herself, struggling against the grip the two of them had on her, but then one of them let go, and she slumped to her knees.

Her mother had come from behind the huge metal tube, swinging a pipe.

Artie ducked, the pipe striking the titanium tube.

Now dropped completely to the floor, Diana tried to turn over.

Rhonda struggled to get her gun into position as it was grabbed. Shoved forcefully back against the tube, Rita Dunphy's grim, hate-filled face filled her world.

That face moved forward, out of her field of view and to her neck. For one panicked second, Rhonda thought, *is this bitch going to take a chunk out of my neck with her teeth?*

Then Rita was flung away. Airborne for a split second, she landed in the front row, her head impacting against the chairs. Artie, half-turned away from her, looking at the body, was now the biggest thing in her world.

"Put one in her head!" Rhonda yelled, lifting Diana once more.

"No need," said Artie, helping out now, "she's gone."

Diana was dropped inside the tube. The dial spun behind her, sealing her in.

"No, no wait..." Diana tried to say, but she felt so tired.

"Now," Rhonda said. "Let's see how much oil we can get out of the skinny little bint." At the controls, Artie grinned, powering up.

*Dad, get up!* Diana thought. *You have to get up, you can't be... Mom, get up! You can't be either! You have to get up and save me from these horrible people! Somebody has to! There has to be a way!*

Diana could barely move, her head hurt so much. *I can get up now,* she thought, *right now, if I just concentrate, but I can't. Maybe if I just lie here a few seconds longer, maybe a minute longer—*

And then the tube began to vibrate. Why was it doing that?

She swallowed, knowing that if she could hear, the tube would be humming. The same humming from before the bright light, from before all the trash had disappeared.

She remembered Craig Farkus sticking his hand into the oil her father had just made. Oil, sticky, gooey oil.

She finally sat up.

She got so dizzy, but she had to find a way out. Hands around the hinges on the back of the door, she used them to climb painfully to her feet.

They were putting something that looked like bricks on the sides of the tube, then sticking wires in the bricks, and the floor's vibration was getting worse and worse, through her feet, then to her knees, then to her spine.

It seemed so much brighter in the tube. Why was that?

Artie was running past her, putting wires into something,

setting something up, but Rhonda? She saw Diana through the window.

Rhonda gave her a little 'bye-bye' wave.

Diana started pounding on the door. She began screaming, not that it could be heard over the thrum of whatever kind of power was needed to open a rift in time. *Make some noise*, Diana thought, *make some kind of a noise before you end up in the oil pan of somebody's Toyota!*

Outside, she saw Artie put the goggles back on and hand a pair to Rhonda, who looked back at her and grinned. Now that she wore the goggles, with their great, smooth, black lenses over her eyes, Rhonda looked like some kind of a bug.

*Like a praying mantis*, Diana thought.

She looked around the tube. *Where was that great, bright light that had taken all that trash away?* Diana thought. *If it was that bright outside, so bright they all had to wear goggles, why wasn't it that bright in here?*

Artie and Rhonda both looked away, shielding their eyes, but to Diana, there was nothing. *To the two of them, outside, am I already gone?*

Diana watched Rhonda look back to the window, look right through her. *To them, she must be vanished already*, she thought, *dead, out with the orange peels, watermelon rinds, dead dogs and cats.*

Artie took a thumb drive out and held it in the air triumphantly. Rhonda looked back to the window and grinned, taking off her goggles. "We're going to be rich!" she announced.

Even with her ears ringing, Diana could tell what she had said. *Rich?* She thought, *Artie and Rhonda rich, on the beach, in the sun, drinking Margaritas while she rotted and compacted for sixty-five million years to become not even a drop of oil?*

*No, that couldn't be.*

Diana watched Artie and Rhonda run away, up the stairs and through the auditorium doors.

* * *

Behind the wheel of the jeep that waited for Artie and Rhonda was a muscular man in a tank top and glasses. He had thinning blonde hair and reptilian eyes that never seemed to blink. Rhonda got into the front passenger seat. The driver passed Artie a grenade.

Artie ran to Rhonda's Cabriolet. Gunter, the driver, asked, "You've got it?"

Holding up the thumb drive, Ronda said, "You won't believe what it is we've got."

Artie pulled the pin and tossed the grenade into the Cabriolet, then sped to the back seat of Gunter's car. "Go!" he yelled.

Gunter floored it out of Gotelle's parking lot.

The Cabriolet exploded, taking out cars on either side, not that their owners would care. They had been shot in the back by Artie as they had fled the auditorium.

* * *

Back in the tube, Diana was conscious only of the awful vibration. She saw her hand, or maybe what she saw was five or six versions of her hand as it moved through the air in front of her face.

She looked outside, one last time. Her heart caught in her throat as she saw her father pull himself to his feet.

There was blood all over his suit, but he struggled to the controls and started working them, using the console to steady himself, looking past her, yelling something at her but the only words she could make out were "don't you worry..."

She saw him break up into dots. Was the world, was everything, just made up of dots?

Was her brain made up of dots?

"Worry...worry...worry...." Her father's lips moved, but hadn't he already said not to worry? Why has he saying it again and again?

She watched her hands float away like they were made of sand, and her wrists and elbows trailed after them. Diana very calmly watched them go. Her legs, too, were vanishing, gone up to the knees except she was somehow still standing there.

*How do you stand with no legs*, she thought, and then another thought came to her: *maybe my legs are still there, it's just that they're still there sixty-five million years ago*!

That's impossible, she wanted to say, and then she remembered the look on her father's face when she was a little girl. "What did I tell you about that word?" he always asked.

*And he really had been right*, she thought, *all along. Nothing was impossible, not anymore.*

She was losing track of herself, except now it seemed like that was okay. Watching yourself melt away, maybe that was not so okay, but wasn't it kind of like diving off the high board? It was scary, but once you were up there, you pretty much had to jump, didn't you?

She heard her father's voice between deep breaths, but it was so odd, she didn't hear his voice with her muffled ears, but somehow knew what he was saying: *We can do it, I know we can do it!*

Then her mother: *It wasn't designed to transport live organic material!*

*Is that how you see me now, mom?* Diana wanted to ask. *Just sixteen year-old live organic material?*

Then she was zipping out, zipping away. The moment changed, and she was somewhere else. Somewhere hot. A jungle.

She was as tall as a house, and she was running.

Not only was she running, but every time one of her feet hit the ground, she was covering enough space to fit two or three cars, and all the screeching animals in front of her were trying to get out of her way, hoping she wouldn't choose them.

Her hearing was back. And her hearing was perfect! Better than perfect! Better than it had ever been...

And when she saw the big creature in front of her, she was hungry like she'd never, ever been hungry before. She bit into its neck, and her tongue tasted blood.

Blood ran down her throat, and it was as if she'd been thirsty her whole life and had finally found water. She had never tasted anything so good, and she continued to tear into that dying thing, gorging herself on chunks of meat, blood splattering everywhere.

And it was sweet, so sweet.

*Her pattern! I've got her pattern!*

*Are you sure?*

*It's the only human pattern, it's got to be her!*

And when she was thirsty, she drank from a nearby stream, washing the blood away, the good, coppery taste of it diluted now.

But her insatiable hunger for meat wasn't gone, it would never be gone, it was part of her forever. It was her old, good friend.

*Are you sure you have her?*

*Damn it, Rita, I have her, I have her!*

She looked down at her reflection in the stream, horrified

and fascinated, the sight so familiar: the huge head dominated by its mouth, a sharp-toothed grin, filled with steak-knife teeth, bits of blood and tissue hanging off of them.

The reflection stood on two feet, tiny arms dangling, covered everywhere with mottled, brownish-green skin. It was a walking, running slaughterhouse, every boy's favorite creature from his elementary school dinosaur picture book.

And she thought: *this isn't so bad, really. This must be what it's like to be good looking. I mean, if you were going to be a dinosaur...*

But the nightmare image broke up, falling away into dots, first the snout, then the huge head the size of a speed boat, then the thick, muscular neck, then the small, clawed, hanging arms...

Birds? Hadn't someone told her at some time that they were like huge birds? Those tiny little arms on this huge body, like the wings on roast turkey, what was up with that?

But then she was out of there, the dots forming back into her elbows, then back into her wrists...

...back inside that tube, where she looked at her hands, which were once more her own.

Diana fell, hitting her knees. She could hear the bump of them against the gleaming floor. She could hear again!

Her mom opened the door, crying and putting her arms around her, forcing her to stand, saying, "Get up, honey, now, right now, get up!" and Diana leaned on her while she walked her out of the tube and down the stairs onto the stage.

She saw dad, holding his side, tearing Artie and Rhonda's bomb off the side of the tube.

"Aaron!" her Mom yelled, "Come on!"

"Keep going," he said, "I'll be right there!" Examining the bomb, he said "looks like maybe Semtex," he said, "but messing with the timer could set it off. We have to get rid of it!" He threw the whole thing into the chamber.

"For God's sake, Aaron," her mother called, "you don't know what that will do!"

"An explosion in the late Cretaceous period isn't going to hurt anyone," he said, and he started punching keys on the computer while Diana and her mother limped out of the auditorium.

That loud hum started again. In fact it was getting louder…

Not two seconds after Diana and Rita had limped through the exit, an explosion blew the rear doors off of the auditorium.

The blast wave threw Diana on top of her mother, and the doors covered them both. Bricks, boards, and debris shot out of the auditorium's smoking ruin, very nearly burying mother and daughter.

* * *

They heard the muffled blast, driving North along state route 315.

Rhonda turned back to Artie. "Let me see it," he said.

Holding the thumb drive out to him, Rhonda grinned.

"We will summer in the South of France," Artie said.

"And winter where?" Rhonda asked, "Malibu perhaps?"

"You are a pair of idiots," Gunter said, his own German accent thicker than Artie's, "once the sale is completed, we must stay away from the United States for a decade at the very least."

"Seriously, Gunter, you big Spaßbremser, if I ever need a party pooped, I'll call you."

# DINOSAUR LIFE

"Behold, his strength in his loins, and his power in the muscles of his belly. He makes his tail stiff like a cedar; the sinews of his thighs are knit together. His bones are tubes of bronze, his limbs like bars of iron. He is the first of the works of God; let him who made him bring near his sword!"

-Job 40:15-24

## CHAPTER SEVEN

Diana had vague memories of sirens, lots and lots of sirens, and then someone in an oxygen mask and helmet digging her out and shouting things like, "Pulse is irregular!" Then she was being strapped down onto something.

Then it was like she was floating away.

"Peter Pan," she said, for some reason remembering when she was a little girl, sitting between her mother and father. They had been happy then, the three of them, and she watched the actor (or had it been an actress?) flying around the stage. She had been amazed in those years, before what appeared on stage or in a movie became separate from what was real. Peter Pan flew. The way she was flying now...

But then, some dim part of her mind told her she was probably being carried.

"Rather fly..." she said.

"What?" someone asked.

"What?" asked someone else.

Then she stopped flying. She slid into something and there were other people looking over her, saying things like "pupils dilating!" and, "she's non-responsive!"

"Tinkerbell..." Diana said, wanting to clap her hands, to keep Tinkerbell alive, but she couldn't bring her hands together.

"Honey," someone said, a woman, Diana thought. Taking one of her strapped-down hands, the woman said, "Honey, are you there?"

"My mom..." Diana said, but her throat felt so dry. She had to tell them anyway, it didn't matter. "Do you have her, too? Don't leave without her, please..."

And a woman's voice replied, "We have her, honey, she's going to be okay. You have to try to remain calm, please," and then she was asking about her father. She felt a jab, maybe more of a sting in her arm, and someone was gasping, saying, "I broke the needle!" and then another jab, and then the feeling of just being out, just drifting in and out for a long while.

Diana thought maybe she was on wheels at one point, in some kind of a van, was that right? And then a scream, a scream like the reptiles that were running before her after she'd been in the Tachyon Chamber.

"The Tachyon Chamber," she said, perhaps out to those in the van, not that it mattered. The siren was louder, and she was out again, and then she was lying on a bed in a white room, with someone sitting her up, getting her to swallow some pill. What kind of pill had she just taken, and did it matter?

No, not a bit. The pill was just so good. It made everything seem so much better. She was floating, going back again, back to the jungle, where she had been, so briefly, happy...

And in that terrible jungle, Diana was free to run, the tree-tops near her face.

Huge herds of panicked lizards ran in front of her, all scared of *her*. It felt so good, the warm wind rushing by her face, keeping her effortlessly warm...

Against her hard, tough, skin. Nothing could hurt her inside such skin.

And her speed. She must have been running fifty miles an hour!

Running. Hunting.

And that hunger. The hunger never left her. It would drive her completely crazy if she let it. If she didn't eat something.

She smiled, and her grin was permanent. A permanent line of steak-knife teeth.

And then she was drifting out of it, sad to leave the jungle. She was drifting awake, or maybe she was dreaming? Perhaps the terrible, fanged grin was real, and she, Diana, the dream? Wouldn't that be something?

"Wouldn't that be something?" she asked.

"What, honey?" someone asked, a familiar voice. Her mother?

Diana remembered, simultaneously, being a baby, her mother feeding her a spoonful of Gerber's banana pear food out of a jar, yes, and she remembered another mother. Another mother, huge and terrible, looking down at her.

Grinning down at her, with her smile of steak-knife teeth.

For that mother, Diana opened her mouth wide. This other mother, this huge one, lowered her head, mouth open like a cavern, but this other Diana wasn't frightened. This other Diana opened her own mouth, ready for the bounty that was going to be regurgitated into her waiting stomach.

Birds, someone had said, every time you saw a pigeon, or a crow, or a chicken, you were seeing one of them, a version of them that had survived to today.

Back in her hospital room, Diana opened her eyes.

And there was mom, her human mom, looking down at her.

"Mom..." Diana rasped.

"What, honey?" her mother asked, taking her hand.

"You gonna puke on me?"

Her mother laughed. "No, Diana, that isn't part of the plan."

"Some mothers...." Diana managed to say, "puke into their baby's mouths."

"Yes, honey, but last I checked neither one of us was a bird."

*But yes, we are*, Diana wanted to say, *or at least I am*. And then Diana realized that wasn't right at all...they weren't birds, but the *ancestors* of birds.

Her mother's face was kind of banged up and there was a cast on her arm. She was in a wheelchair, and she used her left hand to touch Diana's face.

"Am I..." Diana said, "is my face--?"

"You look fine, honey, as beautiful as ever," Rita said. "I somehow took the brunt of it. In spite of *you* landing on top of *me*. I'm so glad you're okay."

"Why wouldn't I be okay?" Diana asked, hearing her own hoarse voice for the first time in... what? A day? A week?

Sixty-five million years?

"Do you know your name?" Rita asked.

"Mom," Diana said, "c'mon."

"I need to know if you know your name."

"Diana Dunphy."

"Where do you go to school?"

"I go to Harvard law. You know where I go to school, I'm not that messed up! Where's Dad?"

Her mother looked up at someone, and Diana looked where she looked, to a guy in a dark suit. The guy was big, built like a linebacker, African American.

The linebacker guy shook his head.

Shook his head why? In answer to her question?

"What?" Diana asked, "Where is he? Where's my Dad? Who are you?"

"Miss Dunphy, my name is Laurence Keyes, I'm with Homeland Security, we should talk when you're feeling better."

"Feeling better? I am feeling better, what's going on here? I want to know where my Dad..."

She heard a squeak as her mother turned around in her wheelchair. Rita started to cry.

Diana looked up at Keyes and said, more calmly than she believed she could, "You've got to be kidding me."

"I'm afraid not, Miss Dunphy," Keyes said.

Everything got very quiet. And very slow. And what really made Diana mad was, in spite of everything, she just felt so...

"Hungry."

Her mother turned back around, looking at Diana as if unable to believe her daughter had just said what she had said.

"Hungry for what?" Keyes asked.

"Hamburger," Diana said, "a big one."

Keyes motioned to someone. There was a guy standing at the door, Diana noticed, dressed in the same style dark suit as Keyes.

"You heard the lady," Keyes said, "get her a burger, and not this hospital crud either, a real burger. You want fries, too?"

"Two burgers," Diana said, "and rare, please, really rare. Make it three!"

The new guy nodded, and he was out the door.

Mom put her hand on top of Diana's hand. "Are you okay, honey?"

"I'm fine, is there..." Diana swallowed, and then finished, "is there a...b-body?"

Rita took her hand away and put it to her face, stifling a sob.

"You have to understand the, uh..." Keyes said. "What your father and mother were working on..."

"He was trying to get rid of the explosive," Mom said, "so he put it into the Tachyon Chamber, and we think, right as it powered up to the event horizon, the bomb must have detonated. And Crock Pot is pretty much an explosion anyway, and with that explosion happening right at that second..."

"The heat was..." Keyes began, but he didn't finish.

"So there's a chance he's still...?"

"He's gone," Mom whispered. There isn't anything left of him."

Diana just sat there.

Nothing left of him? Nothing? "Are they sure he isn't...somewhere...in all that wreckage?" she asked.

"Reasonably sure," Keyes said. "We've sent in..uh..."

"What?" Diana asked.

"Corpse sniffing dogs, Miss. Dunphy," said Keyes. "They would have found him if...but he's not in there."

Diana got quiet, just leaning back in the bed. "Rhonda?" she asked. "Artie?"

"We've alerted the media and put out a BOLO." Keyes said.

"I'm sorry," said Rita, "a BOLO?"

"Excuse me, it's a law enforcement acronym for 'Be On The Lookout,' it goes to police, highway patrol, sheriff's agencies, it features descriptions of the suspects, their real names, all of that."

"Their real names?" Diana asked.

The woman you know as Rhonda Bolling is actually one Andrea Fain, originally from Great Britain, she's a deep cover operative who works for the highest bidder. Artie Urlin's real name is Thomas Orton, we're not sure where he's from originally.

"I heard him speaking with a German accent," Diana said, looking out the window.

"Really?" Keyes asked, taking out a notepad and jotting it down.

"So they just found me," Diana said, "became my friends, for a year, just so they could do this?"

"That's the most likely scenario, yes," Keyes said.

"So it's my fault Dad's dead?"

"Honey!" Rita exclaimed. "No!"

"It is!"

"Miss Dunphy, you musn't blame yourself," Keyes said.

"Who do I blame, then?"

"These were highly trained, professional deep cover agents."

"Me and Rhonda used to watch Bob's Burgers!"

"These are expert con men and women who establish elaborate false identities," Keyes explained, "willing to wait for years, if necessary, to accomplish their objectives."

Diana's jaw clenched. Her muscles tightened.

*Artie and Rhonda*, she thought, *with their fakeness, and their laughter as they left me to be erased from existence!* She was suddenly so angry, it was as if something moved within her. And then, just as suddenly, she thought, *my dad...* and calmed to the point that she wasn't so much furious as terribly sad. "Mom!" Diana said.

Rita took her daughter's hand. "What, honey?"

"Dad can't be dead!"

"Oh, honey..."

"All I ever gave him was crap!"

"That's not true!"

"It is! I was always giving him a hard time, whenever I could, I never gave him any breaks!"

There was a tearing sound. Diana looked down. The IV had popped out of her arm.

"Nurse!" Rita called.

"I don't want any nurse, I want my Dad! I want my Dad so I can be better to him!" Diana said.

The nurse came in and looked at the IV.

"I don't want any more drugs!" Diana yelled, pushing the nurse away.

The nurse sailed away from the girl as if she had vaulted away on a trampoline. Keyes caught her before she hit the wall.

"Diana," Rita said, not in admonishment, not exactly.

Now every eye was on her, and Diana looked around guiltily.

"I'm so sorry," she said to the nurse, who held out a hand as if to say, 'it's all right.' Diana started crying, but at the same time, something had changed, she knew it, she could tell.

The agent was going to be there soon with her hamburgers. Diana could smell them, that rich, meaty, bloody smell, only he wasn't in the building yet. He was still on his way over in the car. She could tell because mixed in with the odor of the hamburgers was...

Gasoline? From the car? And was that...Axe body spray? How did she know the guy wore Axe body spray?

She should have told him to get four burgers, three would never be enough. Why hadn't she told him to get four burgers?

Everyone was frowning at her. "Uh?" she asked, before realizing she had been sticking her tongue out.

Smelling with her tongue...

"Nurse," Rita said, "I'm an M.D., I can put the IV back in. I'm so sorry about my daughter's behavior, please understand, she's suffered a terrible loss."

The nurse nodded and walked out as her mother took the IV. Diana wasn't paying much attention to her mother because that wonderful beef smell was getting closer and closer. He was on the elevator now, Diana could tell, coming up.

The burger smell was so strong that Diana didn't even notice her mother trying to stick the IV back in and never quite getting it to. Rita finally broke the needle off on the inside of her daughter's elbow.

Diana looked down, watching the tiny metal tube roll under the bed.

Rita and Diana stared at each other, unasked questions on each of their faces, but it didn't seem like anybody else had seen it. Rita finally put tape over the IV so it at least stuck *to* her daughter's arm, and then the agent came in with the burgers.

Those burgers, which were all Diana could see.

*The meat...!*

"Give them to me!" Diana said, grabbing the bag from the agent, ripping the burgers out of their buns. She tore into the first patty, then the next, gorging herself on chunks of meat, grease splattering on her hospital gown. The hamburger was gone in an instant and she started to lick her hands, afraid she'd missed some little bits, afraid some of the slaughtered, ground-up cow might not have ended up in her mouth.

Diana didn't realize her eyes were closed until she opened them and saw everyone looking at her.

Embarrassed, Diana gave a little, breathy laugh and shrugged.

They all looked shocked except for Rita. Rita's eyes were narrowed, studying her daughter.

"Mr. Keyes," Rita said, "I think that's enough for now, don't you?"

"Of course, Mrs. Dunphy," Keyes said. "I'm very sorry for your loss, both of you. We'll have a man outside during your entire stay at the hospital. If you need anything else..."

"Burgers!" Diana shouted. "Just like those, done just like that, only maybe a little less well-doe, and more of 'em, five or six this time!"

The agent who had brought the burgers looked to Keyes, who nodded.

Diana watched the agent leave, thinking, *he's a big guy, I bet he works out, all these Homeland Security government agent types do, it's probably a requirement, some weight requirement. They probably have to be in good shape to stay on the job.*

Diana closed her eyes, sticking her tongue out. She caught the Axe spray, so close to the departed agent's body, the smell getting weaker as he got to the elevator and waited.

She imagined him getting out of the shower, spraying it on, muscles rippling beneath his skin.

*Meat. Two hundred pounds of USDA choice...*

*Stop it*, Diana thought. *What are you thinking?*

Rita stayed until everyone had left the room. When they finally closed the door, she felt under the bed until she found the broken IV needle.

Rita stared at a drop of blood on the end of the needle. "Do you remember who put this in originally?" she asked.

"No," Diana said softly.

"Must have either been the E.M.T's or one of the nurses, so... five or six hours ago? But now we can't puncture your skin."

"What's happening to me, Mom?" Diana asked, her mind still on the agent. *Specifically, on his bicep, on biting into it like it was an apple...*

"Not sure," Rita said as she got out a blood pressure cuff and wrapped it around her daughter's arm.

Diana stuck out her tongue.

The agent was just leaving the building, she was pretty sure. Yes, there he was, leaving the building, getting into his car...

"Blood pressure's on the high end of normal," Rita said before getting out a thermometer. She was going to stick it in Diana's mouth, but saw her daughter's tongue was already out.

"What are you doing?" Rita asked.

"Ah, oh no."

"Put your tongue back in your mouth," Rita said.

Diana did so sheepishly.

"Why did you have your tongue out?" Rita asked.

"I don't know," Diana said. "Because I can...smell better?"

"Smell better?"

Diana nodded.

"With your tongue out?" her mother asked.

Diana nodded again. Then she started to cry.

"It's all right," Rita said, patting her daughter's hand. Frowning once more at the broken-off IV needle with the tiny drop of blood on the end, Rita said, "Everything's going to be just fine."

## CHAPTER EIGHT

From that day on, Rita always made sure she was there to *not* put in the IV needles, although it didn't matter all that much.

"Whatever they're giving me wasn't helping anyway," Diana whispered to her mother.

"They don't have to know that," Rita said softly.

"What's the big deal?" Diana asked.

"Your skin is breaking needles, honey," Rita said. "I don't know that that's information we want out there right now."

"Okay," Diana said, "you're the scientific genius."

"Some genius," Rita said, "I just blew up a city block and now..."

"Now what, mom?"

"Now we have to get out of here."

"That wasn't what you were going to say."

"Yes it was."

"No it wasn't. You were going to say something about me becoming a freak."

"I wasn't going to say anything of the sort! Everything is going to be all right, you'll see.

Right, mom, Diana thought, wanting to simply lie there in the hospital bed. Every minute that passed she could feel herself getting better.

The worst thing was the hunger. It was always with her, a constant emptiness. Luckily for Diana, the tall, muscular Homeland Security guy kept her in nice, beefy, thick, undercooked burgers. *God bless him*, Diana thought. He would make two or three runs each day, bringing back five or six hamburgers each time.

"I've never seen a girl your size with an appetite this big," he said once as she was licking burger bits off of her hands.

Diana grunted at him before noticing the pulse in his neck.

It was so small, that pulse, but she could see it if she looked hard enough. She didn't know why she'd never seen that before in people, but now she was noticing it all the time.

Had she never seen it simply because she'd never looked hard enough? The pulse showed that blood was pumping from his heart to his head, to his hands and feet and back again, over and over. Diana wondered just how many times a day that happened, heart to head, hands and feet, then back again, and again, and again...

"Huh," she said, trying to smile at him, but continuing to stare at his neck.

That thick, sinewy neck. Filled with all that pulsing blood.

The Homeland Security guy seemed a little disturbed. He backed out of the room, but Diana could hear him outside.

She could smell something too.

Diana stuck out her tongue. Yes, it was her mother's scent...

"Oh, hi, Mrs. Dunphy," the Homeland Security guy said, and then he lowered his voice. "Is your daughter...is she okay?"

"Oh, sure," Rita said, "she's just a little, uh, she's been through so much."

"So it's normal? For her to be this hungry? For really rare burgers?"

"It's probably the...iron deficiency."

"Really?"

"Mm-hmm."

"You're not eating like that...I mean...are you?"

"Uh, well...iron deficiency doesn't affect everyone the same way."

Diana smelled someone else now, a new scent that had her frowning. The scent was unfamiliar, and it was mixed with something, another scent, something that wasn't human or animal.

Something that wasn't meaty...

In the hallway, Craig Farkus walked around the corner holding some flowers.

"Craig," Rita said, "hello."

The Homeland Security agent walked off.

*Who was Craig?* Diana thought.

"Rita," Craig said, "I'm so sorry. I tried to come by a couple of days ago, but they said no visitors. Here..."

*Whoever this Craig is*, Diana thought, *he had brought...*

*Flowers.* She took in another breath. *Craig brought mom flowers. He was the guy in the hard hat who had been outside on the video monitor when the demonstration happened, the one sticking his hand into the oil.*

"Thank you very much, Craig," Rita said.

"If there's anything I can do, I mean anything, just let me know," Craig said.

"I certainly will."

"What about the software?"

"Software?" Rita asked.

Craig looked around, then lowered his voice. "Crock Pot's software? Shouldn't someone take charge? I hate to bring it up especially now, but..."

"No, it's all right..."

"...I'm sorry, with Aaron gone, to say this, but shouldn't we...?"

"We'll have to figure it out later, okay?"

"Okay. If you're sure."

"I'm sure. We're going to need some time. I'll be in touch. Thank you for the flowers."

Craig nodded, then waved and walked on.

Rita limped in to Diana's room, placing the flowers on the night table.

* * *

*It sure is nice to see Mom out of that wheelchair*, Diana thought. They had her using one of those canes, the ones with a square metal base and four little rubber pads on the end so it was more stable. "How are you doing?" Rita asked.

"I'm okay," Diana said.

Rita sat near her daughter and took the tape off of the IV. Then, looking Diana in the eyes, she gently stuck her with the needle. "Can you feel that?" she asked.

"Yes."

"Does it hurt?"

"No, not exactly."

Rita frowned. "Still on the all-beef diet?"

Diana nodded, wishing her mother hadn't asked her about food. It made her stomach growl. Loudly. "Excuse me," Diana said.

"Oh, please," Mom said, leaning on her cane. She paced to

the window. "You spit up on me how many times when you were a baby? Two of those times it was right in my face in front of company. You don't have to excuse yourself to me, not over a little gas."

"What's happening to me, Mom?"

Her mother was quiet.

When the silence continued to stretch, Diana thought, didn't she hear me? Or is she just so freaked out she doesn't want to even try to answer? She was about to ask again when her mother spoke. "Crock Pot was always supposed to be a one-way trip. A way to break matter down to its component elements and send them back through time so they could become oil. If an orange peel wasn't exactly an orange peel when it arrived back sixty-five million years ago, why would it matter? All we cared about was that whatever arrived back there was organic material that could get covered with sediment and rot away."

Rita turned toward her daughter. "Your father and I only started working on a way to bring things back because we started to get nervous. What happened to you was our nightmare scenario, but industrial accidents happened all the time, in the safest environments. What if something or someone was accidentally placed in the tube and needed to be brought back? We had barely perfected being able to do that when it was time for the test. We never thought we'd need it for the test, we knew everything in the Tachyon chamber was trash."

"What are you saying, Mom? That what came back isn't exactly me?"

"Oh, honey," Rita said, walking up and putting a hand on her face. "It's you, I can tell it's you. What I can't tell is how *much* it's you." Putting both hands on her cane, Rita lowered herself into the chair near Diana's bed. "Think about what was going on sixty-five million years ago. And think about what just happened to you. Your molecules were broken down and sent back there. You may have been streamed back while you were *inside* of something."

"Inside..." Diana remembered her dreams of running, running so fast, head near the treetops...

"And it's entirely possible that your atoms were mixed with whatever you were inside of when we re-assembled you."

Diana swallowed, taking it in. "Who did this, Mom?" She asked.

"I don't know, honey. Keyes has been asking me that for the past week."

"Who else knew about Crock Pot?"

"Your father and I, Ed Notch, who heads up Gottelle, Cordwainer Stansfield, who runs Monolithic Oil...but it was going to mean big money for them if it worked. I can't imagine any of them telling anyone else about it, let alone terrorists."

"Well," Diana said, narrowing her eyes, "somebody said something to someone."

\* \* \*

"Why weren't you at the rendezvous point?" asked their contact.

Gunter Harvack held the satellite phone to his ear, confident the signal was being scrambled. If their contact tried to trace their whereabouts, they would come up as Peking, China--at least for the next five minutes.

He, Rhonda, and Artie were in a farmhouse in the middle of nowhere, Ohio, a place between Columbus and Delaware Gunter had rented using a false name.

"The terms have changed," Gunter said.

"Your deal was extremely generous," replied their contact.

Holding up the thumb drive, Gunter studied it. So much

money in such a tiny package... "This technology is priceless," he said, then looked at Rhonda and Artie who exchanges smug grins. The silence on the other end of the phone stretched on. "Are you still there?" Gunter asked.

"This is unwise," their contact said.

"Meaning we should take this to the open market?"

"No," the contact quickly replied. "How much more are we talking about?

"I shall think it over," Gunter said, then clicked off.

* * *

"Is there any chance it was you, Miss Dunphy?" Keyes asked.

"Mr. Keyes," Rita said, a warning tone.

"I'm sorry, but the question has to be asked. Could you have let something slip to someone, anyone?"

"I had no idea what my Mom and Dad were working on," Diana said. "I didn't want to have any idea what they were working on."

"So the answer is no?"

Diana hated the question, but thought about it, really thought about it because if there was any way for Rhonda and Artie to get caught, she wanted them caught, but... "No, Mr. Keyes," she said, "there's nothing. At least there's nothing I can remember."

"All right," he said, disappointed.

"What about Rhonda's parents? Or the people pretending to be her parents?"

"By the time we got to their houses they had been cleaned out. Everyone and everything was gone. Every surface wiped clean of fingerprints. Like no one had ever been there."

"They didn't find anything? Anything of Rhonda's?"

"No."

"What about her locker at school?"

"Nothing in there either."

Then Diana remembered Rhonda's Flirt shirt still in her locker. If she could get to that T-shirt and smell it...

"Mom," Diana said, "how much longer do I have to stay here? I mean, aren't I okay?"

"One more night," Rita said, "for observation."

\* \* \*

"Do you need a sleeping pill?" Rita asked while they watched Stephen Colbert.

"Do you have one?"

"Have you been sleeping?" Rita handed her a pill.

"Some." A lie. All she could think about was her father and who killed him and why. What sleep she had gotten was light and hadn't lasted long.

Diana popped the pill and took a swallow of water, and for the first time in a long time, actually started to get drowsy. Colbert was talking to Julia Roberts about something when it all finally faded out, and then she was dreaming again.

She ran through the jungle. It was hot. The hunger was driving her crazy, until she saw what she had been chasing.

It was huge, this new creature, with a tiny, sour-faced head at one end, and a sharp, whipping tail at the other.

Between the head and the tail, all that meat! Lots and lots of meat!

And with that terrible, wonderful, sweet smell...

She roared at the moving meat, but the tail whipped up and smacked her with such force that she staggered back, almost falling. She tried to circle around, to get the sour-faced head in front of herself, but it kept its whipping tail in the way, kept moving with her, and finally the tail whipped out again, wrapping around her neck like a noose.

She couldn't breathe.

How? How was a moving pile of meat going to kill the great Tyrant King?

And when Diana awoke, her mother was gone. She panicked at first, wondering where she was. Then she took a breath, forcing herself to calm down.

*You're not a little girl anymore*, she thought, *you don't need your mommy in the middle of the night to keep the monsters away*.

Getting out of bed, Diana went to the window.

*They're out there*, she thought, *out there somewhere*. She frowned, noticing her own reflection in the window. What was up with her arms? She could see them both through the sleeves of the hospital gown, but they seemed different. Bigger. Thicker.

Rolling up her right sleeve, Diana made a fist and tensed, bringing her arm toward her shoulder in a classic bodybuilding pose.

The muscle had gotten tight, 'cut,' they'd have called it in her gym class. She checked the other arm and found it the same.

What the hell was going on?

Looking back at the window, she thought once more of Rhonda and Artie, gleefully putting a bomb on her parent's greatest triumph, obliterating her father, hurting her mother, and laughing uproariously as they sent her back to become not even a drop of oil.

Flexing her new arms, Diana thought, *I won't be the one having to worry about monsters coming after me in the middle of the night.*

*I'm the monster now.*

# CHAPTER NINE

"M om," Diana said from the bathroom when her mother walked into her hospital room, "can you close the door?"

"Why?" Rita asked, "Is everything okay?"

"Everything's okay," Diana said, "I just...I need you to look at something."

Seeing the slightly open door of the bathroom, Rita said, "Something you don't want other people to see?"

"I don't know," Diana said, a slight laugh to her voice.

Frowning, Rita backed out of the hospital room and took a look down the hall. A Homeland Security agent nodded at her. She smiled at him before the door to her daughter's room was pulled closed.

"Mom," Diana said, "I just... look at this, okay?"

*Oh, God*, Rita thought, *has she sprouted sharp, rending teeth? A long, whipping tail?* Calming herself down, she walked into the bathroom to find her daughter in her underwear, posing in front of the mirror as if she were a competitive body builder, and her physique was so tight and corded that she could have been, provided there was a lightweight division. "Diana..." Rita said.

"I know, right? I'm like some gym rat now!" Diana posed, checking herself out in the mirror. "I might not like a lot of things about this whole... thing?" Diana said. "But I like this. A lot."

"Diana, this is... extraordinary," Rita said, approaching her daughter.

"Hey, Mom, underestimate much?"

"I'll get you some clothes," Rita said.

"Like a tank top? And some bicycle pants?"

"Some nice, loose-fitting clothes," Rita replied.

"Mom?" Diana whined, drawing the name out to a two-syllable word.

"Forget it!" Rita said, wagging her finger in her Diana's face. "Until we know for sure what's going on here, low profile!" Rita walked out of the bathroom and looked back to see Diana posing again. "You want the producers of The Biggest Loser shoving you into a lab somewhere?" Rita asked. "Taking blood and tissue samples until they figure out how to bottle whatever happened to you and sell it to every fat lady in America? Stay here."

"Mom..."

"I said stay here!" Rita ordered, holding up a finger, "And stop all this... posing!"

"Yeah," Diana said, striking another pose and checking its look in the mirror, "that'll happen."

Rita sighed and shook her head, then walked back into Diana's room and stuck her head out into the hallway. The Homeland Security agent immediately looked in her direction. "You know we're leaving today?" Rita asked.

"Yes, Ma'am," the agent said.

"It just now dawned on me that my daughter doesn't really have appropriate clothing. And she's a little sensitive," Rita dropped her voice to a whisper, "about her weight. Or, more correctly, her lack of weight. Could you find a sweatshirt and some sweatpants? The looser fitting the better."

The Agent nodded and began speaking into his wrist.

Rita smiled and mouthed, 'thank you!' before ducking back into Diana's room.

They brought an Ohio State sweatshirt and a pair of sweatpants that were two sizes too big. As the nurses wheeled Diana and Rita out of the hospital, Diana pulled the sweatshirt away from herself and let it drop, then stuck her tongue out at her mother.

Smiling thinly at her daughter, Rita got into the back seat of the Homeland Security car and settled in for the drive back home.

* * *

*It sure was good to be out of there*, Diana thought, lying back on her bed in her room. She found a picture of her with her father when she was eight and they had gone on a fishing trip. It had been shoved back there by other photos; one of her and Patrice at a dance recital, another of Diana and her mother at the Golden Gate Bridge...

The photo of Diana and her father was of the two of them, smiling at the camera, a small fish on a hook between them.

Not one photo of Rhonda. How had that happened?

Diana thought about it, remembered Rhonda always ducking down or looking quickly away whenever a lens was aimed at her. "Don't," she would say, "I look awful!"

Except Rhonda never looked awful, and she knew it.

*She had been prepping*, Diana thought, *for the day after she had destroyed lives*. Rhonda hadn't wanted any pictures taken because she wanted to keep her identity as hidden as possible.

But really, what was the point? Between security cameras at McAuliffe High's entrances and hallways, yearbook photos, even the school newspaper, there would certainly be enough images of her.

Unless she changed her appearance, just enough, after the job was done. She could cut her hair, wear glasses, even got a nose job, re-shape her eyes, get chin implants, who knew what she might do with all the money she would make?

*Maybe she just didn't want ME to have a picture of her*, Diana thought. *For whatever reason. Who knows how a scumbag thinks?*

Diana studied the photo of her eight-year old self and her father for a moment. Then she moved it in front of the other pictures as her phone dinged. She picked it up.

Hey, hey! Patrice.

What's up, Crazy Woman? Diana texted.

The soap opera goes on at McAuliffe High, Patrice texted, following up with, How is it being back home?

Diana smiled with a furrowed brow. How you know we're home?

I have my ways...winking smiley Emoji.

Diana laughed, then texted, Stalk much?

So sorry about everything, Patrice texted back.

Enough with the Emojis, Diana wanted to say, but she knew it would hurt Patrice's feelings. Can't really talk about it, she typed back.

Just glad you're okay. Thumbs Up Emoji.

Thanks.

I always knew she was a B-word!

*Yeah*, Diana thought, *you sure called that one right, honey*. But she didn't type anything.

After a minute, Patrice texted: Someone at school has been asking about you, with a mouth to ear Emoji.

Diana frowned. Who?

Wouldn't you like to know?

A guy? Diana typed.

A small picture of Justin Bieber appeared, looking soulfully at the camera, lips puffed out.

Very funny, Diana texted

Someone a lot cuter! Patrice texted back, no Emoji that time, meaning her friend was serious now.

Who? Diana texted.

Not gonna tell!

Why not?

'Cause you could use a pleasant surprise. Diana sighed.

\* \* \*

"When do you think I can go back to school?" Diana asked later, as Rita slid two barely cooked hamburgers onto a plate.

"I don't know, honey," Rita said, presenting the burgers, "why don't you take it easy for a while?"

Diana greedily ate the burgers, then licked the plate clean. She looked at her mother. "How long of a while?"

Rita looked at her daughter, nodding. "How about we wait at least till I get some idea how much barely cooked beef I should pack in your lunch? You know, do I pack it in a paper bag or a five gallon bucket?"

"Mom..." Diana said.

"And anyway, since when are you in such a hurry to get back to school?"

"My friends are all there, I want 'em to know I'm okay." A lie. All she could think about was getting to Rhonda's old shirt in her locker. To take a whiff. See if she could track her down.

*Track her down. And then what?* Diana thought.

It was as if another voice answered, a voice deeper, rougher... *Then... you KNOW what!*

"Can't you talk to them on Facebook or something?" Rita asked.

Snapping out of it, Diana said, "You don't talk to people on Facebook, Mom."

"You know what I mean."

Diana sighed.

"I made you an appointment with a therapist," Rita said. "Her name is Dr. Siddons. She's one of the best child psychologists..."

"Mom!" Diana said.

"What?"

"I'm not a child!"

Rita sighed. "You're under eighteen..."

"I'm sixteen," Diana said. "Sixteen is not a child!"

"Well, you're *my* child..."

Diana sighed. "Mom!"

"...and I want you to see Dr. Siddons!"

"I don't need any child psychologist. I need to get back to school and..."

"I want you here, okay?" Rita said, looking at the carpet. "I don't want you...out in the world. I just want you here with me. Just for a little while, all right?"

"All right," she said in surrender. *When Mom really wanted something*, Diana thought, *she was always going to get it. She was kinda like Dad in that way.*

* * *

"How are you doing today, Diana?" Dr. Siddons asked.

*She's short,* Diana thought, *diminutive might even be the better word. Was she a successful child psychologist because she wasn't much bigger than most of her clients?*

*Claws in now,* Diana corrected herself, an image of a Patrice cat Emoji in her mind's eye...

"Mom says you're one of the best child psychologists around," Diana said.

"That's very nice of her," replied the doctor. She smiled, and it was very warm.

Diana, however, didn't feel very warm. "I'm sure it's very nice to hear, but I'm not sure how to take it. My mom thinking I'm still a child."

"To a mother or a father, their child is most likely always seen as a child," Dr. Siddons said. "When you're thirty-five, your mother will still be saying, 'there's my child.' "

"Okay, but still...why didn't I rate a regular psychologist?"

That warm smile again. "It's not as if I haven't seen adult patients, it's just that I specialize in..."

"Children?"

"I think of them as..." She looked up as if calculating, then back to Diana. "Young people."

"What's the youngest patient you've ever had?"

"Four."

"Four?" Diana laughed. "What kind of problems could a four-year-old have that would send them to..."

Diana saw Dr. Siddons get very sad. *Great job there, Clueless,* she thought. *What kind of problems could a four-year-old have that would send them to a psychologist? Really, really bad ones, what else?*

"I can't really talk about that," Dr. Siddons said. "What I can talk about is you. How are you doing?"

"I'm okay," Diana answered.

"How are you feeling? About your father?"

"Crappy," Diana said.

"Crappy how?"

"Pissed off."

"Were you and your father on good terms?"

"I don't know."

"Did you talk?"

"Not much."

"How often?"

"I didn't talk to him as much as was possible to not talk to him was how much I didn't talk to him." Diana said.

Dr. Siddons nodded.

Diana felt tears coming. "And then he wanted me to come to his demo and I did, and look what happened! Everything went to Hell. And he died, and what do I say to him now?"

"What would you say to him if you could?"

"I can't!"

"But if you could..."

"That I was really sorry. That I'd try to be a better daughter."

"I'm very sorry for your loss. But I'm sure you were a good daughter."

Diana shook her head. "I wasn't."

"Children from divorced families...there can be a lot of anger."

"He died saving me and my Mom and probably a lot of other people too! He could have just run out with us, but he didn't. Instead of that, he tried to get rid of the bomb."

And there it was. In spite of everything, Dad had died saving her and her mother, and what had she ever done for him?

"I'm so sorry," Dr. Siddons said, "have you been sleeping?"

"Yes. No. Well, sometimes..."

"Any bad dreams?"

*Sure, Doc*, Diana thought, *I dream I'm a dinosaur. And not only that, I actually might be one, in some weird way.*

"No," Diana said, trying to make it sound good. "At least, none that I can remember. Sometimes I wake up thinking I dreamt something, but I can't remember what it was."

"What about eating?"

Diana froze. For some reason, she couldn't even look at Dr. Siddons now. "What do you mean?" she asked.

"Have you been eating?"

*Did raw ground meat count?* "Sometimes I eat fine, other times no."

"Do you think you can go back to school?"

"I—I think so. I don't know."

"Do you think you'd be ready for other students talking about you, about what happened? Asking you all kinds of questions? Some about your dad, some about these people who were pretending to not only be friends of yours but friends of theirs?"

Looking down, Diana said, "If you put it that way, that could be kind of bad. You know—" but she couldn't say anything else. She didn't know why.

"What?" Dr. Siddons asked.

"They fooled all those people, all my friends, all their teachers, a big two-year long game they played, and it was all because of me."

"I think that's making a bit of a leap. Remember, your Mom and Dad were..."

"My Mom is and my Dad was smart, both of them trying to do this big thing, they had this big smart plan to improve the world. How did they end up with someone like me for a daughter? That's what I'd like to know."

Diana didn't realize she'd been crying until Dr. Siddons handed her a box of tissues. "What am I supposed to do now?" she asked, taking one.

"What do you think you should do?" Dr. Siddons asked in reply.

"Lay low. Keep out of sight, stay away from people," she said, before immediately closing her eyes.

*What was it with me?* Diana thought. *I want to go back to school! Why can't I just keep my mouth shut?*

# CHAPTER TEN

"This is a nice one," Rita said, looking at the caskets.

*And just what are I supposed to say to that?* Diana thought.

They were at the Parker and Kent funeral home in North Columbus. The casket was a sort of silver blue, with a four-thousand dollar price tag.

"Mom," Diana said quietly.

"We can have the ceremony this Friday," Rita said, "at the Pinegold cemetery. You can see Gotelle from there."

"Mom," Diana repeated, walking to a small pine box, the cheapest casket on the floor, at six hundred fifty dollars.

"I think he'd have liked that," Rita said, "it was where he was most comfortable, where he was happiest."

Diana turned around, finally facing her mother. "Mom," she said once more.

"Yes, Diana?"

"Mom...are you sure you want to do this?"

"Yes," she answered.

"There's...nothing to bury."

Rita nodded, a slight twitch at the corner of her mouth.

"And...we're talking about a lot of money, aren't we? Just to bury...what? An empty box?"

Jane Kent, the heavyset, brunette funeral director, hair shot with grey and a pencil behind her ear, cleared her throat. "What sometimes has been done," Jane said, "in cases like this, is, uh...a suit of the decedent's clothing."

"Oh," Diana said, "the decedent. What a nice word. Almost sounds like a profession, you know, 'what do you do for a living?' 'Well, actually, I don't do anything at all for a living, I'm a decedent.' "

"Diana," Rita said, a warning tone.

Diana turned to the funeral director. "A suit of clothing?" she asked.

"Yes. And a picture?" The funeral director looked from Diana to Rita. "An eight by ten perhaps?"

"What, sticking out of the buttoned up shirt collar of the suit?" Diana asked.

"Diana, that's enough," her mother admonished.

"No, really," Diana asked, "can we get photos of his hands while we're at it? Have them sticking out of the empty sleeves?"

"Diana, stop it!" Rita commanded.

Pointing at the cheapest casket, Diana said, "If you're going to do this, for God's sake, at least pick the cheapest one."

"Oh, come on," Rita said, "look at that thing, it's just a pine box!"

"Yeah," Diana said, "and your problem with that is...?"

"It's just a pine box!"

"Mom, he won't be in there! And even if he was, he wouldn't know the difference!"

"It's so...primitive! It looks like what Moses was buried in!"

"Moses?" Diana asked.

"Well, actually, Moses was buried in a cave on Mt. Nebo, not a box, but... "

Diana sighed loudly.

"What I mean is it's ancient!" Her mother said.

"Mom!"

"It is!"

"It's a casket to bury a suit of clothing and a photo!"

As if on cue, Craig Farkus came down the stairs carrying something wrapped in burlap. All three women turned to him. He looked from Rita, to Jane Kent, and then to Diana before asking, "Did I come at a bad time?"

"Oh, thank you, Craig," Rita said, walking toward him, "is that it?"

"Uh...yeah," he replied as Rita put her arms out for the burlap wrapped package.

"It's kind of heavy," Craig said.

"What's kind of heavy?" Diana asked.

"Did you have trouble getting it?"

"No, the investigators already cleared that part, and..."

"What's heavy?" Diana repeated.

"It's okay," Rita said, still holding her arms out.

"You sure?" Craig asked.

"What's heavy, God damn it?" Diana didn't realize she'd yelled until it was already out of her mouth.

Craig, Rita, and Jane Kent all looked in her direction. Then Rita turned to Craig and nodded. He handed over the burlap wrapped object.

Walking over to Diana, Rita unwrapped the top. It was a terribly twisted, burned and melted piece of metal. "Titanium," Rita said quietly, "from the top of the Tachyon Chamber. From Crock Pot."

Diana nodded, knowing what was coming, but not wanting to admit it. "Okay," was all she could come up with.

"That's... ?" asked Jane Kent.

Rita nodded.

"Could we take that to... ?" Jane Kent asked.

"Take it where?" Diana asked. "Back to the funeral parlor so you can...what? Embalm it?"

Rita turned to Craig, handing over the titanium. "Could you... ?" she said to Craig, who nodded and turned to Jane Kent, who motioned for him to follow.

Rita stood with her daughter for a moment, first looking at the floor, and then into Diana's eyes. "I want someplace," she said.

"You want someplace?" Diana asked. "Someplace for what?"

"Someplace I can go. To remember your father. And I think you do, too. You may not realize it now, but you do. Or you will."

"And you think burying a piece of metal burned and twisted by the creeps who killed him, you think that's going to help?"

"I do," Rita said.

"Mom..."

"It will help me."

"This is not what Dad would have wanted."

"How do you know what he would have wanted?"

"Okay," Diana said, "this is going to cost, what? Four thousand dollars? Six thousand? Ten thousand? Dad was way too cheap to not have been horrified by what you want to do. My God, if there had been a body, he'd have wanted to be cremated and spread over the back yard, just to save money!"

"There will be a grave marker," Rita said, "with his name on it..."

"And a piece of the crime scene those miserable, awful people were responsible for, buried under it!"

"You can't think of it that way!"

"Then what way should I think of it, Mom?"

"It was his dream."

"No, it's the exploded, twisted remnant of his dream!"

"It's what we have, honey."

Diana took a deep breath and shook her head. "If you're doing this," she said, "you're doing it on your own." She walked out of the casket room.

"Diana," Rita called, but her daughter was already outside and walking. She watched her daughter's shrinking figure.

"Mrs. Dunphy?" Jane Kent asked softly.

Still watching after Diana, Rita said, "Yes?"

"Do you still want to, uh...proceed?"

"Yes," Rita said. "Please proceed."

The funeral director nodded and walked away. Rita opened the glass doors to the outside world and got into her car.

\* \* \*

It didn't take long to catch up to Diana, who was walking, head down, arms folded beneath her chest. Rita rolled down the car's passenger side window. "Get in the car," she called.

Diana kept walking.

"Come on, Diana, get in."

Rita continued cruising slowly next to her daughter. "You're going to freeze me out over this?" Rita asked.

"I'm not freezing you out."

"Then what are you doing?"

"I'm walking."

"Okay," Rita said, "well, then I'm cruising."

Diana gave a little laugh, shaking her head.

"Cruising for daughters," Rita said. "You seen any daughters around here might need a halfway decent mother?"

Diana rolled her eyes and stopped walking. Her mother stopped the car. "You're a whole lot better than halfway decent," Diana said. Then she got in the car, and they drove off.

\* \* \*

Diana looked at herself in the full-length mirror.

She had on a black blouse and short black jacket. Her black leather skirt was also short. Too short, she knew her mom would say, but if they were really going to do a fake funeral, she wanted at least some good part of what had happened to be on display.

Rita opened the door, looked at Diana, then said, "You're not wearing that."

"Yes, I am," said Diana.

Rita wordlessly went to Diana's closet and picked out a black pair of slacks. She held them out to Diana, who crossed her arms beneath her chest.

They each stood there for a moment, intractable.

"Diana," Rita finally said in a warning tone.

"No," Diana replied, shaking her head. "You want me to go to this thing, fine, I'm going to your quasi-funeral. But this is the way I'm going."

"You can't."

"Why not?"

"You know perfectly well why not."

"No, I don't."

"Diana, in that outfit, with your legs, it makes you look like..."

"Makes me look like what?"

"Like some dirty old man's Lolita fantasy."

"Some dirty old man's who fantasy?"

"You never read Lolita? Or saw any of the movies? Never mind, that's probably a good thing, plus never mind, you're not wearing that, it's your father's funeral, and..."

"It's a piece of metal's funeral."

"And we want the attention on him, not on you."

Diana looked at her mother for a moment. "You know, you don't get everything you want," she said. "You and Dad, you think you always get everything you want, well, no one gets everything they want. You want that," Diana said, flicking her chin to indicate the outside world, "well, I want this."

Eyes still locked with her daughter, Rita lowered the slacks. "Fine," she said, hooking the coat hanger back on the rack in Diana's crowded closet. "Fine! Whatever! Every guy's tongue can hang out while we read the eulogy."

"Every guy's tongue is not going to hang out."

"Right," Rita said, walking out, "like you know."

\* \* \*

"Damn," said Len Marcus, one of the Homeland Security agents assigned to guard the house, as he watched Rita and Diana get into the car, "you gotta see this."

The other agent, Ken Brantley, looked over and whistled. "Girl's got some legs on her," he said, "that's for sure. Better start the car."

"Wait," Marcus said, staring.

"Oh, come on," said Brantley, "she's, what? Fourteen?"

"Yeah, yeah, sorry."

Marcus started the car and they followed after, all the way to the cemetery, parking at a discreet enough distance that they could watch over everything. "You know," Brantley said, "you have to look at the whole area for potential threats."

"Right," Marcus said, still staring.

"The Dunphy girl's skirt isn't a potential threat."

He watched Diana standing at the gravesite. "If that isn't a threat, I don't know what is," Marcus replied.

* * *

Diana's father's parents had died before she was born, and her grandparents on her mother's side, who both suffered from dementia, were in assisted living, but the funeral would have been sparsely attended regardless. Craig Farkus showed up, along with some people Diana didn't recognize. Patrice and her mother showed up just in time, and her friend looked her up and down before giving her a big 'okay' sign.

Diana rolled her eyes and smiled.

Rita looked around, checked her watch, and then said, "Thank you, all of you, for coming. This won't be a long speech. As many of you know, Aaron was the talker in the family..." that got a few small laughs, "but this has been a very hard time for my daughter and I, as I'm sure you can appreciate. But we just wanted to have this little ceremony to...commemorate Aaron and his work."

*Commemorate him?* Diana thought. As her mother continued to speak, Diana backed away, words like 'dedication,' and 'forthrightness' wafting out of the din of Rita's speech.

Seeing her back away, Patrice moved forward, but Diana held her hand out in a warding off gesture. Turning around, Diana looked out at Gotelle, and past it, to the city and beyond.

*They're out there*, Diana thought.

She put her hand on a nearby headstone as if for balance.

Perhaps her mother was right about a funeral, but seeing Gottelle from where they were wasn't a comfort, just a reminder of how and why he had died. They were in sight of her father's dream, but the dream, the hard work and dedication, had been turned to poison.

*They* had turned the dream into a nightmare.

*They're out there. The people who did this.*

The rage built in her, stoked by her mother's speech, the people standing around, the casket with the wrecked metal waiting to be lowered into the ground...

That piece of tortured titanium, the remains of the work of genius that they had blithely destroyed before skipping off, giggling. It meant nothing to them, the end of more than just her father's life, but of what he had lived for.

And her? Who and what was she, Diana, now? What had they made when they had stuck her in that chamber only to have her parents bring her back?

But had they brought her back? Or had they brought back something else?

The rage built, and then something gave way.

The right edge of the tombstone Diana held in her hand fell away, crushed in her grip. She looked down at her hand, now coated in a fine, grey powder.

* * *

"Hey," Marcus said.

"Hey, what?" muttered Brantley, intent on the Facebook page he'd accessed on his smart phone.

"The Dunphy girl..."

"Will you stop staring at her? It's creepy."

"I'm not! I mean, I am, it's just..."

"Just what? Knock it off!"

"I think she just...crushed a tombstone."

"What?" asked Brantley, watching the scene.

But now Diana was walking back to join the group.

"Don't you see it?" asked Marcus, passing over the binoculars. "That corner of that tombstone."

"What corner of what tombstone?"

"That one, right there, by the tree?"

He took the binoculars away from his face. "They're all by the tree!"

"You don't see the one with the corner broken off?

Brantley gave the binoculars back. "I don't see anything but a bunch of old tombstones."

"She broke off the end of it!"

"She didn't break off the end of anything, maybe something fell off on account of it being so old, ever think of that?" Brantley went back to his phone.

"I *saw* her!"

"You saw her, okay, great, now shut up."

Marcus frowned, putting the binoculars back up to his face. Maybe his partner was right, after all. Maybe it had just been some old masonry, finally giving way.

Diana watched the casket being lowered into the ground.

Her mother took the first handful of grave soil and tossed it in to the grave. It made a hollow tap on the coffin's lid.

Everyone looked expectantly at Diana. She looked back at them, confused. When they kept staring, she asked, "What?"

"Do you want to—" her mother asked, indicating the soil.

Giving a small nod, Diana walked up and grabbed a handful

of soil. She stood over the grave for a moment. "Piece of twisted, busted-up metal," Diana said, "you meant so much to me. I only wish we could have had more time before you became a piece of twisted, busted-up metal, before you..."

The open grave swam before her eyes. Why was she having trouble seeing it all of a sudden? What was happening?

It all came rushing in: the time she had wasted, the time she could have been with him instead of angry with him and holding out, knowing he wanted to see her.

Diana wasn't even conscious of the first huge sobs to escape her, didn't even know about the tears leaking down her face.

Rita watched her stand there, crying, the grave soil in her hand, and then walked up, taking her daughter by the shoulder and leading her away.

"No, no," Diana said, turning away from her mother with surprising strength. Walking back to the edge of the grave, she tossed in the soil. It landed in one crushed together mass on the casket's lid, and then she went back to her mother.

For the first time, Diana was conscious that a tight hug could hurt her mother, and so she let Rita hug her instead. They walked all the way back to the car that way, Rita holding her wounded daughter.

# CHAPTER ELEVEN

D iana was in her room, still staring at the ceiling, when her smart phone dinged.

What did you do to your legs? Patrice.

Nothing, Diana texted back.

Can you teach me how to do nothing?

Diana shook her head. You have very nice legs, she texted back.

I have big, fat thighs, Patrice texted.

Will you stop it? You're NOT fat!

Doesn't matter. Someone's coming to SEE you! Harry Stiles photo.

Harry Stiles isn't coming to see me, Diana texted.

Someone better!

Eye roll, Diana texted. Then her mother knocked on the door. "You can come in, Mom," Diana said.

Rita opened the door. Diana noticed she was using the door-knob to lean on.

"Leg still hurt?" Diana asked.

"Little bit," Rita answered.

Diana sat up.

"It's okay, honey, really. I'm fine. Just wanted to tell you someone's here to see you."

"Who?"

"Some young man."

"A young man?" Now Diana stood up.

"I thought that would get your attention."

"Mom..."

"He's on the front porch."

Diana picked up her phone, texted 'later!' to Patrice and headed downstairs.

The phone dinged. Told ya, it said, with a silhouette Emoji of a boy and girl kissing.

* * *

*Who's the tall guy?* Diana thought as she opened the front door.

Once he turned around, she saw it was Rhonda's old boyfriend Chuck Leadingham.

She and Chuck had never really talked all that much, because really, what did you say to the hottest guy in school who was also involved with your best friend?

*Only now*, Diana thought, *she's your former best friend, who was never actually your best friend, but some twenty-eight-year-old terrorist-for-hire witch from England.*

Diana immediately thought to correct that statement. What Rhonda was only rhymed with 'witch.'

"Hi," Chuck said, "I brought you some, uh..." he had some magazines rolled up in his hand. Diana smiled slightly at the covers of *People, Glamor, Self*, all the magazines a guy would think a girl would want to read. "I was really sorry to hear about your Dad," he said.

"Thanks," Diana said softly. Not really knowing what to say, she just stood there.

"Can you take a walk?" Chuck asked.

"Yeah, okay," she said, then opened the door, waiting till he turned away before sticking her tongue out to smell him. "Mom," Diana shouted as she opened the door and threw the magazines inside, "I'm going for a walk!" She slammed the door shut before her mother had a chance to reply.

Chuck was quiet for a while. Then he said, "I'm sorry to even be here, with your Dad gone and all, and if you want me to go, I will, except there are a lot of things that have been bothering me lately, and I just didn't know who to talk to about it except for you."

"Is this about Rhonda?"

"Yeah," he said, as if he were surrendering something he hadn't quite wanted to surrender. "You know, she and I were so, you know, breaking up and getting back together all the time, and now, knowing what was going on, now I just feel like she was laughing at me, this high school boy. Not to mention it kinda grosses me out that she was almost thirty, I mean, I never would have known. Plus even though she put me through all that stuff, I still feel like I miss her or something."

They walked for a while, passing a lawn sprinkler that had wetted down the whole sidewalk in front of them. They waited while the water passed toward the lawn, and then Diana said, "I'm sorry, I just don't know what to say to you. But if it makes you feel any better, she fooled us all. I mean, the stuff I told her? You know, the stuff you tell to a best friend? And to have her do what she did with it? Use it to hurt me, hurt my family?"

A FedEx truck rumbled past.

"She killed my Dad," Diana said, "almost killed my Mom. I'm not supposed to say too much about it to anyone, but, I'll tell you it all sucks, the whole thing. And I wish I had something better to say to you than that, but I don't."

Chuck was quiet for a while. "She ever tell you anything about me?" he finally asked.

There was a minute when Diana almost said, "I can't tell you any of that! She was one of my best..." and then she had to suppress a laugh. *Besties*, Diana thought, *right*.

"She said she thought you were...a really nice guy, that you were hot..." and really good at sex, except Diana didn't say that, him being, like, sixteen or seventeen, and her being twenty-eight, and really, if you thought about it, just pretty much using him. Diana knew if an older guy had sex with a girl under eighteen it was considered a rape even if the girl was willing, but if it was an older woman having sex with a guy under eighteen, was that a rape, too?

But then it started to creep her out, all that breaking up and getting back together that the two of them did. Was Rhonda just into having a hot, younger guy? And then, when it was over, thinking they didn't have anything to talk about, telling him to get lost because she was like, old enough to be his mother? Well, old enough to be his mother if she had him when she was twelve and gave him up for adoption.

*And if she didn't have anything to talk about with him,* Diana thought, *what did she have to talk about with me, who she pretty much had no choice but to talk to as part of her job? How silly and stupid I must have seemed to her, blathering on about where*

*I wanted to go to college, what I wanted to do when I got out of college, guys I liked or didn't like... and there was Rhonda, all smiling and listening patiently all the while looking for a way to get to my mother and father, to stop the great experiment.*

Now she, Diana, was the great experiment.

"I should have kicked that Artie Urlin's ass when I had the chance," Chuck said, pulling Diana out of it. He stopped walking, so Diana did, too. "Do you think the two of them, Artie and her, were..?"

"Who knows, Chuck?" she answered. "The truth is, I don't know, and I don't want to know. And you'll be a lot better off once you don't want to know, either."

"Yeah? When's that gonna be?"

"You'll get there. There'll be a day when this will just be a memory of some weird thing that happened when you were sixteen."

"Seventeen, and what, I'll be some dad with a beer gut driving my kids around and that's when I'll forget about it?'

She wanted to say, well, heck, Chuck at least you'll have kids, I'll probably be laying eggs, then sitting on top of 'em like a chicken till they hatch. Yeah, won't that be nice? Her Mother wouldn't ever have to bake brownies or cookies, she could just throw the grandkids a chipmunk or a mouse every now and then for their special treat.

"I don't think you'll have a beer gut," Diana said.

"Not if I don't drink beer." For a minute, it looked like he was thinking about something. He started walking again. "And how do you get through life if you don't drink beer?" he asked.

Diana was going to argue with him, except the more she thought about it, the more it seemed a legitimate question.

* * *

Rita signed for the envelope and the FedEx man nodded, got back in his truck, and pulled away.

Tearing away the sealing strip, Rita sat on the front porch and read the report.

When she was finished, she closed her eyes and put her hand to her mouth, something she would never have done if Diana had been with her when the envelope arrived. As it was, she could see her daughter down the street, talking to the tall young man. She saw him wave and walk off, watched Diana look after him before moving down the street toward her.

"What's going on?" Diana asked.

Rita held up the envelope. "Your DNA test, honey."

Diana looked stricken, just for the tiniest of moments, but covered up by clapping her hands and jumping up and down. "Oh, great!" she said, "like opening presents at Christmas!"

* * *

"Montana, two thousand five," Rita said later in the kitchen, handing her daughter a cup of tea, "some preserved soft tissue from a Tyrannosaurus Rex is found in a cave. They make some genetic tests..." she held up an envelope, "of which I got some copies. They find T. Rex DNA is very similar to that of, uh...the DNA of an ostrich."

"Ostrich," Diana said, "great."

"Now," Rita went on, holding up another envelope, "your DNA and T. Rex DNA show a lot of common genetic markers."

Something about just hearing that, flat out, calmed Diana down somehow.

"So," Diana said, "I finally have something more in common with ostriches than skinny legs, huh?"

"Your legs aren't skinny anymore," Rita stated, "judging from the stares you got at the funeral."

"Mom," she asked.

"Yes, honey?"

"Do you think I can be cured?"

The question hung in the air.

"Honey," Rita said, sliding her chair up next to Diana's and taking her daughter's hand. "We've talked about this. I'm not the genius your father was. Re-creating the Tachyon Chamber, it would take years, and more dollar bills than anyone can count. Not to mention that it's a miracle we got you back at all. Science says it's impossible to manipulate the DNA of a mature organism..."

"Mom," Diana said, facing her mother again, "I watch cartoon network, I still have a teddy bear, and my favorite movie is The Princess Diaries. I'm hardly a mature organism."

"What I'm trying to tell you is we shouldn't look a gift horse —or a gift dinosaur—in the mouth."

"Some gift."

Rita hugged her daughter.

"Even if we could rebuild Crock Pot, and even if we could send you back through, even with what we know now, there wouldn't be a way to control how, or even if, you'd come back. What I'm trying to say is, I think...this is you, now."

Diana could hear her mother's heartbeat, could feel the blood rushing around in her veins. She stuck her tongue out, smelling her mother's good, meaty smell.

Alligators ate their own young, and even though everybody said dinosaurs were mainly like birds, Diana didn't feel anything like a bird, she felt more like an alligator, and hoped she wouldn't be the first alligator who, instead of eating its young, ate its own mother.

Yet her tongue stayed out, smelling the aroma...

"Current research says dinosaurs were a lot like birds, but

they shared traits with lizards, too," Rita said. "Did you know lizards smell by sticking out their tongues?"

Diana immediately put her tongue back into her mouth.

Rita broke the hug, looking her daughter in the eye. "And they think the T. Rex could smell its prey from miles away. And then run after it. At close to sixty miles an hour. Imagine something that big moving at sixty miles an hour."

"You telling me to join the track team?"

Rita gave a little laugh, then shook her head. "No," she said, standing up, taking the tea mugs to the sink, "I am not telling you to join the track team."

A slow smile spread across Diana's face while her mother looked away. *Okay, Mom,* she thought, *no track team.*

*But it's about time I did some running.*

# CHAPTER TWELVE

Diana went to bed at eight thirty. Although she really did her best to sleep, at first she couldn't.

After about twenty minutes, she did fall under, and soon dreamt again.

Head once more near the treetops, she roared, telling all that she was in charge.

She could hear them answer, some with bleating screams, others with low bellows, some scattering through the underbrush, tiny and unseen, others lifting up their heads on their long necks before moving away as quickly as they could.

But how quick would that be, with the very earth moving when they walked?

Diana roared again, and then she heard another sound in the jungle, a human voice, soft yet insistent, calling her name, "Diana?"

And when Diana looked down, she saw her.

It was her mother, she could tell even from thirty feet up. Her mother stood there with an apron on, hands on hips.

"Young lady," her mother said, "it's time for dinner, you get down here this instant."

She said it the way she had said it to Diana when she was a child and hadn't come down the first few times her mother called because she was too busy playing with Colorforms, Spirographs, or Barbies.

When Diana tried to answer her mother, tried to say, "Coming, Mom!" all that came out was another roar.

She wanted to be a good daughter, but couldn't do what was asked of her, not in the jungle, even though she was moving forward now, coming toward her mother, lowering her great head while Rita stood there, unafraid.

"Diana," her mother said, the way she said it when she was frustrated with her daughter because she had just finger painted the walls or broken a glass.

Yes, mom, Diana wanted to reply, but as her lips pulled back from her steak-knife teeth, all Diana could think was, *I will not eat my own mother, I will not eat my own mother...*

Diana woke.

Sitting up in bed, a huge, hitching breath tore its way out of her throat. It took her a moment to calm down and check the alarm clock.

Eleven twenty-two.

Getting out of bed, Diana walked downstairs and parted the picture window curtains. Outside, the Homeland Security car was parked in front of the house. It looked like one agent was sleeping while the other was drinking out of a thermos.

Walking back upstairs, Diana changed into some bike shorts and a T-shirt, then got a hoodie out of the closet before looking in on her mother, who was sleeping with a red, frilly sleep mask on.

Going back to her bedroom, Diana climbed out of her

window, which led her behind the house. Hopping over the fence, she got through her neighbor's backyard and onto the sidewalk. She headed for school at a slow jog.

When she got to the school, she wasn't even out of breath, and it was a good two miles away. Now looking at McAuliffe High, it looked smaller somehow.

*How long had it been since I was here last?* Diana thought. *A week? Two weeks?*

*Sixty-five million years?*

She picked up a rock and broke one of the windows in the front door. She reached in, pressing the bar to open the door.

At her locker, she spun the dial on the combination and found the shirt at the bottom of a pile of books, pencils, and crammed-in papers.

Putting the shirt to her face, Diana stuck her tongue out and took a deep breath.

It was a little confusing since she, Diana, had briefly worn the shirt, and Rhonda's actual scent was mixed with her perfume, but then, it became like focusing the lens of a camera. All of a sudden she got it. She had Rhonda's smell, picked out under her own smell, and under the perfume. There it was.

She stuffed the shirt back into her locker and slammed it closed.

Standing there for a minute, Diana closed her eyes, trying to pick Rhonda's scent out, and she caught it, faintly, just faintly on the breeze.

Could she still be in the city? Diana headed for the door where she'd broken the window, but flattened herself against the wall once she heard the squawk of a police radio and saw the cruiser glide past.

\* \* \*

"Silent alarms," said officer DeMarco as officer Stutz put the cruiser in park and they got out. "Every damn thing sets 'em off. What do you think? Raccoon or opossum?" They approached the door. "I'm bettin' on opossum."

Stutz was already shining his flashlight in through the broken window. "Not this time," he said.

They opened the door. When Stutz swept his light across the hallway, he caught a furtive movement. "Is that a..."

"Freeze!" DeMarco yelled. "Put your hands where I can see 'em!"

But Diana was already running down the hall.

"Halt!" Stutz yelled.

The hoodie flew off Diana's head while they yelled again, "Halt!" She looked back once, but when she turned back around, it was as if another chained exit door was suddenly just *there*.

Diana slammed her body against it, taking the door completely off its hinges. She landed on top of it, prone, and slid a good ten feet, as if she had been on a surfboard.

Shocked now, Diana thought, *Am I really that strong?* Then she was up and running, the door sliding back as she took off.

Arriving at the doorway, DeMarco's reaction to the torn-off door was open-mouthed shock. Stutz, seeing Diana was almost off school property, said "C'mon!" Stutz ran back through the hallway to their car.

"She's sure..." DeMarco said.

"C'mon, damn it!" Stutz called.

"Going fast!" said DeMarco, running after his partner.

"Get back here, my Grandma moves faster than you!" Stutz called.

By the time DeMarco and Stutz got back to their cruiser, Diana was well off school property.

"Halt!" she could hear them on their bullhorn, or on their

microphone, or whatever they had, could hear the car's engine pick up speed, so she just kept going as fast as she could.

In the squad car, Stutz watched the speedometer climb past thirty-five, past forty, past forty-five. He tapped his partner on the shoulder.

"If you're trying to tell me this kid is really freakin' fast..." DeMarco said, "I already know!"

DeMarco floored it.

The word "Halt!" crackled electronically from the squad car, but Diana didn't slow down. *No way am I getting arrested*, Diana thought. *Mom would kill me!*

She tugged the hoodie back up in time to hear Stutz say, "You see that? It's a chick!"

"Halt!" they called again and then swung the car ahead of Diana, directly into her path. They opened their doors and got out their Tasers.

Diana jumped.

Her foot landed in the middle of the squad car's hood, denting it in. Springing off, she landed on the other side of the cop car and kept on running.

"Did you see that?" Diana heard one of the cops yell. "Did you see that?"

"Yeah, I saw it," DeMarco said, "get..." He got in the car but the engine wouldn't turn over. "You gotta be kidding me, you gotta be *kidding* me..."

Stutz opened the hood and saw an engine smashed almost flat. "Hey, DeMarco," Stutz said.

"Yeah?" DeMarco tried the ignition again.

"Give it a rest, huh?"

\* \* \* \* \*

Diana was still running as hard as she could, still smelling Rhonda on the air, trying to get closer to her.

And she was getting hungry. She don't know if it was all the exercise, or all the excitement, or what it was. When she saw something moving up ahead, she immediately stopped in a crouch.

It was a raccoon, a nice, big, fat one, looking at her, about to go back through a sewer grate. She moved toward it without even thinking, catching it by the scruff of its neck before it got back in the sewer. It snarled and scratched at her, pulling one of its claws down her cheek, but Diana barely felt it. She headed into the bushes, where, in some deep, barely conscious part of her mind, she hoped she'd be hidden.

When she was done and had thrown the raccoon bones out onto the grass, she felt physically better than she had in a long time.

Why, then, did she suddenly feel so sad and angry?

*Maybe because you just killed and then ate a raccoon?* Diana thought.

She sank to her knees, panicked.

"Okay," she whispered to herself, "okay, keep it together, you're not a freak, you're not a freak..."

*Right*, Diana thought, *not a freak. 'Cause freaks don't eat raccoons!*

She stuck out her tongue and kept after Rhonda's scent. It got stronger and stronger as she neared the city.

Diana never realized, living where she lived, how nice everything was. *No matter what anybody said*, she thought, *the suburbs were the place to be.* Once she got to the bridge that went downtown, Diana made sure no one was around, then ran across it.

She didn't know whether to feel bad or good about getting across faster running than she would have in a car.

Rhonda's smell was stronger across the bridge, and it was

driving her crazy. *What was this, anyway, this excitement?* she thought, *the thrill of the hunt? It made sense. Aren't I now, at least in part, one of the greatest hunters that ever stalked the Earth?*

*Keep it together*, Diana thought, *I'm lucky that Rhonda, and hopefully those other creeps, are still in town, only who knew how long they'd stay in town?*

*Have to get them before they leave!*

The smell was even stronger as she ran out of the city and into the countryside.

Buildings thinned out. Roads became less paved.

The scent got even stronger.

Diana stopped, tongue out. She could see it, just near the horizon. A small farmhouse...

That was it! Rhonda was there!

Diana began to run again.

She had to be there, but her smell was mixed with another one. There was someone else with her, and Diana hoped to God it was Artie.

Getting closer to the building, she heard voices.

"...Zurich," somebody said, a guy. Was it Artie? "Where in Zurich? Yes, I know how much it's worth, everyone knows how much it's worth, everyone but, until recently, the three of us..."

And then something was pressed to the back of Diana's head, something cold and round. "Do not move," said someone with an accent. "Do not even breathe. And then someone's hands ran quickly over her, searching for a gun, she supposed.

*Yeah, right*, Diana thought, *like I'd even know how to shoot a gun, let alone have one with me.*

"Turn around," the person said, and Diana obeyed, her hands up. It was a tall guy in a long coat, holding a large gun.

Rhonda stepped up beside the tall guy, smirking. In an English accent, Rhonda said, "I can't believe it!"

"Nice accent, Rhonda," Diana shot back, "trying out for the school play? I didn't know they were doing 'My Fair Lady' this year."

Rhonda laughed as she came closer. She was dressed in a leather motorcycle jacket and jeans, wearing a blonde wig, her eyes all done up punk-like. "How ever did you get out?" she asked. "I should think you would be a tiny, little drop of oil by now. She found a way to bring you back, your mother?"

"My father," Diana said.

"Your father *survived?*"

"Till your bomb killed him!"

Rhonda smiled at Diana, that same ugly smile she had when she left her in Crock Pot and waved. "Looking for your revenge, is that it? How very 'Hamlet.' Diana, really, you hated your father, I should think you'd be thanking me."

Forgetting everything, Diana ran right at Rhonda.

And Gunter shot her.

# CHAPTER THIRTEEN

I t felt like someone had fired a hammer out of a cannon and it had hit her right in the stomach.

*Getting shot sucks*, Diana thought.

In fact, as she smacked into the wall, Diana came to the conclusion that getting shot double sucked, because first: it hurt when the bullet hit you, and second, it hurt when you hit whatever the bullet knocked you into. In her case, the outside brick wall of the little farmhouse Rhonda, Artie, and Gunter were staying in.

Diana was against the wall, stunned. She slid down and sat there, legs splayed out, wondering what had just happened.

Alerted by the gunshot, Artie came running outside.

"Look who paid us a visit, Thom," Rhonda said, "your girlfriend."

"She...survived...?" Artie, or Thom, or whoever he was asked.

"What happens when you try to get creative," Gunter said, looking first to Artie, and then to Rhonda, "when you don't simply shoot someone and be done with it."

"I'll remind you," said Rhonda, "that with the thumb drive in while she was sent off, the value of the asset has substantially increased, to the point..."

"Shut up now," said Gunter.

"What do we do with her?" Artie asked.

*　*　*

*They're talking like I'm dead*, Diana thought. *Why aren't I?*

As Gunter got his hands under her armpits and dragged her away, Diana didn't see any reason to have these three think she wasn't dead. She knew she didn't want to get shot again. She might have survived the first one, who knew know what would happen if they decided to pump bullet after bullet into her, or if they shot her in the eye or something?

"Little bitch," Artie said as shovels dug into the ground near her head. "God, all that time trying to get her to think I wanted her to like me. And all the time loathing her..."

"Really, Thom," Rhonda said, "you loath everybody, don't you?"

"Less talking," Gunter said, "more digging, yes? We must accelerate."

"Of course," Rhonda said, "bury her and—" she imitated Gunter's accent, "accelerate!"

"Yes," Thom said, "the quicker we bury her, the quicker she rots away, the quicker we get our money, the quicker we get to summer in the south of France."

When there were no more sounds of shovels on the earth, someone, Gunter, she thought, got Diana under the armpits again.

She was dumped into the shallow grave. Then shovels full of

dirt began landing on her. Diana thought of the rusted piece of titanium under the marker 'Aaron Dunphy, PhD.'

The dirt covered her face, but she was still.

"A meal for the rats," she heard Gunter say.

"Don't you mean the worms?" asked Artie, no, Thom, Diana reminded herself.

Their laughter shrank into the distance.

The three of them had acted fast. But how had Keyes described them? Professionals, he had said. They were good at killing.

That's all she was to them. All her, and her mom, and her dad were, just one more job, and a month from now, after they'd assassinated some Prime Minister or blown up a hospital somewhere, they'd be on to the next thing, and the next, and pretty soon they wouldn't even remember silly little Diana Dunphy from Columbus, Ohio.

Under the dirt, her anger built.

Her father was obliterated, his very atoms scattered away. They had deprived her of even a dead body. The substitute was a rusted hunk of metal.

She, Diana, would have to be the dead body for both of them now. And if her father couldn't rise from the dead to claim his revenge like a character in a bad horror movie, well...

The pile of earth stirred.

Diana sat up, dirt cascading off of her body.

Standing up out of the grave, she put her finger through the hole in her shirt where the bullet had hit her. Pulling the shirt up, she noted a bad bruise on her stomach, but nothing more. *T. Rex must have had one tough skin...*

Lowering her shirt, Diana looked toward the farmhouse.

The windows were lit.

It seemed so cozy. If there was snow on the ground and somebody took a picture, the scene could be a Christmas card.

Then she saw Gunter on a funny looking phone, moving from one window to another.

Diana narrowed her eyes.

\* \* \*

Inside the farmhouse, Thom had his headphones on, listening to the new album by Exhumed Infant Corpses, his favorite American punk band.

Rhonda was thumbing through an old copy of *Glamour* magazine.

Gunter, on his satellite phone, was pacing back and forth as he spoke. "Yes, the Dunphy girl," he said. "Yes, she survived." He paused, and Rhonda looked over at him. "I know because I saw her," he said very deliberately, "I saw her, I shot her, I buried her."

"*We* buried her," Rhonda said, offended.

Gunter gave her a flat, dead-eyed stare and waved her quiet. "I don't know what this has to do with our business," Gunter said.

The front door burst into the room, tearing off its hinges.

Diana stepped on top of the ruined, torn-off door.

All of the color drained out of Rhonda's face. She half stood up, pushing on the arms of the easy chair until she, and it, fell backward. Rhonda hit her head on the floor.

Artie, the one nearest Diana, his hearing impaired by his headphones, saw Rhonda fall and turned to the intruder.

Noting the satisfying fear on Artie or Thom's face, she grabbed him around the neck with both hands, lifting him out of the chair.

Behind her, Gunter calmly took aim. The gunshot was impossibly loud in the enclosed space.

The bullet seemed crazily to hurt a little bit less this time, although Diana was knocked forward, landing on top of Artie.

Diana grunted, stunned, shaking her head as Gunter approached, once more taking aim.

*Not this time, Adolph*, Diana thought, getting to her feet as quickly as she could, taking Artie up with her.

"No," Artie said, "wait!"

Throwing Artie, Diana watched his body sail through the air.

Artie hit Gunter at his midsection. With both of them in a heap and lying still, Diana picked up Gunter's gun and studied it for a moment.

*Shoot them?* Diana thought.

She knew sometimes in movies people aimed and tried to fire, but the safety was on, which the villain knew but the person about to fire the gun didn't. Was there a safety on the thing that she had to flick on or off? If so, where was it?

She looked at Artie and Gunter and thought, *they're lucky they got the dumbest member of the Dunphy family*.

Pinching the gun's barrel in her thumb and forefinger, Diana dented it just slightly. *Enough not to fire*, she thought, then turned to Rhonda.

She heard an engine turn over outside and dropped the gun. When Diana got to the window, she saw a car driving away.

Looking for something, anything to throw, Diana found her fist closing around a small statue of a cartoon guy in an easy chair. 'World's Greatest Dad,' it said beneath.

Running to the door, Diana heaved the statue at the car.

In the car, Rhonda screamed as the windshield shattered. Obliterated might be closer to what happened. Glass shards flew into her face, accompanied by a fine white powder.

Unable to see, Rhonda steered into a tree. The airbag inflated, and she sat there, face imbedded in nylon fabric.

* * *

"You have Kevlar?" someone said, a German accent. Gunter, or Artie?

Diana turned, silent.

Gunter, having picked up the gun she had dented and dropped, had Artie behind him. Artie nodded, grinning stupidly.

"I asked if you have Kevlar," Gunter repeated.

Diana said nothing.

"No matter," he said, aiming higher, "for a head shot."

"Yeah, that's right, just do it. Do it!" Artie said.

Gunter fired, the gun exploding in his hand.

Artie backed away, toward the fireplace.

Gunter stood there stupidly, holding his right arm by the wrist, blood jetting out in streams.

Diana watched. The blood fascinated her.

She rushed forward, grabbing Gunter by the wrist and elbow. He said "no, no, you... no, no---"

Diana sank her teeth in just below the wrist, tearing out a good chunk of meat. Blood spattered on the floor, and poured down her throat. She didn't even hear Gunter's screams as she took another bite, then another, swallowing the meat and bone with minimal chewing.

*It's so good!* She thought.

Then something hit her on the back of the head. Something hard.

She turned in time to catch another strike, fully in the face. Artie had grabbed a log from a pile near the fireplace. He cocked his arm back for another strike.

Grabbing his arm, she shook until the log fell out of his hand. "Uh...ahh..." Artie whined.

"I was *busy* Artie!" She yelled. "Couldn't you see I was in the *middle* of something?"

She threw him past the knocked-in door and over the porch. Artie landed just past the stairs.

Looking around the living room, she thought *where is he? Where did he go?*

A trail of blood led outside.

She followed it past the door and over the porch.

"Whuff," Artie said as she passed.

The body was face-down in the path to the driveway, blood in a huge pool around his ruined right arm. Turning him over, she saw a face pale with blood loss, eyes wide open.

"Nerdy Artie," she said, tracking back to the stairs. "Still got a crush on me? Now I got one on you." Bringing her leg up, she delivered a short, decisive stomp to his face.

As she wiped the bottom of her shoe in the grass, a faint voice began crackling electronically. "Harvack?" the voice asked. "Where are you, Harvack? What's going on over there?"

Diana walked into the cabin. She picked up Gunter's satellite phone.

"Harvack?" it was a man's voice asking, clearer now.

"He's dead," Diana said.

There was a pause on the other end of the line. Finally, the man asked, "Who is this?"

"I was about to ask you the same thing," Diana said.

There was a sharp intake of breath, followed by what might have been a laugh. Then: "My God, is this the Dunphy girl?"

Diana didn't answer.

"It is, isn't it?" whoever it was asked, astonished. Then he said, "How extraordinary."

"Dude," Diana said, "you don't have a clue."

"All right. Listen to me, listen very carefully. Harvack had a thumb drive. I need that thumb drive!"

"Sure, I can bring it over right now. What's your address? We can have a talk. A nice, *long* talk."

He clicked off.

Diana went back outside. Patting down Artie, she found nothing. When she went to Gunter, she found the thumb drive in his inner jacket pocket.

*Was this the one*, she thought, *the story of my trip back through time?* She looked at it for a moment. *Could it be a way to cure me?*

Diana pocketed the thumb drive.

She ran to the car, disappointed. The air bag had gone off, but Rhonda was gone.

*Not for long*, Diana thought, turning away from the car and sticking out her tongue.

Too late, Diana saw the cord passing over her head. "I don't care how strong you are," Rhonda said, "or how many bullets you can shrug off..."

Diana struggled for breath. Rhonda got her mouth near Diana's ear. "You still have to breathe," Rhonda said, giggling

And Diana remembered Rhonda's beautiful, awful face, grinning at her as she began her long journey back, where her atoms would be mingled with a monster's, so she'd return a monster herself.

Diana grunted, backing toward the car, smashing Rhonda between herself and the ruined vehicle. Feeling something give in Rhonda's body, she leaned forward. The chord fell to her shoulders.

Turning, Diana heard Rhonda gasp. She had slid to the ground. A thin stream of blood was running from the side of her mouth.

Diana took the chord off of her shoulders and rubbed her neck. She bent down, grabbing Rhonda's leather jacket at the lapels, pulling her up.

"Who hired you?" Diana asked. She could see now that Rhonda's nose *and* mouth were bleeding.

Her former friend took a huge, hitching breath. She coughed, then spit blood into Diana's face. Her eyes closed on reflex, but that didn't stop some of the blood from getting into her mouth.

It tasted *good*.

Diana's stomach rumbled. "Spitting blood in my face might not have been the best idea you've ever had," Diana said.

"Go to hell with your father!" Rhonda yelled.

Diana pulled her closer.

"You're afraid," Diana stated. She heard her own voice rumbling, like a growl. "You should be." Diana brought Rhonda's face in even closer to her own. "Who hired you?" she asked again. "Tell me who hired you, and I'll make it quick."

"Can't tell you," Rhonda said, "can barely breathe...I think... you broke...my ribs..."

Diana ran her hand down until she felt bone protruding and squeezed.

Rhonda screamed as Diana felt a rib give way. "You got plenty more ribs to break, honey, you better tell me who hired you." She held Rhonda away from herself, ready to listen.

There was another hitching breath. "We never...know...their names!" She coughed, "My God," she gasped, "what did we do to you?"

A grin passed between them, rows of perfect white teeth gleaming in the moonlight. "Let me show you what you did to me," Diana whispered, opening her mouth.

In spite of her broken ribs Rhonda found the ability to scream

* * *

Finished, Diana sat on the front porch of the little farmhouse. She wiped her mouth with the sleeve of her jacket.

What remained of Rhonda was against the wrecked car, limbs splayed out, a rag doll tossed away by a careless child.

Diana looked at the thumb drive and the satellite phone. As a light rain began to fall, she put them both in her pockets and began the run back home.

## CHAPTER FOURTEEN

Diana's clothes were sopping wet. She took off her shoes before sneaking back into the house.

Two forty-seven, she noted on the glow-in-the-dark digital kitchen clock.

Diana looked in on her mother first. She he was asleep, mask still on, snoring a little.

Diana took a shower and brushed her teeth.

Then she brushed her teeth again.

After she flossed, she started to worry about how much they could find out with DNA testing. Could they look at their drain, or take the dental floss out of the trash and find what they'd need to convict her?

Diana hoped not, but put a match to the dental floss all the same, watching it burn like a fuse in the bathroom sink.

All of her clothes went into the washer with a bit of extra bleach. She waited, wrapped in her bathrobe in the basement while the clothes spun, then put them in the dryer.

Pouring bleach over the bottoms of her shoes, she washed them off in the basement sink.

Trying to just enjoy the feeling of not being hungry, Diana got into bed and began staring at the ceiling, wondering what to do next.

Not really falling asleep until close to sunrise, she dreamt of running down a street, but she was huge, her head some thirty feet off the ground. Rhonda, Artie and Gunter were fleeing ahead of her, terrified.

Plucking Gunter off first, she had him half swallowed, then tipped her head back and he was gone. Artie was next.

Artie really did taste like chicken.

She looked around for Rhonda, but she had hidden herself somewhere.

Diana narrowed her yellow eyes with their oblong pupils, looking for Rhonda, but she was too big to get into some of the tiny places the woman could hide.

Finally, she pulled back her head and roared, surprising herself with the sound of it, like metal being stressed to the point of breaking, mixed with a lion roaring, a pig squealing, a jet engine...

That's when Rhonda came out from behind a car, holding her ears and screaming, and Diana was on her like a cat on a chipmunk. Rhonda's foot fell out of Diana's mouth when she was done chewing, but then she bent and licked up the foot, too hungry not to have it all.

All of the meat.

It was easy, when her mother woke her, for Diana to think that what she had done last night had been a dream, but when Rita said, "You should eat breakfast. I got a pot roast, and no, I didn't cook it." Diana let go of that idea.

* * *

Kate Froughton got into her jeep.

She was driving to her rental property, a small farmhouse that had been taken by an odd trio. They had been there for a week so far, two guys from Germany by the sound of them, and a woman who was English. They were remote, but they paid well and on time, and were, after all, renters and not friends. They could be as stand-offish as they wanted to be as long as the money kept coming in.

Frowning, Kate drove up to the gate and pulled on the emergency brake. She got out of the jeep and opened the gate, then got back in and put it into gear.

She could feel it, driving up to the farmhouse. Something was off, but what? What was making the hairs on the back of her neck stand up?

With the place in sight, she stopped the jeep and simply looked at it.

A body was in the driveway. Another was near the stairs.

The door was open. No, not just open...

The door had been pushed inside the place somehow. It had actually been torn off of its hinges.

Opening the Jeep's glove compartment, Kate took out the .38 revolver her father had given her. She placed it on the passenger seat, then continued slowly.

It wasn't until she pulled up and parked beside the wrecked car that she saw the last body.

Kate had seen death before. Prior to her retirement, she had been an Emergency Room nurse, but she'd never seen anything quite like the corpses on display outside her cottage.

It was the woman, it looked like, but she must have been outside for at least a few days for animals to have done what they did to her. The body near the stairs looked headless. The one on the path to the driveway looked like its arm had been chewed off.

Swallowing, trying to keep her breakfast from coming up, Kate put the Jeep quietly into reverse. When she was far enough away from the farmhouse, she slammed it into drive and spun the wheel, screeching off, Sheriff Teagan's speed dial number already pressed.

* * *

"Okay," Agent Keyes said to the coroner, lifting the sheet on what was likely the remains of Thomas Orton, "walk me through this."

It had taken the sheriff's office a couple of hours to make a positive I.D. on the three bodies outside the house. They had called Homeland Security, and Keyes and his people were on the scene before the sun rose.

Keyes knew the coroner, a tall, thin woman named Janet Grismer, from a school shooting that happened a few years ago. The shooter, who was currently in a County Mental Health facility, had scrawled "Long Live All Kayda!" on his copy of Strunk & White's *Elements of Style* in red magic marker. Keyes suspected the investigation would go nowhere, the random musings of a disturbed kid meant only to shock, and he had been right. Nonetheless it had to be checked out and verified that young Connor Muldoon had not frequented radical websites before shooting four of his classmates and misspelling 'al-Qaeda.' "

Jane Grismer lifted the sheet on Gunter Harvack. His face was frozen in a relatively peaceful expression.

"Okay," she began. "Note the right arm. Mangled, we're

about positive, when a gun he's holding explodes, we assume upon discharge."

"An exploding gun did *that*?"

Ms. Grismer shrugged. "We don't know yet how old, or how well taken care of the weapon was. It happens, but no, an exploding gun certainly did not do that. Looks like his arm was chewed."

"By what?"

"Might not be a what."

"You're saying---"

"Uh---" Jane said, "hang on. It gets better." She led him to a car, where another sheet covered another body sat. "We're pretty sure this is your Andrea Fain."

"Pretty sure?"

"Reasonably sure." The sheet was pulled past the corpse's head and shoulders.

"Good God," said Keyes, "how long has she been out here?"

"While that's hard to say conclusively, I would bet that she died somewhere around the same time as the two male decedents."

"Then why the..."

"Again, it's hard to come to a definitive conclusion based on what we have here, but my guess is this isn't the result of animal predation."

"What then?"

"I think," the coroner said, looking down, pointing to the body, "this happened while she was alive. I think you may be looking at the cause of death."

"The *cause* of..."

"Don't quote me on that just yet. Let me get her on the table so I can be more accurate, but...yes, I think it's certainly in the realm of possibility."

"What tears through a body like that? Cougar? Grizzly?"

"This is hardly grizzly country. Mountain lion is a possibility I suppose. An extreme possibility"

"Wolves then?" he asked. "Coyotes?"

"Wolves? They certainly have a presence in Columbus, but in small numbers, usually either coming from or going to Michigan, which is one of their largest natural habitats, so not out of the question. But I've seen bodies that wolves or coyotes have gone after post mortem, and from this admittedly cursory examination, it doesn't seem likely to me."

"So if you don't think it's a grizzly, a mountain lion, wolves, or coyotes, you think what?"

"Well," Grismer said, giving him a sideways smile, "That's the real question, isn't it?"

Keyes looked at her incredulously. "You're thinking a *person* did this?"

The coroner shrugged. "Coyotes have sharp teeth, canine incisors. These wounds? Look like they come from small, flat teeth."

"So...like a human being?"

She nodded. "You may have to expand your definition of the term 'human being' in this context, but yes."

"That's crazy," Keyes said.

"We're in law enforcement," Grismer responded, "we are always working either with, for, or in opposition to the crazy. Whoever did this," the coroner pointed skyward, "rain did 'em one hell of a favor. You can forget DNA evidence, at least in saliva, although hair might still be present. But in there?" She pointed to the cabin, "a rental property, and who knows how often or how well it's cleaned. Gonna be random DNA stew in there, good luck making anything stick."

"Terrific," said Keyes.

"Wait, I have more good stuff," Grismer said, crooking a finger at Keyes, then walking past the front porch to the window. He followed her to where a small yellow flag was planted near a spent shell casing.

He knelt near it, then looked up at Grismer. "Nine millimeter," he said.

Grismer nodded, then led him to the next yellow flag. Kneeling once more, Keyes saw a bullet, smashed down as if it had been fired into Kevlar.

"So you think somebody was shot?"

She nodded.

"Somebody standing here?"

She nodded again.

"And then, because they were wearing Kevlar, the bullet bounced off..."

Grismer held her hand parallel to the ground, waving it back and forth in a 'maybe' gesture, then crooked her finger again, leading him to a shallow grave.

"Okay," said Keyes, "you think somebody was shot, the bullet bounced off, and they buried the body?"

Grismer nodded, then pointed to a pile of dirt near the grave's bottom.

"And then the individual got up out of the grave," he pointed to the cabin, "walked in there and...?"

She nodded. "Which would suggest that whoever shot this person didn't know they were dead."

Keyes looked from the grave to the cabin. "Keep me informed," he said, walking past the grave and onto the road. He got into the Homeland Security car next to his driver, Ames. "Where to, boss?" Ames asked.

"Dunphy home," Keyes answered.

# CHAPTER FIFTEEN

Diana lay on her bed in a tank top and boxer shorts, her head hanging over the edge, studying the satellite phone and the thumb drive, the third time she had looked at them since she'd come back from the cabin.

*Back from the cabin*, she thought *is that what you're calling it? Don't you mean back from committing murder?*

"Dispensing Justice," she said softly, out loud.

*So this is who you are now*, she thought, *Batwoman?*

"No," she said, "I guess I'm Dyna-girl."

*They killed Dad like he was nothing. Why should I feel bad about what I did? I shouldn't. Not a bit. Not at all.*

The truth was, she had been on...a kind of a roll, hadn't she?

It started, or more accurately, she had started it, and once she had started it, she had to finish it. Sure there was Homeland Security, and cops, and judges, and trials and courts, but who knew if Rhonda and Artie, and whatever real name that third one had, would ever be caught? They were good at what they did, those three. Keyes had called them professionals, and they *were* professionals. Artie and Rhonda, but especially Rhonda, had gotten her trust so easily.

Keyes seemed like one of the good guys, but what did they have? What leads? Even backed by whatever governmental power he had, could he have found them? The way she did? Found them and *acted*?

"It's about justice," she said out loud, but something moved in her. It moved in her mind and in her chest, she could feel its huge heart beating, could see the steak-knife smile just at the edge of her perception.

What was she supposed to have done, sniff Rhonda's T-shirt, then go to Keyes and say, "I think I know where they are?" Get in the front passenger seat of a Homeland Security car, roll down the window, and stick her face, and her tongue out, like a dog? Yell, "You're getting warmer, warmer!" as they sped through the city, then out into the country, then to the farmhouse where they would perform a raid, lead the three of them out in handcuffs?

"You won this time, but we'll be back," Rhonda would say, as she, Artie, and the other one were led out of the cabin.

"The world is safe again," Keyes would say. Thanks to you, Miss Dunphy!"

Diana could salute him with a big grin on her face. "We're all part of the same team," she'd answer, before running off into the countryside and her next adventure, pausing only to catch a squirrel of woodchuck a quick lunch.

Suppose she had just tracked down Rhonda and Artie, then run back home again? She could have simply told Keyes where they were, an anonymous tip. The anonymous tip, she was certain, had been responsible for catching plenty of guilty people. That would have worked, wouldn't it? Why hadn't she done that?

Because that wouldn't have been any fun. Because she wanted to get them herself. She wanted to kill them herself.

She wanted to eat them...herself.

And there it was, wasn't it? She wanted the ultimate triumph. She wanted to eat her enemy. She wanted her enemy's flesh to fuel her along.

"Good God," Diana said out loud, "gross..."

And just as fast, she knew it wasn't 'gross,' not anymore. 'Gross' was a word for the 'before' Diana, not the after. Wasn't 'gross,' as a concept, kind of meaningless once you'd eaten most of a former Bestie?

Staring at the satellite phone and the thumb drive, she knew it was never going to be that way, Diana Dunphy as the stalwart, rule-following hero, not now or ever. She wasn't the same girl who'd been sent back to when dinosaurs ruled the earth. She was lucky that she hadn't come back with greenish-brown skin or a tail, or tiny little useless arms, very lucky, but science and nature had still changed her into something else.

*Okay*, Diana thought, *enough of that. Maybe now there was a way to find the mastermind behind it all.*

She studied the thumb drive thinking, *there also might be a way to...what? Cure myself? Make myself normal again?*

When Diana heard her mother turning the doorknob, she had just enough time to slip the phone and thumb drive under the covers.

"Put something on," her mother said, "Mr. Keyes is here."

* * *

When Diana came downstairs in the sweatshirt and sweat pants Rita had insisted on, Keyes was looking very serious.

Immediately standing, he said, "I have good news and bad

news, Miss Dunphy. First, the good news. We found Thomas Orton and Angela Fain along with another fugitive, Gunter Harvack, who is wanted in connection to recent bombings in Salerno and Tel Aviv. The bad news is that all three are dead."

"And that's bad news because--?" Diana asked.

"Diana!" Rita admonished.

"What?" Diana asked innocently.

"It's bad news because now they can't be questioned," Keyes answered. "We won't know if this started and ended with them, or if it's part of some larger conspiracy, and those are things we need to know. It's highly unusual that we found them here since Columbus wasn't really the focus of our search. Usually, in cases like these, with outside contractors, they leave immediately, yet these people stayed. We haven't yet figured out why."

"How did it happen?" Rita asked. "How did they die? Was it during the arrest?"

"No, Mrs. Dunphy, but I'd rather not go into detail pending autopsies. The bodies were, uh, well, cause of death has yet to be determined. Even positive identification was...tricky."

"Tricky?" Rita asked.

Keyes nodded.

"Tricky why, can I ask?"

"The, uh..." Keyes looked at Diana. "Perhaps we should talk later?"

"You can say it in front of me." Diana kept the smile off of her face.

Keyes looked back to Rita, who nodded. "Harvack's arm, Keyes said, "and Andrea Fain's face," looks like there might have been some...small animal predation?"

"Animals always did like Rhonda," Diana said.

Keyes shot her an immediate look.

*God*, Diana thought, putting her hand to her forehead, *why can't I just keep my mouth shut?*

"We'll be in touch," Keyes said.

\* \* \*

Walking out onto the front porch, Keyes thought of Gunnery Sergeant Novato who had taught him survival skills when he'd first entered Camp Lejeune.

Novato, a squat man whose high, tight haircut did little to help the naturally square shape of his head was fond of saying, "The single most important detector any marine will ever have is the Bullshit Detector!"

*The Bullshit Detector*, Keyes thought, pulling a pack of Wrigley's from his pocket and finding the catch. This particular detector, honed from five years in the armed forces, ten years in the Chicago P.D., another five at the F.B.I., and the past seven at Homeland Security, was going off.

Taking a stick of gum out of the sleeve, he unwrapped it, careful to stick the paper in his pocket. Keyes began to chew.

The Dunphy girl hated Orton, Harvack, and Fain, and had every reason to. Her reaction wasn't anything but completely normal. Too wise-ass by half, but she was a teen, so completely normal, right?

Right.

Then why did the Bullshit Detector go off? Was it just too many years studying, questioning, and chasing after terrible people?

Keyes chewed as he crossed the street. The window of the Homeland Security car slid down as he neared. It was Marcus on the driver's side, and Brantley, it looked like, on the passenger's.

"What's up, boss?" Marcus asked.

"Time to pack it in, gentlemen," Keyes said, "everyone we can prove to be a threat is dead."

Marcus paused, looking up at him for a moment. "What about the daughter?"

"Never mind him, boss," Brantley said, "he just likes her legs."

"Will you shut up?" Marcus asked.

Now Keyes frowned, the Detector going off a little louder. "What about her?" he asked.

"You don't think she's in this somewhere?" Marcus asked.

Keyes looked down at Marcus. "Three highly trained, professional operatives, veterans of terrorist activities in Europe, Japan, and the Middle East, and you think they were, what? Killed? By a sixteen year-old girl with no combat experience who weighs, what? A buck ten? A bit far-fetched, isn't it?"

Marcus shifted uncomfortably. Brantley gave him a barely perceptible 'partners-only' shake of the head.

"What?" Keyes asked.

"Well..." Marcus said. He didn't elaborate.

"Well, what, agent Marcus?" Keyes asked.

"I think I saw something," Marcus answered.

Keyes shrugged. "Okay. What?"

"At the funeral. The Dunphy girl. I saw her break off the end of a tombstone."

Keyes stared at Marcus, who immediately rubbed his forehead.

"How old was the tombstone?" Keyes asked.

"I don't know, boss."

Keyes leaned down to the car window. "What about you?" he asked Brantley.

"What, boss?"

"You see this?"

"No, uh, I didn't, Marcus was, uh...he was watching closer than I was."

"He was more concentrating on the perimeter," Marcus said.

"The perimeter?" Keyes asked.

"Yeah, the, uh...see if anyone was going to be coming at them."

"Gentlemen," Keyes said, "I won't be angry, I promise, and there will be no repercussions no matter your answer, you have my word. I just have to know something."

"Sure, uh, what?" Brantley stammered.

"What is it, sir?" Marcus asked.

"Is it possible you missed any unusual activity at the house last night? Is it possible you were both asleep at the same time?"

Marcus shook his head. Brantley simply said, "No, no way."

"She didn't drive the car out of there, at night, and then drive it back in again, sometime early this morning. The only way out in a car is through the front of the home," Marcus explained.

"We'd have seen it," Brantley added.

"Definitely," said Marcus, "I mean...one of us."

"If someone was waiting for her in a car," Keyes said, "you'd have seen her leave and be picked up?"

Both men nodded.

Keyes looked down, then back toward the Dunphy home. He stood up. "You go home now, gentlemen," he said, "and have a good night."

"Thanks, boss," Marcus replied, starting the car.

As they drove off, Keyes noted the house. A shadow moved in the window of one of the upper floors. Was it the mother, or the daughter?

He began a slow walk up the driveway to the back of the house. Three windows. If the girl's room was one of them, she could have gotten out that way, landed on the roof, climbed down the tree...

At his left was a not particularly tall fence, then another neighbor's back yard. The fence could have been hopped by a reasonably athletic young girl, who could have made it through the rear neighbor's back yard and to a waiting car, but that still meant she'd have to have known, somehow, where Orton, Fain, and Harvack were before making the...what? Hour and a half drive out there?

"Doesn't hold much water, does it?" Keyes asked out loud.

*But that doesn't mean it's entirely out of the realm of possibility*, Keyes thought. If he were going to pursue this, what he'd have to know was who the Dunphy girl's friends were. Specifically, which of her friends was a good enough friend to pick her up very late that night, drive her out to East Jesus, and at best, stay in the car while she murdered three people, or at worst, help her murder three people, and then drive her back home.

As Keyes walked back down the driveway toward his car, he dialed Pete Bogosian at the lab.

"Bogosian," came the greeting.

"Pete," Keyes said, "it's Keyes."

"Oh, hey, what's going on?"

"The Dunphy girl have any fingerprints on file?"

"The Dunphy *girl?*"

"Yeah."

"You don't mean the *daughter* of the guy that got blown up?"

"That's exactly who I mean."

"Isn't she like...fourteen?"

"Sixteen, she have fingerprints on file or not?"

"She in school?"

"Yeah."

"Then she must. Shouldn't be too hard to get."

"Then get 'em, will you? And then match 'em against any unknowns you might find at the crime scene."

Silence came on the line as Keyes sat behind the wheel of his car. There was laughter in Bogosian's voice when he answered, "Come on!"

"I know it's unconventional..."

"Try crazy."

"But indulge an old guy and do it, okay?"

"You're the boss, boss," Bogosian said.

"Damn right I am," Keyes said and clicked off.

## CHAPTER SIXTEEN

Diana was looking through a "Fitness Land" catalog when her mother knocked on the door.

"Yes?" Diana answered, studying a photo of a sinewy guy with a big smile on his face, doing one-handed chin-ups on a pressure-mounted chin-up bar lodged above his door frame.

Her mother opened the door, then leaned against it, arms crossed at the chest.

Diana sighed. It was mom's 'see here, young lady' pose, so Diana flipped the catalog toward her mother, pointing to the photo. "Can I get one of these?" she asked.

"I don't think attractive, physically fit young men get sold through catalogs."

Diana clicked her tongue. "Mom," she said, drawing out the word, then pointing at the chin-up bar.

"I suppose so," said Rita, "as long as it doesn't damage the paint"

Diana sighed. "It's not going to damage the paint, and if it does, I'll re-paint, how's that?"

"All right, fine," mom said, but she stayed leaning in the doorway.

"Hello?" Diana asked, flipping the page. "What now, I'm very busy."

"Did you have to do that?"

"Do what?" Diana flipped another page.

"You know what," mom said.

"Sorry, mom, but I don't know what."

"Young lady..."

"I don't! I don't know what you're asking me, I'm a dinosaur, remember? Slow and dumb? So dumb they needed two brains?"

"Diana..." it was a warning tone.

"You mean with Mr. Keyes?"

"Of course with Mr. Keyes!"

"What?" Diana looked up. "What did I do?"

"You called attention to yourself!"

"How did I call attention to myself?"

"By being a smart-ass! With a professional investigator!"

"Okay, sorry, my 'stop talking' brain just wasn't engaged."

"Young lady, your 'stop talking' brain hasn't been engaged since the day you were born. And while we're on the subject, there were no dinosaurs with two brains, that was a myth."

"And speaking of brains," Diana said, "can I go back to school?"

Rita sat on the bed beside her daughter. "You really think you're ready?"

"Why wouldn't I be?"

Rita reached up, taking some errant strands of hair out of her daughter's face. "I don't know. Rage issues?"

"Really, Mom? Keyes just brought me some great news. How was I supposed to contain myself?"

Rita sighed. "That's what I mean, honey. Whoever they are and whatever they did, you can't call the deaths of three people 'great news.' "

Diana became serious. "Why not? It's not like it's just us that they messed with! All we are is the latest they messed with! Professionals, remember? That's what Keyes called them!" She leaned toward her mother. "Which means *this is what they do for a living*! Or what they used to do, anyway. How can it not be a good thing for people like that to be someplace where they couldn't hurt anyone else?"

"You mean like...prison?"

"No, I mean like...hell."

"Oh, Diana," Rita said, turning away from her daughter. "I know how ugly it is, what happened. But the world is just so filled with ugly. Sometimes I think the only thing we can really do is keep the ugly out of ourselves. And it's a constant fight, I get that, but we really don't have another choice. It's the only way to remain a decent human being."

*But Mom*, Diana wanted to say, *to be a decent human being, you first have to be a human being, and I'm not really a human being anymore. Those three saw to that. And now they're exactly where they belong.*

Rita put her hand to her forehead and stood up. Now Diana felt bad. *I've put more sadness in Mom's life*, she thought. *And if there's anything she needs right now, it's less sadness, not more.*

"Mom?" Diana asked.

He mother looked at her.

"What if we could build another Tachyon Chamber?

"Diana," Rita said, "I told you..."

"But what if we could?"

"Well, we can't. So stop thinking about what we don't have and start adjusting to what we do."

Diana looked away.

"I'd like you to see Dr. Siddons again," Rita said. "At least one more time before you go back to school. Okay?"

Diana nodded. "Sure, Mom," she said, "whatever you want."

Rita returned her daughter's nod with one of her own. "Okay," she said and walked back to her bedroom, closing the door behind.

Taking the thumb drive out again, Diana put it into its slot in the computer. Incomprehensible code filled the computer screen.

If she could find someone smart, someone who really knew that stuff...

And wasn't her mom...

Diana clicked the 'close' button, then removed the thumb drive. She placed it in the drawer under her diary and turned off the light. She got into bed, pulling the covers up to her neck.

* * *

Diana had another dream.

She took down one of those big dinosaurs, a brachiosaur, she thought they called them now. She had read somewhere that they used to be called brontosauruses until someone found out that when they were first discovered, some archaeologist had put the wrong skull on the wrong body or something.

She was chasing one of them, chasing that huge moving wall of meat. She was almost sick with anticipation of the feast that awaited, watching the creature's muscles shift under the skin and fat.

'Chasing' was the wrong word, Diana thought. You couldn't really chase these things, they moved so slowly.

But she got one.

She got one and she sank her teeth into its neck, just below its confused little head. Diana felt the good, sweet blood run into her throat, and the huge, pitiful thing gave a confused blat, sounding incongruously like the noise that comes from one of those big, plastic horns people blow into during football games.

The huge mobile meat pile closed its eyes, its mouth open and struggling for air. Blood ran from the wound, and spit dribbled out of its mouth. When it came down on its side, its huge whipping tail striking the ground, the earth shook.

The brachiosaur's whole flank exposed, Diana lowered her head, ready to dig in, and then her father walked out of the jungle.

Now unable to think of food, Diana wanted to cry.

Dad looked like he'd been there a long time. His clothes were ragged, his hair was long, and he had a beard. He looked up at her and he said, "It's coming, you know."

Diana wanted to ask, 'What's coming?' except nothing came out but some kind of a huge grumble.

Her father pointed at something, something far away, and Diana looked up, keeping her foot on the brachiosaur, perhaps so something else couldn't come along and eat it, but what if they did? There was more than enough here, why be selfish?

Something streaked across the sky.

Big and glowing hot, it left a trail of smoke and fire behind it.

She was shocked. Was it all coming to an end? Would we dinosaurs be less than a memory? Our buried fossilized bones would become the only evidence that we had eaten, mated, raised our young...

We, Diana thought, I am one of them now! The last true survivor!

When the chunk of rock hit, the earth shook again, shook

much deeper, shook with the end of an age. A stampede had begun, dinosaurs of all shapes and sizes on the run, but Diana just stood there dumbly, tongue out, smelling the odor of cooked tree, roasted meat, flash-fried bone.

The flames were coming for her, but really, why run? Where was there to run *to*?

Why fight it? She would only face starvation once the plants died, and the plant eaters died, and then she died. There would just be a bony shadow of the way she had been, the barest remnant of the Tyrant King.

Flames roared out of the jungle.

She opened her great mouth to roar back, but the fire struck her face, peeling back eyes, nostrils, and jaw, taking her to cinders with very little real pain.

But somehow, all through that terrible roar, she could still hear her father's voice, "It's happened before," he said, "it will happen again. It's only a matter of time."

Diana woke with a start, sitting up in bed, taking in a huge breath, looking at her hands in front of her. Her five fingered, human hands.

Lying slowly back on the bed, she took a deep breath. She closed her eyes and tried to get back to sleep.

* * *

"What does it mean to you to be a dinosaur?" Dr. Siddons asked.

"Scares me." Diana answered.

"Why?"

"Why aren't I dreaming I'm an astronaut or an Olympic athlete or a super-model?"

"At the moment, your subconscious isn't seeing you as an astronaut or an Olympic athlete or a super-model."

"You mean the subconscious doesn't take requests? Because I'd much rather dream about being a super-model."

"What does it mean to you to be a super-model?"

"Everybody takes your picture all the time. You're on magazines everywhere. Go to all the cool parties. You're Taylor Swift's BFF, you can marry Zac Ephron, go to all the best parties..."

"And to be a dinosaur?"

"I don't know. They were such freaky things. They looked like big lizards, except lizards are cold-blooded, and they were warm-blooded, like us. And the closest thing we have to 'em today is birds. How can you look like a lizard, but have blood like people, and be like a bird? They were all freaks of nature."

"Only from our point of view."

"But isn't our point of view the point? Dreaming I'm a dinosaur makes me feel freaky."

Dr. Siddons made a little noise in her throat. Then she said, "Freaky, yes, but what else?"

Diana thought about it. "Dead," she said. "No, not just dead, long dead, deader than dead, extinct, as a species. Gone. That's it, done."

"Is that the way you feel?"

"Dead?"

Dr. Siddons didn't answer, but remained looking at Diana until she had to look away

Did she feel dead?

"No," Diana said, "I can't really say I feel dead, not personally. I might feel a little extinct as a species."

"But we're not extinct."

"No."

"And you're a person, not a species."

Diana wanted to say, 'I wouldn't be too sure about that,' but she didn't.

"How do you feel about those people being caught?" asked Dr. Siddons.

Unable to help herself, Diana laughed.

"Is that funny?"

"They *weren't* caught," Diana said, "somebody killed 'em!"

Dr. Siddons appeared grave. "I didn't know that," she said.

"Oh, yeah," Diana answered, "gone, cancelled, out of here! Now it's *their* turn to be extinct. Extinct with the dinosaurs."

Dr. Siddons raised her eyebrows and nodded.

"What?" Diana asked, "You think I'm a terrible person now?"

"Therapy isn't about judgement, Diana."

"Really?"

Dr. Siddons nodded. "Really," she said.

"What's it about then?"

"It's about perspective. Gaining perspective on what brought you here."

"Yeah," Diana said, almost wishing she could tell Dr. Siddons everything. But would it be a good idea to tell a psychologist something that would make her think you were really and truly nuts? Diana thought that for the kind of person she was (not very mature) being able to do the things she was able to do—destroy things, kill people—it felt like what she mainly needed was to become a better person, and fast.

But could you become a better person if you weren't even exactly a person anymore?

"How do you become a better person?" Diana asked.

Dr. Siddons leaned back. "In what way?"

"I don't know. Every way?"

Dr. Siddons smiled and shook her head. "That's been the aim of religion, philosophy, psychiatry, for thousands of years. I don't think I, or anyone else, as far as that goes, could answer such a huge question in the time we have left today."

"Then how about this: how do I not become a revenge-crazed psychopath?"

Dr. Siddons grinned, then nodded. "Thomas Jefferson said, 'When angry, count ten before you speak; if very angry, a hundred.'"

"So count to ten? Even if someone killed your dad?"

"This is an awfully tough thing you're going through, but in essence, yes. You know who Benjamin Franklin is, or was, right?"

"What's with all the Founding Fathers? Is this psychiatry or American history?"

"Maybe it's both. Because Franklin said, 'whatever is begun in anger ends in shame.'"

Diana opened her mouth to say something, but whatever she had to say seemed pretty unimportant after that. She thought about it for a moment. "I guess you really did have to be pretty smart to found a country," Diana finally said, "because Benjamin Franklin sure was right when he came up with that one."

# CHAPTER SEVENTEEN

Keyes stood behind Pete Bogosian, who was staring at his computer screen with a squinting frown that was far more pronounced than usual.

On Bogosian's screen was a hugely magnified partial fingerprint.

"Where'd you find this?" Keyes asked.

"Off of a little statue."

"Statue?"

Bogosian nodded. "In the dead woman's car," he said. As far as we can tell, it was thrown through the rear window, most likely causing her car to strike the tree."

"What kind of statue was it?"

"Hang on...one...second," Bogosian said, clicking on another file, and then on another box. A photo of the statue taken in the evidence locker filled the screen.

"You've got to be kidding me," Keyes said, looking at the little cartoon man in the easy chair, 'World's Greatest Dad' emblazoned beneath.

"Woman who owns the place said renters leave stuff behind all the time, she usually just leaves it there, figuring they'll come back," Bogosian explained.

"Yeah, but this?"

"What do you mean?"

"The Dunphy girl. These three are responsible for the death of her father."

"But even on the million-to-one chance this was her, it could still have just been something she grabbed."

"Something she grabbed to throw hard enough to smash through the window of a car?"

"Not that hard to break a car window, boss." Bogosian turned back to the computer screen, then moved his hand around on the keypad, high-lighting some areas on the fingerprint. "Not enough here to match up with the Dunphy girl anyway. Only a partial, and smudged."

Keyes frowned.

Bogosian swiveled around in his chair. "You don't honestly think these three were killed by a sixteen year-old girl, do you?"

"Don't know," Keyes said. "You find any other unidentified prints in there?"

"It was a rental cabin, there's probably prints in there from before the Battle of Gettysburg."

"Then get me Abe Lincoln's prints, I don't care. Keep me posted."

"You got it," Bogosian said. He watched Keyes nod then turn away, taking out his phone before heading out of the lab. It wasn't until Bogosian could no longer see Keyes in the hallway that he walked into the corridor and entered the men's room.

"Hello," Bogosian called, "anybody in here?"

Even though there was no answer, Bogosian checked all of

the stalls before walking into the last one. He took out his smart phone and hit speed deal on an entry marked 'Udall, Connie.'

Bogosian waited.

"Yes?" came a man's voice. It was a voice Diana would have recognized from Gunter's satellite phone.

"You said to call with anything weird? On the Dunphy kid?" Bogosian asked.

"Yes."

"I got some weird for you. Capital W weird."

"I'm listening," the man replied.

* * *

Diana stood at the entrance to the girl's locker room, hearing laughter, locker doors slamming, the occasional scream...

*Okay*, she thought, *it's all going to be okay.*

Pushing open the doors, she tried to concentrate on the walk to her old locker. She spun the dial, opening the lock, trying to ignore how quiet everything became. Finally, she turned to them, hands up. "Yes, I'm back, okay?" she said, "can we not make a 'Real Housewives' episode out of it?"

Some girls nodded. Others rolled their eyes and went back to getting dressed. Patrice walked up to her, already in her gym clothes. "It's good to have you back, Diana," she said.

"Thanks, Patrice," Diana answered, "I mean, really." Diana turned to her locker and took off her shirt.

Patrice's mouth hung open as Diana changed into her now too-tight gym uniform. "My Gawd," Patrice exclaimed, "what have you been doing?"

Diana sat on the bench, pulling on her socks, trying to think of what to say.

"Easy on the male hormones, Double D," Frannie Lightfoot

said, breezing past Diana and Patrice with two giggling acolytes trailing behind her.

Looking after Frannie, Diana felt the anger stir.

But then the thought came to Diana, unbidden: *It's more than anger*, she thought, *you know that. It's the T. Rex challenged, stirring....*

"Diana?" Patrice asked. "Don't pay any attention to her."

She turned to Patrice with a bit of a terrible grin. *It might be past time to pay some attention to Frannie Lightfoot*, Diana thought.

"So?" Patrice asked, indicating Diana's body.

"Oh, uh..." Diana said.

Patrice held out her hand, indicating that Diana should go on.

"Oh," Diana said, "this psychiatrist Mom has me seeing, she said, uh, exercise would be a good way to, you know, work off anger?"

Patrice laughed. "You must be really, really angry!" she said. "Lucky for Rhonda she never ran into you the way you are now, huh?"

"Yeah," Diana said, "heh, heh, heh."

"Was that a fakey laugh?" Patrice asked.

"No," Diana said, standing up and heading into the gym.

"I think it was," Patrice said, following her.

"It wasn't."

"I know fakey laughs."

"You obviously don't, or you'd know I hadn't just given you one."

Patrice stopped, turning to Diana. "I'm *so* glad you're back," she said, "you don't know." Then Patrice hugged her.

Patrice was a hugger, always had been, and that was fine except when *everybody seemed to be watching*! But Patrice was a friend, perhaps her truest, and if she'd been taught anything by recent events, it was that you stuck by true friends.

And so Diana put her arms around Patrice, and the dinosaur seemed abated. It seemed to settle into the background...

...until Frannie Lightfoot shot past dribbling a basketball, dark ponytail trailing after. "Knew it!" she said, pointing to Diana and Patrice. Some of her acolytes laughed even as Mrs. Mallard put her whistle to her lips and blew.

"Okay," Mrs. Mallard said, clapping her hands above her head, "let's choose up sides and go!"

Diana and Patrice knew better than to go to Frannie's side, so they went to the crowd that was already coalescing around Tori Linares. A tall, thin, African-American girl, her brown hair styled into a short bob for as long as Diana had known her, which was pretty much since grade school. Tori and the rest of the girls not on the basketball team always did their best against Frannie, but they were like the Washington Generals against the Harlem Globetrotters, their destiny to lose.

"Hey, Tori," Diana said, "I want to guard Frannie."

"You..." Tori said, a little confused.

"C'mon," said Diana.

"Uh..." Tori stammered, putting her hand on Diana's shoulder and leading her slightly away from the group. "Diana, Frannie's nine feet tall, the only person anywhere near capable of guarding her is, well, me."

"C'mon," Diana said, watching Frannie free throw a basket, make it in, then hold her arms up, and scream, "Whoo!"

"You seem like you're in excellent shape, Diana," Tori said, "and that's great, but she's going to tower over you..."

"Let me try it. Just for this quarter, if you don't like what happens, you can put someone else in the position, huh? What do you say?"

Tori was quiet for a moment, watching Frannie run around the court as if she owned it.

Because Frannie pretty much *did* own it.

"Yeah," Tori said. "Okay. Do your best out there, huh?"

"Nothing but," Diana said, "nothing but."

Frannie smirked when Diana showed up for the tip off. "This should be quick," Frannie said, the four players behind her starting to laugh.

Diana just grinned.

Mrs. Mallard held the ball up for the tip-off. Diana charged in, slapping the ball toward her team. Frannie's face went from the quickly hurtling ball to Diana, who just grinned at her. Frannie ran to Tori. Tori began dribbling down the court toward their basket.

Inserting herself between the two players, Diana gave Tori time to plant her feet. Tori threw outside the arc. As Frannie tried to intercept, Diana jumped.

When she could look Frannie directly in the eye, Diana splayed her fingers out, placing her thumbs in her ears and sticking out her tongue.

Catching a whiff of Chanel mixed with sweat, Diana saw Frannie look confused, just for a moment.

The basketball sailed up from behind Diana. It struck the rim of the basket and took some twirls around the rim before dumping inside.

"Go, go go!" Patrice, their team's self-appointed cheerleader, screamed from the sidelines.

"Three points!" said Mrs. Mallard.

Frannie walked toward the gym teacher, pointing to Diana. "Isn't that a foul?"

Mrs. Mallard looked confused. "Isn't what a foul?"

"This," Frannie said, imitating Diana's face, hand splayed out, thumbs in her ears.

Mallard looked at Frannie as if she had just shown her a huge pimple in some sensitive region. "How long have you been playing basketball?" Mrs. Mallard asked. "She didn't shove, elbow, or touch you."

"Yeah, but...come *on*!" Frannie said.

"No rule against making a face," Mrs. Mallard answered, tossing the ball to Frannie, "you got three points to make up, let's go!"

Frannie nodded in her direction.

*Damn*, Diana thought, *if looks could kill...*

Diana took a theatrical bow.

As Frannie took the ball away, Diana motioned Tori over. "Get to the arc," she said.

"Diana, are you serious?" Tori asked.

"Serious as a forehead zit, get down there!"

Tori shrugged and headed down to just outside the arc.

Now dribbling down the court, Frannie dismissed her guard with a brief exhale of breath.

*I've ran at...what?* Diana thought. *Forty miles an hour? Maybe sixty miles an hour? But that's running. A T. Rex could run that fast, but it was a big, lumbering thing, wasn't it?*

Diana ran beside Frannie, watching her opponent's hand as the ball dropped and bounced up, dropped and bounced up...

*There's a pattern*, Diana thought, *Frannie's dribbling has a pattern...a rhythm, and I can't let her get much further down the court to her basket...*

*Wait for the moment*, Diana thought, *wait for it...*

*The T. Rex might have been big and lumbering*, Diana thought, watching the ball leave Frannie's hand, bounce to the floor, and back to her hand, *but you're not. You're a little human being with subtler talents...*

*Subtler ways to move...*

Frannie approached her team's basket. The ball struck the floor, bouncing up.

Diana shot her hand inside, catching the ball.

And then Diana was gone. Someone—most likely Patrice—screamed and began clapping as Diana reversed course, charging down the court past Frannie's shocked teammates.

Seeing Tori's open hands as well as the big, beautiful grin on her face, Diana got a little closer and passed the ball forward. *Not too hard*, she reminded herself, *Tori has to be able to catch it!*

Tori caught the ball, Diana barely noticing Frannie running up and stopping beside her. The ball began its journey, flying high over the hoop, bouncing slightly off the backboard, and then dropping perfectly in.

Frannie sputtered, looking to Mrs. Mallard. "That's a foul!" she said, pointing to Diana. "Those are points scored off of a foul!"

"She never touched you," Mrs. Mallard said.

"She was inside my zone."

"Your *zone*?" Mrs. Mallard asked. "I wasn't aware you had a zone."

Diana raised her hand. "Do I have a zone?"

"Do I?" Tori called.

"I know I do!" Patrice yelled.

"There was no touching, therefore no foul," Mrs. Mallard said, bending to pick up the ball. "But the good news, for you is, that you get the ball." She threw the basketball

Tori ran up to Diana, a big grin on her face. "She's not used to losing," Tori said.

"Let's *get* her used to it," replied Diana. "Think you can make it back to the arc again?"

"Most definitely," said Tori.

"Woo-woo!" Patrice called from the sidelines. Diana glanced over and got two thumbs up. She nodded and ran up beside Frannie, who began to dribble down the court.

*I could steal again*, Diana thought, *but that's been done. It's in the computer...*

Frannie stopped suddenly, planting her feet for a shot, Diana behind her.

And an elbow shot directly into Diana's mouth. She stood there for a moment, thinking stupidly, *Frannie elbowed me! That bitch!* Then she thought, *it should hurt!* Except it really didn't hurt. *But I better make it look like it hurts.* Diana thought. *I'm calling too much attention to myself as it is.*

Diana fell quickly to the court floor making sure she banged her head.

Mrs. Mallard's whistle stabbed the air, drowning out all noise.

All Diana saw was ceiling, the gym's bright lights filling her field of view.

"You want to know what a foul is?" she heard Mrs. Mallard say. "*That* was a foul!"

"I didn't see her!" Frannie whined.

Mrs. Mallard's face came into Diana's field of view. "You all right?" she asked. Diana saw more faces. Tori's, then Patrice's...

"Diana," Patrice said, "you okay?"

*How do I answer that?* Diana thought, " '*Of course I'm okay, I've stopped bullets?*' " She stood up grinning.

"You cut anywhere?" Mrs. Mallard asked, "You bleeding? Want to get some water?"

"No," Diana said, "I'm okay."

"Are you sure?"

"I'm okay, really," Diana said, looking Frannie in the eye. She tried not to let herself grin. "It didn't hurt," she said. "I'm sure Frannie didn't mean to elbow me in the mouth, right, Frannie?"

"No," she said, rubbing her skinned elbow, "I didn't. Of course not."

"Sure," said Diana, "we're both players here, right? Little student athletes just trying to do our best, right?"

"Sure thing," she answered.

"It's still a technical foul," Mrs. Mallard said, picking up the ball and handing it to Diana.

Nodding, then running back beyond the foul line, Diana noted the basket before bringing the ball up into view. *Okay, T. Rex*, she thought, *no way you can do this, your arms were too damn short. But you were a hunter... you had to see what you wanted to eat and then go after it...I can see where I want this ball to go...*

Shooting the ball up and into an arc, she watched it, praying.

The ball sailed perfectly into the basket.

A small cheer went up from Diana's team. She ran up to the ball and picked it up.

She held it out to Frannie. "Why don't we get back to it?" she asked.

"Sounds like a good idea," said Mrs. Mallard, "but why don't you back up a few feet, Frannie?"

Frannie did, shadowed by Diana. "How 'bout a few more feet?" Diana asked softly. "You're gonna need it."

Frannie tried to ignore her, but Diana could tell she was rattled.

Mrs. Mallard blew the whistle, and Frannie began to dribble.

Approaching the arc, Frannie took a stance, Diana coming up from behind. She got in front of Frannie just as the ball sailed toward the basket.

Jumping in front of the ball, at least four feet separated the bottoms of Diana's shoes from the gym floor. Her catch ruined Frannie's basket.

There was only silence as Diana landed, the whistle leaving Mrs. Mallard's open mouth.

Diana dribbled all the way around her opponent once, then moved for Tori.

Seeing one of Frannie's acolytes heading down the court toward Tori's position, Diana got as close as she could and shot the ball forward.

Catching the ball, Tori planted her feet, the acolyte still coming toward her, and shot.

The ball hit the backboard, then fell through.

Tori ran to her, wrapping Diana in her long, graceful arms.

Patrice gave Diana a big 'thumbs-up.'

"Okay," Mrs. Mallard yelled, clapping her hands over her head, "get showered and changed, ladies, period's over, score ten-zero, favor of Tori and her Terriers!"

Tori's team cheered. Diana looked over to Frannie, but she was turned away, talking to her teammates.

*That's fine*, Diana thought. *I don't need Frannie Lightfoot telling me I'm a badass, not now that I've PROVED I'm a badass! In front of everyone! Time to take a shower and get to the next...*

"Hey, Dunphy," Mrs. Mallard called. "Come here a minute, huh?"

Diana jogged over.

"Nice moves out there," Mrs. Mallard said. "Ever think about going out for the team?"

"I'm not really a team player, Mrs. Mallard."

"You did okay with a team out there," Mrs. Mallard said, "you positioned Tori, you had your strategy, you executed it..."

Diana shook her head, deciding to play her trump card. "The way things are right now with my Mom... I was lucky she even let me come back to school. She really wouldn't like me having anything that keeps me in school longer than I have to be, you know? She wants me back with her after all the...well, you know about what happened, right?"

"I know," Mrs. Mallard said sadly, but then hiked her thumb in the direction of the hoop. "But that's some real talent out there, you should think about it"

"I will," Diana said, trotting off to the locker room.

* * *

They stared at her as she undressed, and they stared at her as she walked toward the shower, and they stared at her as she turned the dial and let the warm water gush over her.

She was soaping up when the shower next to her came on.

It was Frannie, holding her hand under the water, testing it for warmth. Without looking at her, Frannie said, "So what do they have you on?"

"What?" Diana asked, showering off the soap.

"What steroid?"

"I'm not on any steroid," Diana answered.

"Yeah, right, everyone could see it: the jumps, the speed, the brand-new bod, nobody who isn't on something looks the way you do."

"Listen, Miss International Olympic Committee," Diana said, "I know you're probably an expert on doping, but I'm not on anything, you're just all pissy over getting your ass beat out there. Why don't you shut up, shower up, and get out of here?"

"No, you listen, Double D..." Frannie said.

That was all it took.

Diana reached over, her hand circling Frannie's neck. She

shoved her against the wall, pinning the taller girl against the tile.

Frannie struggled to breathe, both of her hands struggling to remove Diana's arm. "That's the last time you're going to call me that," Diana said, struggling to keep the growl out of her voice. Do you understand?"

Frannie continued struggling. Diana slackened her grip. "Do you understand?" She repeated.

Giving the smallest possible nod, Frannie acquiesced, but Diana came forward anyway, getting her face near the other girl's neck.

She could feel Frannie's blood pumping, could smell it in fact, that good, rich, meaty smell...

"The healthiest thing you can do for yourself," Diana whispered, "is pretend you don't know me, or any of my friends, just walk on by when you see us. Because if you don't do that..."

Diana put both hands on the sides of Frannie's face and began turning her head. She kept going, Frannie gasping, until Diana said, "If you don't do that, I'm going to twist your head right off, and we'll play basketball with *that*."

Sticking out her tongue, Diana smelled the blood, smelled Frannie's utter and abject fear.

*It would be so easy*, Diana thought, *to bite into that right now...it would taste so good!*

Her eyes widening, Diana abruptly let her victim go and stepped away.

Frannie coughed and choked, getting under the water.

Diana was pulling on her T-shirt when Frannie walked out of the shower, still rubbing her neck.

Out of the locker room and into the hallway, Diana joined the late morning student flow, confident she'd be called into the office sooner rather than later. She panicked briefly, thinking of her mother's face as they sat together in the principal's office. It would be Diana, her mother, along with Frannie and her mother. "We have a zero tolerance policy for violence," the principal, Mrs. Anson would say. Diana would look at the floor, avoiding mom's gaze, just wanting to die.

How would mom take it, after everything she'd already been through?

How could she have been so stupid? Drag mom though all that because of Frannie Lightfoot? Frannie Lightweight? Frannie Lightbrain? She wasn't worth it.

*It was the dinosaur*, she thought. *He's in there. And I can't let him have the driver's seat.*

Diana ducked into her history class.

# CHAPTER EIGHTEEN

Janet Grismer said "Blunt force trauma, for lack of a better term, killed Thomas Orton."

"For lack of a better term?"

"His skull, his face, was completely crushed. As if somebody just stomped on him."

"Harvack?"

"Bled out, and pretty fast. Traces of metal in what was left of his hand, but also bite marks, not quite as dramatic as those on Andrea Fain, and there was some secondary small animal predation to the wound.

"And Andrea Fain?" Keyes asked, indicating the body on the table. "What killed her?"

Pulling the sheet up to cover the remains, the coroner said, "She had very hard blunt force trauma both to the back and ribs, almost as if..." Grismer took down her mask and began peeling off her gloves, "almost as if she were perhaps choking someone from behind. And whoever she was choking backed up and pinned her against something. Most likely the wrecked car."

"Pinned her with enough force to break a rib?"

"Ribs," Grismer corrected.

Keyes raised his eyebrows. "How many?" he asked.

The coroner held up two fingers. "One tore into a lung while another punctured the vascular wall. Only a matter of time after that."

"How much time?"

"Minute maybe. Two minutes tops."

"And the...?" Keyes pointed to his face.

"Isn't *that* the question?" Ms. Grismer asked. "It's complicated by the fact that there was definitely small animal predation, but I think that was secondary. I think those initial wounds were made fairly quickly after the blunt force trauma. And while the secondary predation makes it very difficult to prove this, I think the bite marks were human."

"So a human being did do this?"

"Remember," the coroner said, "I can't be one hundred per cent conclusive, but, yes. As near as I can tell."

"Could you tell...the age of the person who did it...from these bite marks?"

Grismer laughed. "That's a tough one," she said.

"Gender?"

She shook her head.

"Size?"

"Too hard to be conclusive with available evidence," she said. "I prefer not to speculate." The corners of her mouth turned up slightly. "But somebody was either really angry or really hungry."

*Or both*, thought Keyes..

* * *

Diana sat in Dr. Siddons' waiting room thumbing through an

issue of *People* magazine. Some politician was leaving his wife for a porn star. Some writer was going to have sexual reassignment surgery. A pop singer had broken up with her latest boyfriend and written a song about it... the world was spinning on. Things were about the same.

She stopped thumbing through the magazine. *Except for you,* she thought.

Frannie had not only stopped calling her Double D, she, along with all of her acolytes, had stopped talking to her altogether. They didn't so much as look in her direction anymore, or in the direction of Patrice, or Tori, or anyone else Diana knew.

*It's not like that's a bad thing,* Diana thought.

There had never been any repercussions from what happened in the shower. She hadn't been called into the principal's office, mom hadn't been called, there hadn't been a suspension...

Everything that had come of the incident had been good.

Diana put down the magazine.

There it was, for all to see. She had always been told, by parents, teachers, even the few times her family attended church, that appeals based upon raw power were wrong.

But were they?

She felt the Tyrannosaurus inside, waiting, poised as ever on its huge hind legs. The beast was ready to run, ready to hunt, to attack...

The door opened, and Dr. Siddons ushered a mother and a very young girl, perhaps five or six, out of her office.

"Yes," Dr. Siddons was saying, "I think that when you're older, you can ride horses."

"But I wanna ride now!" the girl said.

"I think you're a little young now," said Dr. Siddons, "but you might be able to ride a pony." Dr. Siddons glanced at the girl's mother, who gave a small nod of her head. "That's something to think about," Dr. Siddons said. She looked to Diana, waiting as the girl and her mother walked toward the door. The girl turned around and waved, and the psychologist waved back. Then she turned to Diana and said, "Ready?"

Diana stood up.

* * *

"Did you tell your mother?" Dr. Siddons asked.

"Are you kidding?" Diana shot back.

Dr. Siddons shook her head.

"That's a rhetorical question," Diana said. "Can't tell her, she'd freak."

"You might be surprised."

"The only question would be, 'how big would the freak be and how long would it last?' She'd ground me till I was thirty."

Dr. Siddons shifted in her chair. "Why did you do it?" she asked.

Picking at the cloth on the edge of her armchair, Diana said, "She'd been calling me that since I was twelve."

"Double D?"

Diana nodded.

"They *are* your initials."

Diana gave Dr. Siddons a 'yeah, right' look. "Sure," she said, "that was always where she could retreat. But everybody knew what she meant."

"Which was what?"

"Don't you need a Ph.D. to get this job?" Diana asked.

Dr. Siddons smiled, nodding. "I want to hear from you what it meant."

"Her way of saying I had tiny little boobs."

"And that embarrasses you?"

Diana shrugged. "I don't know." Diana thought for a minute.

"Obviously it bothered you. Why?"

"Frannie Goddam Lightfoot, you know?" Diana said.

Dr. Siddons shook her head. "No," she said, "I don't know."

"Tall, beautiful...right down to her name. Frannie Lightfoot, how do you get a name like that? She even sounds like somebody who's going to go out there and everyone will be talking about her. Who am I? Diana Dunphy. Even my name just sounds ordinary. Dumb."

"Diana," Dr. Siddons said, in a 'come on, really?' voice.

"Dr. Siddons, it's true. It's a name that should be buried in the end credits of some movie, 'Production Accountant, Diana Dunphy.' " Diana shook her head. "And there's Frannie Lightfoot, stepping right out of McAuliffe High and into a basketball scholarship at Rutgers. Probably go the Olympics. Probably play professionally. Not just play professionally, but with her moves and her looks, finally make Women's Basketball into something that people will actually watch. Probably endorse every basketball, basketball shoe, and basketball jersey out there, not to mention perfume, her own fashion line, who knows what? Now let me ask you, with all that going on, why would she care about making someone like me feel bad?"

"Someone like you?"

Diana nodded.

"What does that mean?" Dr. Siddons asked.

"It's not like I'm the most hated person in school, I'm okay, I've got friends, I've won a couple of awards, I get pretty good grades..."

"A three-point eight average, your mother tells me."

"Yeah, okay."

"So that's a lot better than pretty good. That puts you in the upper third of the class, right?"

" 'Upper third of the class,' that's a real ringing endorsement of my academic career."

"It's possible you're being too hard on yourself."

"The point is I'm kind of just *in* there somewhere. Always have been. And here's this...I'm sorry, this bitch, with this incredible talent, how did someone like me even get on her radar? Why would I matter enough to her to constantly be calling me that? Double D."

"You don't know her."

"I know her enough."

"I'm not so sure about that."

"So what now? I should try to be her Bestie? Not gonna happen."

"I'm hardly saying that. I don't know her either," said Dr. Siddons, "but if someone needs to denigrate another person, it usually speaks to some need."

"What need could someone like Frannie Lightfoot possibly have?"

"She might seem this way to you, this sports star with the halo and the bright future, but she obviously isn't that way to herself. She feels like if she can put someone else down, she'll be elevated."

"Elevated to what? She's already so elevated she can't see the ground." Diana couldn't help but smile. "Until two days ago, anyway."

"That's when you and your team beat her?"

Diana nodded. "God, it was great."

"And the incident after, in the shower?"

"You really want to know?"

Dr. Siddons nodded.

"It was great. too. A different kind of great."

Dr. Siddons said nothing. The silence stretched.

"What?" Diana finally asked, looking at her therapist, "no quote from the Founding Fathers?"

"I'm curious. Do you have any idea why you were able to beat her this time? When you weren't ever able to before?"

*And how do I answer that question?* Diana thought.

"I think we worked better as a team," she said after a moment. "And I think..." She stopped talking, looking at Dr. Siddons, who raised her eyebrows as if to indicate that Diana should go on. "I think that ever since my Dad died, it's like I've had a monster inside me."

"A monster?"

Diana nodded. "A big, mean one," she said softly.

"Anger?"

Diana nodded.

"And it helped you win against this amazing athlete?"

"She elbowed me in the mouth and knocked me to the ground, and I didn't care. She lined up and shot this perfect ball at the basket, and I didn't care. I intercepted it and it became *my* ball. *My* basket."

"Well," Dr. Siddons said, "I would say sports are not a bad way to channel this anger, this...monster."

"Really?" Diana asked.

"Physical exercise has been used as a way to curb aggression for centuries. And most sports are a kind of substitute war, so a basketball game? Yes. It sounds like you played well and played by the rules."

Diana felt relieved but tried not to show it.

"You were doing fine," Dr. Siddons said, "until the incident in the shower. That's what concerns me."

Diana shrugged. "Frannie didn't tell anyone, or at least I don't think she did. If she has, I never heard about it."

"Then maybe you were lucky. This time."

"This time? It's not like I'm going to be playing against Frannie ever again..."

"That doesn't matter. There are always going to be people or situations that might set this monster of yours loose."

Diana felt a stinging at the bridge of her nose. Were her eyes watering? Was she going to start crying? "What...what do I do about him? About It?"

Dr. Siddons leaned forward. A box of tissues had somehow appeared in her hand. She stretched her arm forward. "Maybe you could start by realizing It's part of you."

"It doesn't seem like It is," Diana said, taking several tissues and putting them to her eyes. "It feels like something in me that wasn't in me before."

"You hadn't gone through such a terrible loss before. Complicated by how troubled your relationship with your father was... it's a recipe for a great deal of inner turmoil. Maybe this monster really is something new for you, and maybe not. Maybe you were just better at keeping It penned up before. Either way, Diana, It is *you*. It is nothing from outside of you, even if It feels that way. And it might feel like you can't control It, but you can. We are obligated, in this life, to own all parts of ourselves. You must own this monster."

"I..." Diana said. She blew her nose. "I don't know if I can do that."

"Yes, you can."

Dr. Siddons started to talk about the work of Carl Jung, about archetypes and what they meant, about the whole idea of the shadow. *No, Dr. Siddons I'm serious.* Diana thought. *It's not an archetype, It really is this beyond ancient apex predator alive in me, and*

*I don't know what to do, but I can't tell you that, mom said not to tell you that, and I don't want to be put away somewhere...*

*But Dr. Siddons is right about one thing.* Diana thought. *It really is a part of me, whatever the new me is. And I've got to own It. All ten tons of It.*

*Own it...*

# CHAPTER NINETEEN

Keyes sat in his office, staring at the college-ruled notebook open on his desk. After a moment, he drew a line down the center of the first page. On the left side he wrote, "Why I think she did it." On the right side he wrote, "Why I think she didn't."

On the right side, he wrote:

1. How the hell did she find them?

Police, FBI, Homeland Security, even Interpol looking for those three, and this young girl somehow tracks them down?

1. No one saw her leave.

He thought about it, then wrote:

1. Even if she managed to evade detection and leave, it's a 50-60 mile trip.

Keyes mulled it over. Then he wrote:

4. She would either have to have gotten a car somehow, or someone would have had to drive her.

*Who?* Keyes thought. *The mother? A possibility, but remote. She seems to want to get on with life, not wallow in vengeance. The Dunphy girl's got friends, but they're all in high school! Of course I got away with all kinds of crap in high school, why couldn't Diana Dunphy and her friends? Question is; could this ordinary seeming girl drive someplace and brutally murder three people? Did she have friends who would either kill with her, or sit in the car while she committed multiple revenge killings?*

Note, Keyes wrote at the bottom of the page, who are Diana Dunphy's closest friends? Then he went back to looking at the right side of the paper.

5. Whoever did it got the better of three highly trained operatives and was most likely shot at least once. Which means she had access to body armor of some sort.

Going back down to 'notes,' Keyes wrote 'Search Warrant.'

It would solve so much. If the Dunphy girl owned a Kevlar vest, that would do it. That might be the ball game. But could he get a judge to sign off on a warrant based on this evidence?

He circled 'Search Warrant,' then circled it again, and again, his pen absent-mindedly drawing over and over those two words.

*What evidence? I really have no evidence of any kind at all. I have exactly zero to take to a judge to attempt to order a search warrant. They'd laugh me out of court. In fact, if he were the judge hearing the case, he'd laugh himself out of court.*

*So what was it? Why couldn't I let it go?*

On the paper's left side, he wrote, simply:

1. Attitude.

And that was really it, wasn't it? Her attitude.

The girl wasn't just unmoved by the deaths of her former friends, however deserving of killing they might have been; she'd been laughing about it.

*No*, he thought, *not laughing about it. Wanting to be SEEN as laughing about it. She was covering up something.*

But a sixteen-year-old girl whose father had just been killed? Whose mother had just suffered a terrible injury? Who had herself just suffered a terrible injury? Wasn't that the kind of reaction to be expected?

Of course it was.

So, back to the original question: what was going on here? Why couldn't he let it go?

It was because of her eyes.

The thought had come on its own, punching through the confusion in his head only to float now as if it had always been there, but he simply hadn't seen it.

BECAUSE OF HER EYES.

What about her eyes?

He'd seen it before, in children in Iraq, after he'd been called up in the wake of 9/11. In a place where everyone was a potential enemy combatant, you couldn't count anyone as safe, not even those under the age of twelve. You could always tell the ones who had experienced death, the way they'd look right at you, not down or away, but right at you as if to say: 'I don't sweat you, my mother is gone, and my father is gone, and when I'm big enough, someone's going to give me an AK and I don't even care if I get killed as long as it means I get to kill some of you.'

And their eyes were like flat disks of obsidian that had not only seen it all, but expected to see a lot more. And a lot worse.

That was the look the Dunphy girl had. Not just that she'd experienced death, but that she'd caused some. And that was a tough look to find in the eyes of an upper middle class white girl in a city like Columbus, in the state of Ohio, in the United States of America.

Now that he had almost cut a hole in the paper, Keyes realized he'd gone back to circling the words 'Search Warrant.'

When the phone rang, he picked it up absent-mindedly. "Keyes," he said.

"Agent Keyes," came the not unpleasant voice on the other end, "Janet Grismer."

"What can I do for you, Ms. Grismer?"

"Well, it might be nothing, but I thought I ought to tell you. When they were towing the car away, we found a muddy footprint that was at least somewhat protected from all the rain. It's only a partial, mainly the heel, and not particularly well-preserved, but we've got pictures if you want them."

"What kind of a footprint?" Keyes asked.

"Looks to be a girl's athletic shoe."

Keyes sat up in his chair. "Say again?"

"Girl's athletic shoe, size in the…maybe five-to-six range?"

Keyes swallowed on a dry throat.

"Hello?" the coroner asked, reminding Keyes he hadn't spoken for a while.

"Can you E-mail me those photos?" he asked.

"Right away," she said.

"Thank you," he replied, "thank you very much."

"Anything to help."

She clicked off. Keyes held his phone in limp fingers, then went back to staring at the notepad in front of him, the first, slightest verification of a theory he realized now he hoped wouldn't be true.

* * *

Right before lunch, Chuck Leadingham came up to Diana's locker. "How you doing?" he asked.

Diana tried to be cool about it, but inside she was trying to control her heartbeat. It didn't help that she was so hungry... and he smelled so good.

And just when it seemed like it couldn't get any worse, Patrice walked by and said, "Ready to go to lunch?"

"Sure," Diana answered. Patrice turned away so Chuck couldn't see her, only showing Diana the huge smirk on her face. "Perhaps you'd like to join us, Chuck?" Patrice asked.

"Well, yeah, sure," Chuck said.

*Great,* Diana thought, *just great.* She had intended to eat lunch somewhere quick, and by herself, but instead she'd be there with Patrice, who was, as much as Diana liked her, a gossip queen, and Chuck, the hottest guy in school, and they could both watch her while she ate the seven barely cooked hamburgers her mom had packed for her.

Later, seated in the cafeteria, not so far away from where she and Rhonda, or whatever her name was, had once been discussing Chuck, he asked, "So how are you, you know, feeling?" Then he popped a French fry into his mouth.

"I'm okay," Diana said, but her voice was a little shaky, and she felt kind of faint. She was hungry, and got hungrier watching him eat, but French fries...

*I used to love French fries*, she thought, Now, it wasn't like she hated them or anything, she just...didn't want any.

Looking around at the burgers, the chicken, all being eaten, the smell of all that meat mixing with the smell of all those people all packed together...

Packed together like cattle.

There was no way she was going to be able to keep her cool. If she didn't eat, she was going to die, or she was going to attack

Chuck or Patrice, and neither was a good option. "Listen," Diana said as she got out the Tupperware container with the burgers, "I'm like, on this high protein diet. And so, that's why, I'm—you know?"

Diana took out the first hamburger and tore into it. She had barely finished when she went on to the next one, only sort of listening to what Chuck and Patrice were saying. She thought Patrice was telling Chuck about her lifting weights and getting buff and all, and before long she was on the third nearly raw burger with no bread.

It wasn't until Diana got to the fourth one, chewing, then lifting her head back to swallow, that she realized they weren't talking anymore, but watching her.

Diana swallowed, then looked at the two of them and said, "I was kinda hungry."

"I think you can take the 'kinda' out of that statement," Patrice said.

*Patrice I could kill you*, Diana thought. *And what's bad is I actually could kill you without all that much of a problem.*

"I'm sorry," Diana said, trying to laugh it off, "but all this food, all these people eating..." She grabbed the next burger and started in.

"So are you bulking up?" Chuck asked.

"God," Diana said through a mouthful of barely cooked meat, "I hope not..." She tilted her bead back to swallow.

"So, uh... you're trying to cut?"

"She's doing both at once, I think." Patrice said.

Finished swallowing, Diana shot Patrice a 'God, shut up!' look.

"What?" Patrice asked, "I mean, what's the big deal?" She turned to Chuck and said, "You should see her in the shower!"

Diana closed her eyes, incredibly embarrassed, and it was a

real achievement to be embarrassed after eating your sixth mostly raw hamburger with no bun, having swallowed them all like a bird.

But even Patrice realized she had crossed a line. "I don't mean you should see her in the shower," Patrice said to Chuck, "what I mean is, uh…"

"I think he gets it, Patrice," Diana said.

At the same time Chuck looked down and said, "It's okay, really. I mean, I get it. Some guys don't like it when a girl gets all muscly, but I think it's kind of cool."

"You do?" Patrice asked, taking a sip of coke and trying to catch Diana'a eye.

"Sure," said Chuck, "my brother has a women's fitness calendar. Some really hot babes on there." He winced. "Sorry! My mom says I shouldn't call women babes! What I mean is, it's nothing to be ashamed of or anything, being a buff chick." He closed his eyes, grunting. "God! Sorry! She says I shouldn't say 'chick' either. Okay, anyway, where do you work out?"

"Oh, I'm just kind of…at home right now," Diana said. She slowed her chewing. Now that someone had brought it up, she had to admit she was starting to wonder just how strong she actually was.

After the lunch bell rang, Chuck, Patrice, and Diana walked down the hall. "So, uh…" Chuck said, "I was thinking maybe, uh, since our houses are in the same direction, maybe, uh…"

Diana's heart started beating into her throat. They stopped in front of Chuck's math class. Diana tried to give Patrice the old 'please get lost' head tilt, but it took her a minute to get it.

"Oh, listen," Patrice said quickly, checking her phone, "I gotta go, I have a class, and, well, I have to go!" Patrice walked quickly away, turning back only to hold her splayed hand up to her face in the universal 'call me' sign.

"So, uh, maybe, uh...what?" Diana asked.

"So maybe...we could, I could, walk you...home?"

"Okay," Diana replied "yeah, sure, that would be okay, we could do that. Walk home. Meet at the front door of the school. Like at three or so. And then just...walk home."

"Yeah, okay."

"Okay."

They stood there nodding at each other, a couple of those bobblehead dolls, Diana wondering what was she supposed to say. Why should someone like Chuck be so nervous around someone like her? He probably just wanted to talk about Rhonda and all of that, she was sure that was it, because there weren't many people who could understand what he was going through, who knew Rhonda was a terrorist, right? It couldn't be anything else, could it?

*Maybe in my dreams*, Diana thought. *But right now my dreams were all about stomping through dinosaur times and scarfing down brachiosaur meat.*

*Mmmm...brachiosaur meat!* She was walking down the hallway with about the hottest guy she could imagine, and all she could think about were the dreams. The hunting...the eating...

Thinking about that warm brachiosaurus blood running down her throat...

And she looked over at Chuck, at that perfect profile, at all that dishwater blonde hair, and there was a perfectly clear voice in her mind that said, "And after he knows all about you, all about the things you now want, and the things you've done, and the things you can do, what happens then?"

And then she thought, *You're getting ahead of yourself, aren't you? This is probably all about Rhonda, right? It had to be.*

"Okay," Chuck said, "well, I'll, uh, I'll see you, huh? At three?"

"Sure, three."

"Okay."

Chuck walked into the classroom.

"Okay, bye." Diana turned around, closing her eyes as she walked away. *'Okay, bye?' Is it possible*, Diana thought, *to be any lamer than you are right now?*

And then Diana remembered the weight room.

*Okay*, she thought, *maybe a bit lamer. What if I go in there, someone else walks in and sees me pumping iron?*

*So what if they do?* she thought, *Guys don't have a monopoly on weight training.*

*You know what I mean.*

Sure, she knew. But she also wanted to know: *how strong was she?*

She not only had a free period, she was sure the place would be empty; it wasn't football season, so anyone inclined to use the weight room would likely be in class.

Walking past the first time, Diana couldn't hear any noise coming from inside. She walked past again, opened the door and ducked in.

Empty!

"Okay," Diana said out loud, "so you got that going for you."

She quickly stacked the bench with three forty-five pound plates on each side and sat down. "Okay," she said softly, "bar's also forty-five, I think, so that's...what?"

Diana laid down on the bench, the bar bisecting her field of view. *Fifty times seven was three fifty*, she thought, *and five times seven was thirty-five, meaning I am about to bench...three hundred and fifteen pounds.*

"Okay," she said to herself, "okay, okay..."

Wrapping her fingers around the bar, Diana cleaned it out of the cradle. It was suspended over her chest for a moment, and then she brought it down and back up.

Effortlessly!

Diana sat up, looking around. Just how many plates were in the weight room?

Five minutes later, she had every available plate on to the bar. Trying to count, she was flustered thinking that any minute someone could walk in. It was easily over a thousand pounds on there though, wasn't it?

*Never mind*, Diana thought, *first see if you can lift it, then add it all up!*

Back down on the bench, staring up at the bar, she wrapped her fingers around the cold metal. She hefted it up.

Even though Diana knew she was doing it, it felt as if the crowded Olympic bar was floating out of the cradle of its own accord.

Suspended over her chest by her own straight arms was an amount of weight that before the accident would have simply come down and crushed her to death.

Not now.

Diana inhaled, taking the bar down to just over her chest. When her breath was out, she punched it up.

Punched it up as if it were ten pounds!

*I could do reps like this all day*, she thought, *but should I be scared or excited?* Standing up, she counted the weights to calculate the poundage.

It was like...what? Was it really twelve hundred thirty-five pounds? Was that possible?

The door banged open. Two guys walked in, one tall, the other squatter, both thick. "She said she might go out with me," the tall one was saying.

"That's what girls say when they definitely, no way in hell will go out with you," said shorter one.

Diana turned around just as they took it all in: no plates on the floor or on any of the racks. All piled onto one bar on a single bench.

And a girl in front of it staring at them.

"My boyfriend was working out here," Diana said, "and he just went to get a coke, so..." She nodded, then pushed past them toward the door.

The two guys stared at the weight bench, then back at her.

She pointed at them. "You...see?" she asked, indicating the bench. Then she wagged her finger in their faces. "So you better not mess with him when he comes back!" she said before ducking out of the weight room.

"If you're going to get a work out," Diana said to herself as she walked down the hall, "you're going have to get it someplace else."

*But where*, she thought. *How?*

Diana stopped dead in her tracks. As Thomas Jefferson and Benjamin Franklin probably both said, and most likely at the same time, "Necessity is the mother of invention."

Now if she could just get home before mom did...

When she walked through the school's front doors, Chuck was standing there, hands in his jacket pockets, staring at the ground.

Diana stopped for a moment, just wanting to look at him. She so badly wanted to stick out her tongue to smell him, but...

"Hey," Chuck said, the left corner of his mouth turning up, "are you all ready?"

"Sure," Diana answered, then immediately thought, *ready for what? For a walk home? What was there to be ready for, they both knew the way.*

*Okay*, she thought, *just calm down*.

Neither of them said much as they walked on, both staring at the sidewalk. "How is it being back?" he finally asked.

"Okay," Diana said, only that was a lie.

Well, kind of. It was kind of a lie. The first day back was actually more than a little weird. Maybe more than a lot weird, but Diana was really not interested in telling Chuck about what it was like now, to not only be back after what happened, but to have such a different body, and to have people staring at her in the shower.

And then to bench every plate in the weight room without even breaking a sweat!

"You know," Chuck said, "about Rhonda, I mean, as weird as it feels... to think you know someone, realize you don't, and then have them get killed... I've never known anyone who got killed before. I've known people who died, but no one who ever got killed. And you say things to people all the time, like 'I'm gonna kill you,' if you're mad at them, but one of the weirdest things is, I can't say that anymore to anyone. And I used to say it all the time, you know, you get a bunch of guys together, pretty soon somebody's gonna say something that will make some other guy say, 'dude, I'm gonna kill you... "

*Sure*, Diana thought, *yeah, you get a bunch of guys together, that's the way it is, it gets a little rough, somebody says something, somebody else says something, pretty soon somebody threatens to kill somebody else, sure, I got it.*

Except she didn't get it, not at all. The truth was, she just liked looking at him.

Then she smelled something.

Chuck was still talking so she turned her head away and stuck out her tongue.

Something was coming.

Diana heard it before she saw it: a deep, loud barking.

She didn't know dog breeds. All Diana knew was that it was a huge dog with a large, flat head, running out of a garage at them, barking like crazy.

There was a time when she'd have been scared silly.

Now she took a step toward the charging dog without even thinking about it.

Diana looked the thing straight in the eyes, and it stopped in its tracks, stopped barking too.

*That's right*, Diana thought, *I am the superior predator! Bow to your queen!*

The dog looked at them and whimpered. She noted the hard muscle around its shoulders and neck. *Yes*, she thought, *you'd be great eatin'!*

The dog ran back to its garage, tail between its legs. The noise was pleasant to Diana's ears.

"All right," Chuck said, "Show him who's boss!"

Diana laughed, then noted the address. Perhaps if she came back on her own, tonight, perhaps she could...

Diana blinked. *Girl*, she thought, *you're not really thinking about coming back here and eating that dog! Disgusting! Except... we are obligated, in our lives, to own all parts of ourselves. Isn't that what Dr. Siddons had said?*

*You must own your monster...*

*And Chuck. He seemed pretty cool about it, but does he think I'm weird now? Doing that to a dog?*

"We used to have a dog like that," Chuck said, "barking like crazy all the time, but as soon as anybody stood up to him, off in the corner, whimpering like a baby."

Diana nodded, and said, "Yeah," like some lame person, except really, once she thought about it, what else was she supposed to say?

They walked on.

"Okay," Diana said when they got to her house. This is my house."

"Okay," Chuck said.

*Was she supposed to invite him in? How would mom take it if she came home and I'm there with a guy? Even if we weren't doing anything, and of course we wouldn't be doing anything, how would mom take it? Would she be okay with it? Especially with everything that had just happened, how could I do that? Invite a guy inside?*

Better not. Better just say, "It was really great to see you, Chuck." Of course, that seemed better before she had actually said it.

"Well, yeah, sure," he said.

"Listen," she went on, "things are gonna be okay, I mean, about Rhonda. You'll get over it, and pretty soon it won't be that big of a deal."

"Oh, yeah," he said, "I know..."

"Are you...I mean, do you need to, uh...see someone?"

"Oh, I'm not seeing anybody, with what happened to Rhonda, I just..."

"I don't mean 'see somebody' like that, I mean, you know...a doctor? Psychologist?"

"Oh, no way!" Chuck exclaimed. "My folks would never let me do that. Know What my dad calls a therapist? He calls him 'the rapist,' get it? Therapist, the rapist? Spelled the same way, you know?"

Diana wanted to tell him she got it, but instead of that, said, "Well, you never know, it could help. I mean, I've been, uh, to see this woman my mom knows. I've been going to talk to her a little bit."

"Really? My mom and dad always say if you weren't crazy before you saw the shrink, you sure would be after."

She looked at him, and he seemed suddenly more like a bag of meat. A very good looking bag of meat, but a bag of meat nonetheless.

Chuck looked uncertain, perhaps even afraid. He backed away ever so slightly.

Diana cleared her throat. "So, anyway," she said, "this is my place, it was nice walking home with you." She started walking down the driveway.

"Hey," Chuck called, "I don't mean I think you're crazy or anything."

"Mm-hmm," she said, waving without turning around. "Yeah, okay, see you tomorrow."

"Okay!" he called, and as soon as she got inside, she was just so mad, and she don't even know if she could exactly say why. She just wanted something to do, something that could be hard to do. Like maybe finding something big and heavy that she could lift.

Diana guessed mom had taken a walk someplace, because there was her Honda Civic, parked in the garage.

# CHAPTER TWENTY

The worst thing about pressing a car up from the bottom, Diana thought, *isn't getting underneath it. It's finding the right place to put your hands. And there's all the grease and oil, because once all that stuff got on, it'll be really hard to get it off, it's going to mean some seriously scrubbing.*

Diana placed her hands at the juncture of the front wheels and the axle. She closed her eyes, concentrating, then took in a breath.

* * *

Rita answered the door, surprised to see Keyes. "Agent Keyes," she said, "hello. Why don't you come in?" Rita moved to the side, and Keyes entered. "Any news on the investigation?" Rita asked.

Keyes looked at her. "Some...strange news," Keyes said.

Rita was confident she had betrayed nothing, but tried to quiet a now rapidly beating heart. Strange news? Her daughter now shared DNA with a dinosaur. Rita had become rather inured to strange news.

* * *

After she had done almost twenty reps with the car, Diana thought she'd see what see could do with her legs, so she lifted the car, drew her legs up, got her balance, and simply traded legs for arms, as if she were a trained seal balancing a ball, only it wasn't a ball, it was a freakin' car, and she could pump out reps with her legs like it was nobody's business. She didn't even get tired.

Then her mother opened the door leading from the living room to the garage.

Diana and Rita locked eyes, and Rita gave a quick sharp 'get in here!' pull of her head. "Agent Keyes," Rita said, closing the door, "I think Diana might be coming home now!"

Diana lowered the civic to the garage floor. Getting out from under the vehicle, She looked around quickly for something, anything to wipe her hands on, found an old rag and did her best. But when she heard her mother call, "Diana?" she thought she better get in there.

"Ugh," Diana said out loud. Then she opened the garage door and walked in.

Keyes was sitting on the couch, but stood up when Diana entered. "Hi," she said, "I'd shake your hand but we were in... auto shop today," Diana said, "it's a new class, to try to teach girls about cars, and it went over the time they had, and, uh, well, I didn't have time to wash up."

"Don't worry about it," Keyes said, his eyes never leaving hers.

"Can you explain to Diana what it is that you'd like?" Rita asked.

Keyes' eyes flicked to her mother very slightly, then went back to Diana. "We've found what we think is a partial shoe print, at the crime scene," he said, taking out a photo and showing it to Diana. "It was hidden, protected from the rain, it was under the car that, uh, Andrea Fain most likely died in the vicinity of. We've made a very preliminary identification as a woman's running shoe. A Skecher's La Boheme, to be specific."

Diana nodded. Something told her to maintain eye contact.

"Now we know it's impossible for you to have gotten out and committed this crime," Keyes said.

"Nothing's impossible," said Diana.

Rita gave Keyes a non-committal smile, then turned to her daughter with a 'say one more word and I'll kill you myself' face.

"Isn't that what Dad always said?" Diana asked innocently.

Furious, Rita was careful not to let it show when she turned back to Keyes.

*Something's going on*, Keyes thought, *they're hiding something.* "What did your dad always say?" Keyes asked.

"He always said very little was impossible. Many things were highly improbable, but most were not impossible."

"So you see where we're going," Keyes said.

"I suppose I'm a suspect?" Diana asked.

"A rather far-fetched suspect," said Rita.

"Why do you say that, Ms. Dunphy?" Keyes asked.

"Rather expensive shoe," Rita said.

"There are knock-offs," Diana offered.

Rita smiled pleasantly at Keyes again, then turned back to her daughter, staring daggers.

*He doesn't know*, Diana thought, *but he suspects. Best to pop this like it was a zit.* "It would probably be hard for you to get a search warrant," Diana said.

Keyes gave the slightest nod.

"I mean, based on this evidence, how would you even do it?" Diana asked. "You'd have to go to a judge, right? And what would you say to the judge?"

"Diana," her mother said, a warning tone.

*Look at her*, Keyes thought, *cool as a cucumber. Sixteen? This kid might be sixteen physically. Mentally and, for lack of better term, spiritually? She's a whole hell of a lot older.*

"But I can let you search my room, right?" Diana asked.

"Diana," said Rita, a warning tone.

"Well, I can, right?" Diana asked her. I mean, it's my room, right?"

"That may be, Diana, but..."

"Go up. I'll take you there. Right now. All my shoes are in the closet, take a look."

"Mr. Keyes," said Rita, "I think my daughter is..."

"Underage," said Keyes.

*Looking for a tell*, Diana thought.

"Technically, legally," Keyes said, "your daughter really can't give permission for a search. Only you can."

Rita crossed her arms, looking at Keyes, wondering what to say to him.

"Up to you, Mom," Diana said, "but I say let him look. He's not going to find anything." Diana smiled at Keyes, who nodded and returned a tight-lipped grin.

"All right, then," Rita said, "all right."

Diana went to the stairway. She took a few steps, then stopped. When she turned around, Keyes was still sitting on the couch.

Diana pointed to her room. Keyes stood and followed her, with Rita a few steps behind.

* * *

"I know that's a lot of shoes," Diana said, "but you know women and footwear."

Keyes was down on one knee, frowning, turning over the athletic shoes, trying to match the photos of the shoe print to the pattern on the bottom.

"I know what you're thinking," Diana said, "what is it with girls and shoes, why are do they have so many of 'em, right? My Dad, he only had two pairs, one nice one for work and business stuff, and athletic shoes for running and working out at the gym."

Keyes stood up. The room was very female; if it was a bit cluttered, it was cluttered neatly. Looking around for anyplace else an athletic shoe might be, he heard Diana say, "Your wife must have a lot of shoes, right?"

Keyes turned to her. "My wife passed on two years ago," Keyes said, carefully watching Diana's face, "she had cancer, uh, unique to women."

Diana's smile faltered, then disappeared. "I'm so sorry," she said, then pointed to Keyes' hand. "I thought, the ring..."

*So she's empathetic*, Keyes thought, *and observant*.

"Some people still wear rings, even after a spouse has...even after they become a widow or widower," her mother said quietly.

Momentarily, Keyes had seen it as she apologized. It was in her eyes, the sixteen year-old girl Diana Dunphy had been before all of this occurred. Vulnerable. Young. But now he could see it slowly making its way back into her face; the weight of the terrible loss; the drag it had put on her soul.

*It was that, and it was more than that*, Keyes thought. *There's something else going on in her face, what is it?*

"No offense, Mr. Keyes," Rita said, "but are you done here?"

*Kevlar vest*, Keyes thought, *ask about a Kevlar vest? But even if she had one, would she simply hang up here for all to see?* Keyes studied the closet full of clothes for a moment, then nodded.

"Then we should probably...?"

"Of course," Keyes said. "I very much appreciate your indulgence."

"No problem," Diana said.

Rita stood at the door, waiting for Keyes to pass, then looked at Diana, who returned a tight-lipped grin. *I get it, Mom*, the grin said, *I'll be hearing more about this later*.

* * *

Later, in the kitchen, looking at Mom, Diana thought *when you came home and found your daughter bench-pressing your car, it could put an odd slant on your day.*

*Oh, don't be such a wench*, Diana thought, *you know it's more than that.*

Mom sat across from her at the kitchen table and asked, "What was that all about?"

"What was what all about?" Diana answered, putting on her best innocent face.

Rita closed her eyes and shook her head. "You know what I'm talking about," Rita said, "Keyes? Letting him search your room?"

"It's not like he found anything."

"The very fact that he wanted to search your room says something."

Diana shook her head. "You heard him," she said, "just routine."

"Nothing about his coming here and doing this is routine. Your friends were, what? Sixty, eighty miles away?"

"They weren't my friends. They were never my friends!"

"You know what I mean! They were counties away from us."

Diana got up to get a glass of water. She was, after all, tired. She had just finished a workout. She needed some water.

"Right?" Rita asked.

Diana downed the glass of water, wishing it were blood.

"Maybe Rhonda, Artie and their Euro-trash friend just crossed the wrong people." Diana said, turning to her mother.

Rita returned a level stare. "Why do you say their friend was Euro-trash?"

"What other kind of trash would he be?" Diana said, turning back around. Had she done it now?

"And how do you know it was a he?"

"Keyes said it was a guy."

*Okay*, Diana thought, *advice to self: never try to outsmart a genius. Especially when you aren't one. Now the question was, how do you tell your mother that you killed three people and had partially eaten two of them?* "What do you want to hear from me, Mom?" Diana finally asked. "Do you really want to hear the details?"

There was no response. Turning around, Diana saw her mother sit heavily in one of the dining room chairs. "Cannibalism, Diana?" her mother said softly, as if barely able to squeeze out the words.

"No, Mom," she said, "Cannibalism is eating your own kind. They weren't my own kind."

"They were human beings!"

"And I'm not a human being. Not anymore, thanks to those pitiful excuses for human beings. So I'm not a cannibal."

Rita turned away, a huge sob escaping her.

Diana moved forward, holding out a hand as if to reach her mother. *I'm sorry, Mom*, she wanted to say. *But am I?*

Rita stood up to grab a paper towel off the counter so she could wipe her nose. "You're my daughter, for God's sake, and I'll do anything for you," she said, "but you have to help me. You have to help me here!"

Her mother turned to her.

"I want to hear that you'll never, ever, do anything like that again. That human beings...that they are off-limits, no matter what they did!"

*No matter what they did?* Diana thought. She turned away.

"Diana?"

What was she supposed to say? *That you don't know what it's like to run faster than a car?* Diana thought. *Or stop a bullet? Or smack Gunter, Artie, and Rhonda around like they were rag dolls?*

*Or see the satisfying look of terror on Rhonda's face just before you pulled her close, opened your mouth, and...*

"Okay." Diana said softly.

"Okay, what?"

Diana turned back to her mother. "Okay, human beings are off limits. No matter what they did."

Rita nodded. Standing up, she walked up to Diana, taking the water glass away from her and putting it on the kitchen counter. Then she hugged her daughter, so tight, Diana could feel her mother's heart beating like it was some little trapped animal.

In that moment, Diana loved her mother more than she thought possible, more, perhaps, than her body might contain. *How are we going to do this?* Diana thought, *how am I possibly going to survive?* Because the hunger, even then, was gnawing at her, and with her face against her mother's neck, feeling her blood pulse just under her skin, Diana was both fascinated and repelled.

Diana closed her eyes, trying to remember a time when she didn't crave the taste of freshly killed flesh and blood. *My own mother*, Diana thought, *and I'm thinking about her as if I were Dracula's daughter.*

Could she be any more separated from people?

Did she feel bad about what she'd done to those three? She didn't know. Did they have to murder her father, and shove her in that chamber, hoping to not just kill her, but break up her atoms and erase her from existence?

Okay, they were terrorists, industrial spies, whatever scum like that were called, but shoving her into the Tachyon Chamber, that wasn't part of their job, that was just plain old ordinary mean.

And it occurred to Diana that what really pissed her off was that now, even more than her parents, Gunter, Artie, and Rhonda had created her, had given her this new body, this new life, these new awful dreams, and this terrible, unending hunger.

They had given her the gift of the Tyrannosaur, always there, always threatening to come out. If anyone was going to have to be victims of that long-dead monster, now given a reprieve from extinction in her body, mind, and heart, Diana was glad it was the three of them.

* * *

That night, when she dreamt of feeding on a brachiosaurus, she looked up as the asteroid streaked across the sky.

Once more, Diana knew what was coming, and as her father stepped out of the jungle, she looked down at him, and he said, "It's not the impact and flash fire that did it. It was all the ash and debris that kicked up into the air, and circulated for years. It kept out the sun, and cooled the planet, and so the plants died, and then the plant eaters died, and then the predators died. Ironic, isn't it? That the asteroid was so much of what made human beings possible?"

This time, when the asteroid hit, Diana looked up and closed her eyes, unafraid as the blast waves swept across the jungle, flash frying everything in its path. When it struck her, it was like being caught in the muffling air of an attic in the middle of the summer, or stepping into a shower that was way too hot. She wasn't conscious of her reptile skin being blasted off, or her muscles being cooked past the bone, there was just heat, and light, and then nothing.

Waking up, Diana sat bolt upright in her bed.

The fire was gone. She was back on her cool planet, with plenty of air to breathe, plenty of water to drink.

And meat. There was plenty of meat.

Getting up out of bed, Diana went into the hallway and cracked open the door to her mother's room.

Rita was asleep, eyeshade on, and Diana thought how vulnerable her mother looked and was thankful she had been able to sleep, knowing what she knew.

Diana couldn't quite bring herself to say she had committed murder, it felt to her like she had only meted out justice, it was simply a justice she'd have preferred her mother had not known she had meted out.

*Whatever you wanted to call it*, Diana thought, *if it causes Mom to cry like that, maybe you shouldn't be doing it.*

But it's not as if she would ever be doing anything like that again. The people who had killed her father, hurt her mother, and turned her partly into a dinosaur were dead. There wouldn't be any need for that to happen ever again, wasn't that right?

*Right*, Diana thought, closing the door to her mother's room.

Walking back to her own room, Diana sat on her bed for a minute. Then she reached under the bed, finding the satellite phone and the thumb drive.

Hitting 're-dial,' she waited.

"Hello?" came the voice, sleepy this time.

"Who are you?" Diana asked.

"Oh, yes," the voice said, "the Dunphy girl. Can't sleep?"

"I can sleep just fine."

"People who can sleep just fine generally don't make phone calls at three o'clock in the morning. Is something bothering you?"

"You're not my friend!" she said bitterly.

"I beg to differ," he said. "I may be your best friend. In ways you don't even know about."

"Really?"

He took a deep breath. "I don't know what happened to you, but I have my theories. My suspicions. I think my rather unfortunate former associates got...creative. They exceeded their scope of work in so many unfortunate ways that it no longer surprises me that one of their mistakes...turned up and bit them. Or is that an unfortunate choice of words?"

Diana's eyes narrowed. She tried to keep the growl out of her voice. "When I find you, I'm going to..."

"I don't think you will at all," he said. "I think that by that time, you and I will be great friends. Why do you think I haven't come after you? Oh, too-smart-for-his-own-good Gunter Harvack had this Sat phone rigged so I couldn't trace it, but you? Do you think I don't know where you live?"

Diana swallowed, thinking now of her mother.

"There's been far too much un-needed unpleasantness between us, the last thing I want is more of that. You have rid me of three terrible and recalcitrant free-lancers who more than deserved what happened to them. The truth is, I would actually pay you for what you did, if I could. The only thing stopping me is, how would I get it to you? I suppose I could find your bank account number and arrange a wire transfer or something, but that would be awfully suspicious. More than likely it would mean a lot of cash in a suitcase or something, and I'd have to arrange to have it dropped someplace you could find it, and blah, blah, blah, how tedious! If you try to put more than ten thousand dollars in the bank at any one time, you get flagged by the Department of Homeland Security, you might not know that, but it means you couldn't easily get it into a savings account without attracting unwanted attention. Worse than any of the process of getting it to you is the amount of money I'd pay. Suddenly infused into your life, it could ruin a young person such as yourself, with little real knowledge of the world." He stopped talking for a moment, and when he started again, he sounded much sadder. "I know that from bitter experience."

What did that mean? That this guy, whoever it was, was a father? And that it maybe hadn't worked out so well?

"And anyway," he went on, "what would you *do* with that much money at your age? Buy a lot of Madonna records? Or take all of your friends to go see Madonna live in concert so you could all sit in the first row? Or just pay Madonna to come to your house and sing at a slumber party?" He paused for a moment. "Do sixteen year-old girls still like Madonna, or am I showing my age? Come to think of it, do you still engage in slumber parties, or does that show my age even more?"

Diana tried to keep from laughing.

"You're about to laugh," he said, "I can feel it. It's okay, you can let it out. You know I actually met Madonna once? At a party in New York? There was this tiny little blonde woman, holding forth on something called 'Kaballah Water,' bottled water blessed by a Jewish Rabbi, and if you drink it, you apparently get 'Kaballah-nated' or something. I thought, how can someone be so gullible and still end up that rich?"

Diana kept her lips pursed.

"Still no laughs? All right then," he said, "that's fine. Just let me tell you something. Just one thing, may I? Something I've learned in life: there are all kinds of power in the world; wealth, intelligence, athletic ability, even beauty, all are forms of power. And one must never feel guilty about the exercise of power to further one's ends. If you have power, you will use it. If you don't have power, you'll go to church. And now, if you don't mind, I'm going to go back to bed."

He clicked off.

Diana turned the satellite phone off and slid it back under the mattress. She kept the thumb drive out, examining it from every angle before pushing it back next to the phone, then lying down for another attempt at sleep.

Tomorrow she would have to remember to take her spare athletic shoes with her so she could switch them with the pair which she had worn when she'd gone to see Artie and Rhonda. Those shoes which were sitting safely, at least for now, in Diana's locker at the school gym.

# CHAPTER TWENTY-ONE

Keyes found a parking spot at McAuliffe High and started walking toward a side door. Under the guise of "looking out for her mental well-being," he had made an appointment with a Ms. Fitzhugh, Diana's guidance counselor.

What he actually hoped to get was find out who the girl's friends were so he could call on them, get some idea, at worst as to whether Miss. Dunphy had been behaving strangely lately, at best as to whether any of them might have waited for her in a car the night Harvack, Fain, and Orton had been killed.

Keyes passed a janitor who was drilling some holes into a new door What was left of the old one was off to the side, its hinges bent, the glass shattered out of the windows as if a rhinoceros had left in a hell of a hurry.

"What's this?" Keyes asked.

The janitor, a balding, grey-haired man with a gold tooth, shook his head. "Somebody busted it right off its hinges," he said.

Keyes knelt, examining the twisted metal. "Somebody?" he asked.

The janitor smiled, nodding.

"How could some*body* do this?"

Shrugging, the janitor said, "Steroids?"

Keyes frowned, standing back up. The janitor slapped him playfully on the arm. "Cops around here gotta lay off the booze."

"Why do you say that?"

"They swear it was some girl."

It took Keyes a moment to register what the janitor had said. "What?" he asked.

"Yeah, they say she ran right outa here, say they chased her, couldn't keep up with her in their car! That's what I mean by they gotta stay off the..."

"This would have been caught on security cameras, right?"

The janitor laughed. "On those cameras? Right," he said. "Go to the office. See if you can check out what those things shot."

Ten minutes later, Keyes was watching dark, grainy footage with the school's principal, a short woman named Virginia Anson. It looked like a shadow passed through the hallway and then out the door. He couldn't even tell, from what he saw, if the door was broken down or simply opened.

"There's nothing here," he said.

"There's something," Anson said, "You can kind of see...something."

"Anything from the camera outside?"

Anson nodded and the shot switched to another grainy shot, this one outside, from above. A hooded figure runs past an over-hang above the door.

"Shot's too high and the overhang blocks anything signifi-cant," Keyes said. "Ever think about an update for these cameras?"

"I think of a lot of things I want to update, Mr. Keyes. But a couple of levies get voted down, and it's between security cams and new geography texts...you'd be surprised how fast priorities get set."

"Okay," he said, "thank you."

Passing the janitor again, Keyes took out his notebook. "What did you say their names were? The policemen on duty that night?"

"Joe DeMarco and Glen Stutz, I play Euchre with 'em..."

Noting the names, Keyes got into his car. Driving out of the high school parking lot, he began receiving directions to the police station from his phone.

* * *

The girl's locker room was mainly empty when Diana walked in. Finding her locker, she spun the dial and took out her old athletic shoes, replacing them with new ones and stuffing the other pair into her backpack.

*The murder pair*, she thought.

Walking toward the exit, she heard a whistle blow, and then the girl's basketball team started trickling in; it was a few players at first, and then Frannie and some of her acolytes walked past.

Diana knew they had noticed her, but they made a show of not letting on. *Fine with me*, Diana thought, *if she never talks to me ever again that will be just great.*

At the end of the line, spinning the ball on her index finger for as long as she could, was Mrs. Mallard.

*God, don't notice me, please don't notice me....*

"Dunphy!" Mrs. Mallard said, letting the spinning ball drop off of her finger. It bounced once and she caught it. "Just who I wanted to see," she said, "you thought any more about what we talked about?"

Diana looked back to where Frannie and company were getting dressed. "I should really get to..."

"Just take a minute, I promise," Mrs. Mallard said, holding the door to the gym open. "If you're late I'll write you a note, how's that? Step into my office?"

Diana nodded, shoulders slumping, and walked through the door Mrs. Mallard held open for her.

In the empty gym, Diana leaned against the wall as Mrs. Mallard started the ball spinning once more on her finger. "I could teach you how to do this," Mrs. Mallard said. "It's actually a lot easier than it looks. I could teach you a lot of things. About life."

*Great*, Diana thought, *here it comes again*.

"About basketball," Mrs. Mallard said.

"Mrs. Mallard," Diana said, "this is really not a good time to be..."

Watching the ball spin, Mrs. Mallard said, "It's always a good time to be..." she let it fall off of her finger again, then bounced it back up, "thinking about your future."

"My mom..."

"Your mom will be just fine. Better than fine! Especially once she has a star basketball player for a daughter, huh?" Holding the basketball out toward Diana, in front of her own face, Mrs. Mallard feinted slightly toward her. "C'mon," she said, "you can't tell me you didn't love it out there, I could see you did, in your moves. In your eyes."

"I may have loved it, but it didn't love me."

Mrs. Mallard exhaled dismissively. "What's that supposed to mean?"

"C'mon, Mrs. Mallard," Diana said, "even if my mom didn't

need me around as badly as she did right now, what about Frannie?"

Mrs. Mallard shrugged. "What about her?"

"She's your star player!"

"A team can always use another star player."

"She hates me."

"She doesn't hate you."

"You know she does. And it's not like *I'm* exactly in *her* fan club either."

"Things like that can change. On my high school basketball team, there was this girl, Patty Lessky. We used to call her 'Pesky Lessky.' Two of us were just like you and Frannie! Then, one time, coming back from Chardon, on the team bus..."

"It won't be like you and Pesky Lessky," Diana said. "Frannie and I have hated each other since..."

"You can't let something like that stop you. Let me talk to your mom, can I just...?"

"No!" Diana said, not meaning to yell.

Taken aback, Mrs. Mallard frowned. Diana looked away, frustrated.

"You're really that dead set against it?" Mrs. Mallard asked.

"Yes, I am," Diana replied.

"Did you know that all because of basketball, Frannie has a free ride at..."

"I'm sure she has all sorts of free rides everywhere. But she's her and I'm me, and the last thing you want to be dealing with is her and me on one team together."

"What if I talk to her?"

"Please, Mrs. Mallard, I know you mean well, but I just can't do it. You have to stop asking me."

Mrs. Mallard frowned. "Dunphy," she said, "it's such a waste hiding that kind of talent. With a little coaching, the world would just open up for you, I know it. I can feel it."

"The world's already opened up. Opened up and swallowed my dad, and almost my mom along with him. I wish the world would close up a little bit."

"What does that even mean, Dunphy?"

Diana averted her gaze, tears already forming in her eyes.

"Okay," Mrs. Mallard said, putting a hand on her shoulder, "I know things are hard with your dad and all…"

"Hard doesn't cover it," Diana said.

"I'm sure it doesn't," Mrs. Mallard added after a moment.

"I'm sorry, Mrs. Mallard," Diana said, "but all I really wanted to do was beat Frannie. That was all! She'd been mean and awful to me for years, 'Hey, Double D,' and all that, and all I wanted to do was beat her, and I did, out of pure pissed offed-ness. Someone like me would be a terrible addition to the team."

Mrs. Mallard shrugged. "I disagree," she said, "but I guess you know what you want."

"I do," Diana stated.

Mrs. Mallard nodded, then went back inside, and Diana walked into the hallway, her stomach already starting to feel empty.

*Feed the beast*, Diana thought, heading to her locker. Opening it, she found the small cooler that mom had packed for her. She took out one of the barely cooked burgers, just one.

The locker's open door shielded her from view on one side. She checked the other way, and when no one was looking, tore into the burger.

The barely cooked patty was over halfway gone with the first mouthful. Diana held up her head, and when the blood and meat had fallen gloriously down her throat, she looked around again and shoved in the rest of the burger, just barely chewing before tipping her head back so the meat and blood could slide down.

*Like a bird*, Diana thought, *everyone said they were like birds...*

"Diana?" someone asked. It was a guy.

Startled, Diana almost choked, but then continued to swallow. *You're committed now*, she thought, *no sense fighting it.*

The meat completely consumed, Diana looked up. It was, of course, Chuck.

"What's...what are you doing?" he asked.

Replacing the cooler in her locker, Diana said, "I was a little hungry." She slammed the locker door and started walking down the hall.

"Well..." Chuck asked, catching up to her, "can I, do you mind if..."

"What?" she asked, looking straight ahead.

"Can I...just walk with you a little bit?"

"Not my hallway," she said, and immediately thought, *I'm such a bitch!*

"Okay, I...I guess I deserved that."

"Deserved what?" she asked, "I don't think you deserve anything." *If only he wasn't so damn cute...*

"I shouldn't have said that, about you and your therapist..."

Diana rolled her eyes and stopped. Chuck walked on a few steps and, once he realized she wasn't with him, glanced back. "Could you say that a little louder?" she asked. The Entire school didn't hear you yet."

Chuck closed his eyes. "I'm really doing well here, aren't I?" he asked. When he opened his eyes he said, "Okay, all I want to do is apologize, that was all I was *trying* to do, for anything I said yesterday that I shouldn't have said. There wasn't any reason for me to even give an opinion on any of that stuff, but..." his gazed drifted off into the distance for a minute, then back to her. "As you've probably figured out by now, I got a big mouth, and I'm not that smart, so...I say things I shouldn't say, that's all. I hope we can still...be friends. Or friend-*ly*, or whatever we are. Or were."

Chuck held up a hand but didn't wave, then turned and walked down the hall, away from her.

*Lumbering*, Diana might have said. *He's more lumbering down the hallway than walking,* but on him it looked good.

She watched until he lumbered into a classroom, and then Diana went to her English class.

\* \* \*

The school was emptying out except for intramural sports and after-school clubs. From a window in the hallway, she watched Chuck talk and laugh with a couple of other football players, then start walking home alone.

*Hope there's no after school computer science club*, she thought.

After closing the door and sticking a chair in front of it, Diana woke the nearest computer. It came on with a whirr and a strange musical tone.

She sat and stuck the thumb drive into its port. A series of clicks followed, and the screen came to life, completely filled, side to side and up and down with the same indecipherable code.

Diana stood up, looking down at the screen. She didn't know what she had expected to see, but for some reason she didn't think it would just be more code!

*He's buried in there*, she thought, *the monster, the T. Rex. That's where he lives now. Not stalking around some prehistoric landscape, he's here. Right here.*

Moving her finger down the touch pad, Diana saw only more

code, and more, an eternity of letters, digits, and squiggles she would never understand.

*Dad could have understood it*, she thought. *And the guy she talked to last night, he could maybe understand it. And if he couldn't, he could probably find someone who would.*

Diana ran her finger down the touch pad again, half expecting the code to form into its awful, fanged, reptile face, half expecting its steak-knife smile to grin back at her.

Could whatever is on here be used to send her back again? Could it sort out her molecules of DNA from the T. Rex's?

Was it possible that she was looking at the key to getting rid of it? The key to being a normal girl again, one who didn't eat raw hamburgers in front of cute guys, or get stares when she got dressed in the locker room, or outran cars?

Clicking on the circle at the far left of the screen, Diana dragged the thumb drive icon to the trash bin, then pulled it out of the computer.

# CHAPTER TWENTY-TWO

"Thank you for seeing me, Officer DeMarco," Keyes said.

"Yeah, no problem," DeMarco answered. "Stutz should be here any minute."

Full dark had settled, the start of the officer's shift. They waited in the hallway of the police station until Stutz swiped his card and walked in. Walking over and slapping DeMarco on the arm, Stutz regarded Keyes. "You really from Homeland Security?" He asked.

"I told you he was from Homeland Security," said DeMarco, but Keyes was already handing over his I.D.

Stutz glanced at the I.D. before giving it back. "Why's Homeland Security interested in this?"

"It's possible," Keyes said, "not likely, but possible, that it relates to the deaths of some foreign nationals who were suspects in the bombing that took place at Gotelle in Columbus last month."

"You're kidding," said DeMarco. "How?"

"Well, that's the thing. We're really not sure yet, it's all speculation, but the details of what happened to the two of you may match up with certain details at the scene."

"What details?" DeMarco asked.

"I'm very sorry, officers, but I can't share the specifics with you at this time. It's like I said, it's not probable that your situation has a bearing on these events, but it is possible. You said you found someone had broken in at McAuliffe High?"

"Yeah," answered Stutz.

"A chick," said DeMarco.

"You're absolutely positive it was a female?"

Both officers nodded.

"Hair long? Short? Blonde, brunette?"

"She had a hoodie," Stutz said.

"Plus it was dark," DeMarco added.

"I checked the school's security camera, and there was nothing useful there. Did you officers have body cameras?"

DeMarco shook his head. "A bill to give 'em to us didn't get through the statehouse."

"What about a dash cam?"

The officers looked at each other and laughed.

"What?" Keyes asked.

DeMarco opened the station door. "We're gonna take you somewhere, that okay?" Stutz asked, motioning for Keyes to go ahead of him.

"Where?" Keyes asked.

"Impound lot," said DeMarco.

* * *

Fifteen minutes later, Keyes found himself with his flashlight out, looking over DeMarco and Stutz's former vehicle.

The hood was completely smashed in near the dashboard, the metal flaring out like two huge, white wings.

"She landed just about right exactly where she had to in order to completely screw up the dash cam and the taping system," Stutz said.

"Our luck," DeMarco said, "sure would have been nice to have some corroborating evidence."

Keyes craned his neck to see past the metal which had shot up around what sure looked like a human footprint.

Every rational instinct Keyes had said no, it wasn't possible. But how much did he know about whatever the hell the Dunphys were doing at Gotelle? It was something related to oil production, but the sponsors of the research had been adamant that no exact details could come out.

But he had a smart phone, which, when he was growing up, was only owned by people on *Star Trek*. It was places like Gotelle, Keyes was sure, that in the sixties had been working on the tech that made smart phones possible today. So what might they be doing now? Hadn't somebody said, "Any sufficiently advanced technology is indistinguishable from magic?"

"So?" Stutz asked. "What do you think?"

"I don't know, gentlemen," Keyes answered, frowning, before looking at the two of them, "I honestly don't."

"Well, do us one favor, huh?" Stutz asked. "When you clear all this up," pointing to the ruined car, "and it gets to a point where nobody cares anymore? Will you come back and tell us exactly who or what we were up against?"

"Yeah, like if she's maybe some prototype super soldier escaped from a lab somewhere?" DeMarco asked.

"I will," Keyes said, but he knew that was most likely a lie.

\* \* \*

The next day, back in the parking lot of the high school, Keyes sat for a moment.

If what he was thinking was even remotely possible, it might also have meant the Dunphy girl wouldn't have even *needed* a friend to drive her to the location. She might have simply...run there.

Problem was, all he had was a story, that, if told out loud, would simply guarantee a psych evaluation. He couldn't accuse the Dunphy girl of...what? Somehow finding out where they were, running sixty miles to their location, wiping up the floor with three highly experienced criminal operatives and then running back? No.

But he could question people around her. See if he could rattle her a little. Let her know that she was being investigated, and see if anything shook out.

Getting out of the car, Keyes walked toward the front doors of McAuliffe High School. Once inside, he went to the front office and flashed his I.D. Soon he was introduced to Audrey Grossman, a thin, grey haired woman, guidance counselor to letters A through F for the junior class.

"Ah, Ms. Dunphy," Ms. Grossman said, "a terrible thing, what happened to her, to her parents."

"Yes," said Keyes. "I was wondering how Ms. Dunphy is getting along."

"Oh," Ms. Grossman said, "I've heard some talk about some more aggressive than usual behavior on her part."

"Really?"

She nodded. "But that's to be expected, considering the situation."

Keyes raised his eyebrows. "What sort of more aggressive than usual behavior?"

"Our gym teacher, Mrs. Mallard, told me she played quite the Michael Jordon-esque game of basketball the other day."

*She played a Michael Jordon-esque game of basketball?* Keys thought. *That would look good on the arrest warrant.*

Keyes relaxed. "Who are Ms. Dunphy's close friends here?" he asked.

"At McAuliffe?" Ms. Grossman frowned. "Well, there was that awful *woman* who *pretended* to be a student." She looked around, as if to check if anyone was listening, then said, in almost a stage whisper, "I was *glad* to find out what happened to *her*."

"Yes," Keyes said, "very unfortunate."

"Not to me."

Keyes nodded. "What about people Ms. Dunphy is in contact with now?"

"She and Patrice Heath have always seemed very close."

"Would it be possible to talk to this Patrice?" Keyes asked.

\* \* \*

"To start out," said Mr. Bidderson, pointing to a map in Diana's history class, "The United States was fortunate enough to be bordered by two very stable allies. To the North, Canada, and to the South, Mexico."

Diana's stomach rumbled.

Next to her, Patrice laughed. "Hungry much?" she whispered.

Trying to smile at her, Diana managed only a tight-lipped nod.

"Hey," Patrice whispered, "you okay?"

Diana tried to nod again, but the truth was she felt almost dizzy from hunger. If she could get out of the class, even for a few minutes, and get to her locker and the cooler... there wouldn't be many people in the hall, she could down a burger and come back.

"Diana," Patrice said, "you don't look so good."

"Ms. Heath," said Mr. Bidderson, "Ms. Dunphy, so sorry to interrupt, but it's a bit hard to stand up here and try to give a lecture with the two of you conspiring back and forth like a pair of mice."

"I'm sorry, Mr. Bidderson," Diana said, "but I'm not feeling so well, do you mind if I just head to the...?"

Closing his eyes and shaking his head, Mr. Bidderson indicated the door. Diana nodded to Patrice and left.

She got to her locker as quickly as she could and spun the dial. Then she took out the cooler and pulled back the white cover.

* * *

Ms. Grossman sat back in her chair. "Why would you want to speak to Patrice?" she asked.

"It's always possible she may know something that Miss Dunphy doesn't know, or overlooked. With an investigation this large, we have to..."

A series of loud banging sounds came from behind Keyes.

He immediately knew what the noise was.

Drawing his service revolver, he stood up. "Dial nine-one-one," he said, "then get under the desk."

Ms. Grossman just stared at him, wide-eyed, all color drained from her face.

Slapping her lightly on the cheek, Keyes said, "Ms. Grossman, please do as I've asked."

She nodded, punching the numbers into her desk phone. As Keyes closed the door he heard her say, "Yes, this is.... this is McAuliffe High, there's someone here. Someone shooting..."

In the outer office, a woman was already crouching under her desk.

Eyes front, weapon at the ready, Keyes moved stealthily into the hallway as two more gunshots reported loudly, their sound magnified off the walls.

* * *

Head tilted back, Diana swallowed the remains of the hamburger. She wondered if she should have eight patties instead of seven in the cooler tomorrow.

Then she heard the first shots.

*No*, she thought, *that can't be...*

Hunger sated at least for the moment, she put the top back on the cooler and slid it into her locker, closing it with the most barely audible click she could manage.

* * *

"Ladies and Gentlemen," Mr. Bidderson said, "please get to the back of the classroom, away from the door."

Some of the girls screamed, but Mr. Bidderson was already getting the emergency locking system out from behind his desk and sliding it beneath the door.

"Mr. Bidderson," Patrice stammered "what about Diana?"

Unfolding the locks, he turned the key, sealing the door. He looked up at Patrice. Tears were welling in her eyes.

"I'm sure Ms. Dunphy will be fine," he said, "she's a smart young woman and she'll find a place to hide. Now please, get to the back of the classroom."

Patrice didn't move.

"Please," Mr. Bidderson said, standing up and placing a hand on Patrice's shoulder. "The very best thing you or anyone can do right now is to get to the back of the class. I'm sure someone's already called the police. Everything will be fine, Ms. Heath, you'll see."

* * *

Diana heard two more shots. *From downstairs*, she thought, *whoever it is isn't up here yet.*

*Yet...*

She knew she needed to keep a low profile, but she was in the situation. She was in the situation and unlike anyone else in the building, she could actually *do* something about it.

*No*, she thought, *you'll give yourself away. Get out of here!*

But then it was as if something else took over. The monster reared its head.

*No, this is not happening*, Diana thought. *Not to my friends and my teachers, not in MY school!*

Diana began to move down the hallway in a crouch.

# CHAPTER TWENTY-THREE

*here were the sirens?* Keyes thought as he moved down the hallway. *Shouldn't I be hearing sirens by now?*

He turned the corner, and there he was, the shooter, bigger than life and twice as ugly.

The guy was broad-shouldered, and he wore what looked like a bullet-proof vest, covered partially by his long, dark, stringy hair. Down the middle of his pudgy face was a vertical white line, possibly make-up, possibly some kind of white tape. Four more horizontal lines crossed the vertical, one over the eyes, another under them, another over his mouth, and another beneath.

*What the hell was the point of that?* Thought Keyes.

Confident he hadn't been seen, Keyes retreated down the hall to a corner formed by a smaller hallway perpendicular to the main one. *Should give some cover*, he thought, *before I have to fire.* Putting as much of himself behind the wall as he could, Keyes extended his revolver toward the shooter.

Tape Face had what looked like an AR-10, and when he fired it into the ceiling, Keyes though the noise alone would kill him.

Keyes yelled, "Drop your weapon and put your hands up."

"Oh," Tape Face yelled, "so it's an agent of Z.O.G!"

*Great*, Keyes thought, *One of those white supremacist nuts.* Z.O.G., he knew, stood for, Zionist Occupational Government.

"Where are you, Agent of Z.O.G?" Tape Face yelled. "Only way I drop my weapon is if I'm dead!"

Keyes wanted to say that sounded like an acceptable proposal, but instead, he aimed for dead center of the bullet-proof vest and fired.

The shot struck Tape Face squarely in the chest, knocking him back against the lockers, AR-10 swinging away on its sling.

Keyes ran toward the sprawled body.

Tape Face held an empty hand out to Keyes, a warding-off gesture, he thought, until he heard the sound of metal-on-metal. Then a gun seemed to appear in Tape Face's empty hand.

The shot BOOMED in the hallway.

All Keyes knew was that one minute he was looking at Tape Face and the next minute he was looking at ceiling tiles.

*Hit*, Keyes thought. *I'm hit.* He managed to get up on one elbow. His gun was just out of reach.

"Uh-uh," said Tape Face, handgun still trained on Keyes. There was a metal slide strapped to his forearm where the handgun had come from.

*This nut is prepared*, Keyes thought.

Hand gun still trained on Keyes, Tape Face said, "Figures. An 'African American' member of Z.O.G." Keyes could hear the contempt dripping from the words 'African American.'

"Well," said Tape Face, training the AR-10 on Keyes, "ain't nothin' like shooting one of the darker hued members of..."

Someone jumped from the stairs, landing on the floor with a sharp thud. Damned if it wasn't the Dunphy girl!

"Miss. Dunphy, get out of here!" Keyes yelled as Tape Face whirled, squeezing off a shot.

*No time*, Keyes thought grimly. Grabbing his gun and turning to see Diana Dunphy take the shot square in the chest, he gasped. The girl flew back onto the floor even as Keyes calmly aimed for the top of Tape Face's head and pulled the trigger.

Hair, blood, and brains appeared in a brief halo around Tape Face's head, and then the AR-10 left his hands, hanging there for a moment by its straps.

Tape Face went down, a marionette shorn of its strings.

Keyes, light-headed now, was losing blood much faster than he cared to, but he had to sit up. He had to get to the girl, he could crawl if he had to, maybe she was still alive, maybe if he could just...

Was he seeing things, or was it the Dunphy girl getting up, walking toward him, looking down at him, concern all over her face?

"Are you all right?" he asked.

Was that her, shaking her head, or was he watching her soul leave her body? It would be so sad for her mother, losing her ex-husband, now losing her daughter. He had to get to her, had to...

Keyes got up on one elbow, but saw only one body on the floor, and it was Tape Face, not the Dunphy girl.

It really was her, standing above him, wasn't it? "I'm so glad," he managed to gasp out, "so glad you're okay..." He reached for her, and she knelt, briefly taking his hand. She had such a pretty young face.

Knowing he could relax, Keyes let his head drop back onto the floor, even though something was under it, the girl's hand he thought, giving his skull a bit of a cushion from the fall. Then loud voices were yelling, and heavily booted feet were running down the hall above.

Keyes felt the Dunphy girl let go of his hand, felt the back of his head on the linoleum, heard her run off somewhere.

He was back to just looking up at the ceiling tile now.

*It's okay*, Keyes thought, *it's all okay. The girl is okay. If the girl is okay, none of the rest of it mattered all that much. I didn't matter all that much.*

*Protection was what it was about. Protection for the girl. Protection for all the boys and girls...*

Seconds later, the SWAT team thundered down the stairs. An officer leaned in to take a look at him. "Man down, man down," was radioed in.

* * *

Diana had made it to the weight room. She rolled up her shirt, checking her discolored bruise. It had looked and felt like a much more powerful gun than what Gunter had used on her. It stung a lot more, but still...it hadn't gone through.

She could hear them screaming and yelling in the hallway, police, no doubt, lots and lots of police. She was sure all she had to do was walk out into the hallway with her hands up, but she'd rather her mother not hear about her involvement. Plus, who knew what the outcome would be, Keyes seeing her take a bullet and survive?

No. It was a much better idea to just get out of there. Diana went to the nearest window and opened it as far as she could.

*Great*, she thought, *no way am I going to be able to wriggle through there*. Reluctantly, she tore the window from its hinges and then, looking to be sure no one had seen her, jumped out. Once her feet hit the grass, she ran for the front of the school.

Diana was just in time to join the groups of kids already forming behind a line of ambulances, squad cars, and police vans, all with their lights turned on.

"Diana!" someone yelled. When she turned about, she saw Patrice and Chuck with Mr. Bidderson behind them, all looking relieved.

"Thank God you're okay!" Patrice said, throwing her arms around Diana. She was in tears, babbling, "I'm so glad, I was SO scared, I didn't, we didn't..."

Diana pushed away, taking Patrice's face in her hands. "Its okay, Patrice, I'm okay, everything's okay."

"I know!" Patrice said, sniffling, "they're saying he didn't shoot anyone, that everybody's fine!"

"Good," Diana said.

"Where were you? What happened?"

"When I heard the shots, I was in the girl's bathroom, I just locked the stall door and stood on the toilet so no one could see me. Did you call your mom?"

"Yeah," Patrice said, nodding.

"I better..." Diana said, "I should call..." she looked at Chuck, "mine..." she finished.

"I'm, uh, so glad you're, uh..." Chuck said, holding out his hand.

Diana looked at the empty hand, as if to ask, 'What is this?'

"I mean, I," Chuck stammered, looking at his own hand as if holding it out to her to shake was the dumbest thing possible to do, at any time, any place, before or since, in human history. "I just, I don't," he said, before wrapping his arms around her.

Diana tensed at first, taken aback, but then she closed her eyes, settling into it. She could feel his heart beating, and she could smell his blood, but it didn't make her hungry.

224 · SHELDON GLEISSER

Letting his arms drop to his sides, he broke the embrace, looking at the ground now.

Diana watched Patrice smile and wave, turning away and trying not to laugh.

"We're all just very glad, very relieved that you're all right, Ms. Dunphy," said Mr. Bidderson.

"*You're* glad?" Diana asked.

Mr. Bidderson rolled his eyes. "Why don't the three of you call your parents, go home, whatever," he said, before turning away. "God," Diana heard him say, "I'm so glad it ended *this* way instead of...some *other* way.... "

Seeing paramedics rushing out, Keyes on a gurney between them, Diana noted that although he didn't look conscious, his mouth was covered by an oxygen mask, which must mean he was alive and unhurt enough that they were going to try to save his life.

The paramedics collapsed the gurney's wheels and slid Keyes into a waiting ambulance. Then they screamed off for the hospital.

"Diana!" someone called behind her. Diana turned in time to see her mother scanning the crowd. "Diana?" she called again.

Diana waved. Her mother's face lit up and she made her way through the crush of people, finally getting to her daughter, embracing her as if afraid to let go.

"Chuck?" a woman was yelling, and then a man's voice, not far behind, yelled, "Charles?"

"Oh," Chuck said, "these are my folks!" Diana, still held in her mother's embrace, saw a tall, broad guy in a light grey three piece suit, a virtual preview of Chuck in twenty years. The older guy embraced Chuck, and then a shorter, pretty woman wearing a housecoat, Chuck's mother, encircled the two of them in her arms.

"We were so worried!" said Chuck's mom.

"Worried..." said his dad.

"Everything's fine," Chuck said, "we're all fine, everything's good!"

"Let's get you home," said Chuck's mom.

Chuck turned to Diana briefly and tried to get a hand free to wave, but then the three of them were moving through the crush of people. Soon they had melted into the crowd.

"Patty!" came a woman's voice, and then Patrice's mother, not heavy, but on various diets since Diana knew her, came charging out of the crowd to hug her daughter. "God," Patrice's mother said, "do they have that cowardly, crazy, murdering..."

And right then Diana saw it, the black, zipped-up body bag on another wheeled gurney heading toward the coroner's transport van.

There was a stunned silence, and then the applause started, lightly at first, then growing heavier as the gurney's wheels collapsed and the body headed into the back of the transport.

Soon, both Diana and Patrice's mothers broke their embraces to watch the transport's doors close.

"It's terrible," Rita said, "applauding *anyone's* death."

"The hell with 'im," Patrice's mom said. "I hope the devil kicks his ass up one side of Hell and down the other, if there really is a devil, I mean."

Rita looked at Diana and shrugged.

The coroner's transport van drove slowly away. *I should know pretty soon if there's a devil, AND if there's a hell,* Diana thought, *all depends on what happens when Keyes wakes up.*

# CHAPTER TWENTY-FOUR

Keyes shooed the oxygen mask away as they tried to lower it over his face. "Mr. Keyes," said the paramedic, a stocky young woman with her hair tied back, "we have to get you on oxygen!"

"Was anybody...." he managed to gasp out, "hurt?"

"Only the shooter," she said.

"No one...else?"

"No," she said, "you can rest. Please. Let us take over from here."

Giving a barely perceptible nod, Keyes let them place the mask over his face. The paramedic injected him with something.

He was going away, he could feel it, floating away to a pleasant place.

"You're a little banged up," the paramedic said. "But you're the hero of the day"

Hero of the day, right, he wanted to say. It was her, the bullet-proof girl, she was the one who was the hero of the day.

He was just an old flabby guy who wasn't even the best they had at the time, just the only *armed* guy they had at the time.

As he sank back into the utter emptiness that came courtesy of whatever the paramedic had injected him with, Keyes tried to hold on to the idea that for both of their sakes, he shouldn't tell people about the bullet-proof girl.

* * *

School had been called off 'until further notice.'

After the first two nights, when Rita couldn't seem to sleep unless Diana was in bed with her for at least the first few hours, things seemed to calm down a little.

On the second night, Diana looked over at her mother, sleeping with her mask on, and thought, *She doesn't know I'm bulletproof. If I told her, would she feel better or worse?*

*Better because I'm a lot safer out there in the world*, Diana thought as she got up, *but worse because she'd see it as one more abnormality. And maybe she'd be afraid it would make me reckless.*

*And maybe it had made me reckless*, she thought as she went into her own room and slid under the covers. She checked the bruise on her stomach where the bullet had struck her, already faded to the barest little outline.

Diana didn't know what kind of gun the nut had used, or what kind of bullets, but had charged in anyway. Was the T. Rex so aggressive it made her crazy?

Luckily for her, mom had instituted a news blackout, not wanting to know what was going on in the world, just keeping her daughter nearby. *Maybe I'll luck out,* Diana thought. *Maybe she'll never know Keyes was there, and I won't have to worry about explaining anything.*

*Right*, Diana thought. *It would come up. It would have to come up. But it hadn't come up yet, so I'll just have to worry about it when it did.*

Diana dialed the hospital.

"Methodist General," came a female voice.

"Hello, can you tell me where a Mr. Keyes is staying?"

"One moment please."

There was a click. A few moments of hiss. Then another female voice, this one older, sounding a little tired. "I.C.U."

"Yes," Diana said, "I'm one of the students who was at McAuliffe High. And I was, a bunch of us were, just wondering how Mr. Keyes is doing."

"I'm sorry, I can't give out that information. Personal privacy rules."

"Can he see visitors?"

"I'm sorry, what did you say your name was?"

"All right," Diana said, "thank you." She hung up.

Pulling the covers over herself, Diana tried not to think about helicopters hovering over the house with black-suited SWAT guys repelling down on ropes or charging up the stairs while huge spotlights lit up the neighborhood.

Would they drag her off to a lab like mom was so worried about? Take skin, hair, and blood samples? Well, not blood samples, how would they find a needle sharp enough? *Don't kid yourself.* She thought. *With enough money and time, they'll find a way.*

Why couldn't she stay away from danger? Why didn't she just run out of the school as soon as she heard those shots?

"Okay, God," Diana said out loud, "I'm going to count on you now. If you can find a way to not have me discovered after all this, I promise..."

*I promise I'll never try to be a hero again*, she wanted to say, but couldn't. It was, after all, God she was talking to, and God would see right through her. Seeing right through people was kind of God's job.

"I just sure would appreciate it," Diana said. "And if there's anything you need me to do for you, just let me know. And keep in mind I'm not too smart, so you're going to have to find a way to tell me what it is so I understand. I mean, you don't have to send me a burning bush or anything, but...*something*. Something pretty direct. I mean, I don't want to tell you your business, but try not to be all mysterious, okay?"

With that, she closed her eyes and tried to sleep.

\* \* \*

Sliding under the car, Diana grabbed the axle and pressed upward.

*It's getting easier*, she thought. *I need more weight.*

After pumping out twenty reps, she got her legs underneath, trying to get the balance right for a leg press.

"Do you *have* to do that?" her mother asked. Diana looked over.

Rita was leaning in the doorway, and the car started to rock on Diana's feet. "Diana..." her mother said, a warning tone.

Diana lowered the vehicle and crawled out from underneath it, her face and clothes grimy. "Sorry," she said, going over to the sink and starting to wash up, "but you did ground me. And I had to do something."

"You could do needlepoint," Rita replied helpfully.

"I suppose," said Diana.

"Scrap-booking?"

Diana nodded, scrubbing the grime off of her hands. "I don't think I'm a needlepoint or scrap-booking sort of a girl," Diana said.

"Macramé?" Rita asked.

Diana sighed, regarding her mother with a kind of a bemused tolerance. Then the doorbell rang.

"Saved by the doorbell?" Diana offered.

Her mother nodded and went to answer it while Diana continued to scrub. After a minute, Rita ushered Chuck inside.

Diana shot her mother a look, then desperately tried to find a reflective surface to see if there was any grime on her face. "Chuck," Diana said, "I, uh," she stared daggers at her mother. "I wish I had some idea you were coming."

Rita shrugged and headed out, pointedly leaving the door from the garage to the living room open.

"I'm sorry if I, uh," Chuck said, "caught you at a bad time or anything. I just had, uh, some magazines again, thought you might be bored or something," he fanned them out, and it was the same array of titles, *Glamor, Vogue, Insight*...

Diana sighed. "Can I ask you something?" she said.

"Sure, anything."

"What about the times we've talked makes you think I'd want to read those?"

"I, um..." Chuck was quiet. "I don't know, uh...my mom likes reading 'em, and uh, well..." he looked down. "Rhonda always wanted to, uh, take a look."

He let the magazines drop to his side.

"I'm sure Diana appreciates the thought," Rita called from the next room.

Closing her eyes and shaking her head, Diana loudly closed the door. She looked at Chuck. "I do, okay?" she said. "I do appreciate the thought. But I really don't care about make-up tips from the Kardashians, or what they're wearing in Paris, or Taylor Swift's latest boy crazy song inspiration."

"Well...oh," Chuck said. "Okay, I, uh..."

Diana sighed. "Chuck," she said, "I don't want you to feel bad, I just—if we're going to be friends, I just want you to, need you to, get some idea about who I really am."

*But not too much of an idea*, she thought, *or you'd run away screaming.*

"Well, sure," he said, "that's okay." He nodded, rolling the magazines up into a tube. He began rolling them up tighter.

*He sure is cute*, Diana thought, *I just wish...*

She wished what? While Chuck's eyes were on the garage floor, she stuck her tongue out, taking in his smell: a shampoo she didn't recognize, shaving cream, Ivory soap, and then...him. Just a *him* smell.

And that smell was the nicest one.

Then her mother opened the door and walked in. Immediately withdrawing her tongue, Diana watched her mother, hands on hips, scanning the garage. "Ah," she said, grabbing a pair of needle-nosed pliers. She brandished them at Diana, then walked out, once more leaving the door open.

Watching after her, Chuck nodded, then looked at Diana. "I think she thinks we're gonna...that we might..."

"You get that idea, do you?" Diana asked.

He rolled his eyes in a 'damn, I'm so lame' way, and Diana thought, *God, why can't you just keep your mouth shut?*

"Okay," Chuck said, heading for the door, "I guess I can..." he walked toward it and Diana moved forward, trying to think of something, anything to say that might stop him.

But Chuck stopped himself, half in and half out of the door, then came back inside. "I already apologized to you about what I said that day. I don't think apologizing again is going to help that much or I would." He took a breath. "Coach always tells me I don't listen enough. 'Leadingham,' he says, 'don't engage your mouth before your brain is in play,' but let's face it, "I'm a foot-ball player, right?"

*Say something*, Diana thought, *anything*!

"So, anyway, that's all okay? If you ever think that maybe I'd be okay to hang out with again, you know how to find me." Chuck walked into the living room.

"You heard anything about when school opens back up?" Diana called.

He didn't come back in. She started to think he hadn't heard her.

*Crap*, Diana thought, But she didn't hear the front door slam.

Instead, Chuck stuck his head back into the garage. "I hear two days," he said.

"Yeah?"

He nodded, standing in the doorway now. "My folks, some of the other parents, they say that should be enough time. I'll tell ya, as ways to get a couple of days off go? I'll take snow days any time."

She smiled, nodding.

He pointed at her face. "So what's with the...?"

"What?"

"You're...you've got some..." he pointed to a spot just below his own eye. "Little bit of grease."

"Oh," she said, retreating.

"No, really, don't worry about it," he said, taking a handker-chief out of his pocket and holding it up. "Don't worry, it's clean." Walking up to her, he said, "Is it...all right? To...?"

Diana nodded.

"I'm not," he said, putting the tip of the handkerchief to her face. "I'm not saying, I mean, you look fine and everything, you look great, if you were working on the car, that's completely cool, nothing wrong with girls, with young women working on cars, I'm not saying that, if you want to keep that on your face..." He withdrew the handkerchief. "Do you want to keep it on your face? 'Cause I'm sorry, if I..."

"It's okay, Chuck," she said, taking his hand and putting it back on her face.

"Okay," he agreed, resuming his work on the grease spot, " 'Cause I don't want you to be mad at me again. I just..." He moved toward the sink, wetting the end of the handkerchief before putting it back on her face.

*I'll give you all day to stop doing that*, Diana wanted to say.

Finally Chuck stopped, inspecting her face. "Okay," he said, "you look good."

She couldn't help but grin.

"I mean, you always look good," Chuck said quickly. "What I mean is, the grease spot..."

"I get it," she said.

Chuck nodded. "You...you..." he said.

"What?" she asked.

"Well you, you just..." He got a little closer.

"I just what?" she asked, while getting a little closer herself.

"Ah-ha!" Rita said, marching into the garage and rifling through another pile of tools.

Diana nodded.

"Needed a hammer," Rita said, holding up a hammer.

"Yes, I think we can see that, mom," Diana said.

"Maybe the two of you would like to watch a movie?" Rita asked.

"Well, actually, mom," Diana said, "maybe we could help you with whatever you're doing?"

"Whatever I'm doing?" Rita asked innocently.

"Whatever you need the hammer and the needle-nosed pliers for," Diana said.

"Oh, I can..." Rita said. "I can do that myself later on."

Diana smirked at her.

Rita beamed back. "I've got that new one with Tom Hanks," she said, "where he lands the plane?" She started walking out.

Chuck shrugged, then followed her mother. "Tom Hanks. I would not want to be on a plane where he was the pilot, or on a ship where he was the captain, you know?" Chuck said.

Rita laughed. "Or in a space capsule with him, trying to get to the moon. Do you want some popcorn?" she called.

"Is the Pope Catholic?" Chuck answered. "Does a bear..."

"That's enough of *that*," Rita said.

Diana shook her head, turning out the light and pulling the garage door closed behind her.

* * *

*This is going about as well as it can go*, Diana thought, seated between Chuck and her mom.

When the movie was over, Chuck stood on the front porch. He waved before walking off down the street.

Diana watched him for as long as she could. Soon he disappeared around the corner.

"He seems like a very nice young man," Rita said when she was back inside.

"He is," Diana said, heading up the stairs.

"Do we need to have a talk?" Rita asked.

Diana stopped. "You mean about your project?"

"Project?"

"Whatever you needed the hammer and the pliers for?"

"Oh," Rita said, waving dismissively, "that can wait."

"I'll bet it can."

"No," Rita said, "what I mean is do we need to have a talk about...young men and young women?"

Diana nodded, leaning back against the stairway wall. *This should be good*, she thought. "Sure, mom. Let me have it."

"Well," Rita began, "sometimes when young men and young women are together, uh, well, you'll have certain...feelings. And these feelings are completely normal, nothing to worry about, they're just...well, teen pregnancy? Not a good thing."

"Mom, are you being serious here or trying to be funny?"

"Oh, honey, I know you know everything you need to know." Rita was quiet for a moment. "You know? What I'm asking you is, you do know, right? We never really sat down and had that talk..."

"You mean the birds and the bees...and the dinosaurs?"

"Diana..."

"Let's face it, mom, you could be worried about nothing, you know? Chuck and I are completely different species. Dinosaurs laid eggs, right? Could be that whatever you're worried about wouldn't be a problem even if, well, even if there was a problem, which there isn't."

"Yet."

Diana rolled her eyes and resumed her march up the stairs. "Don't worry about it, mom," she said.

Rita called, "Easy for you to say! You're not a mother! Wait 'til you're a mother!"

*Sure*, Diana thought, *I'll just sit on that egg 'til little Godzilla Jr. hatches and say, 'I sure wish I hadn't messed around with that cute velociraptor, he only wanted one thing! Mom warned me this could happen! Why didn't I listen to mom?'*

\* \* \*

"Dad?" he whispered.

Jarrod Keyes watched his father's chest rise and fall, accompanied by the beeps of the various machines he was hooked up to. As soon as Homeland Security had notified him, he had flown into Columbus. He told his teachers about what had happened on the Uber drive both to and from the airport.

His father had been in surgery when Jarrod arrived. The doctors had been cautiously optimistic. It seemed the bullet had nicked an artery, but they'd been able to patch him up. It looked like he'd pull through.

But of course, you never knew. There had been doctors who said his mother would pull through.

"Okay, dad," Jarrod said, "I'm right here." He took his father's hand.

The elder Keyes' eyes opened, and he looked at his son, confused for a moment, and then happy.

"Dad..." Jarrod whispered.

There was the smallest bit of pressure on Jarrod's hand, and then his father's eyes closed again.

Jarrod settled into the chair beside the bed, thinking now that he'd seen a sign of life, he could go to sleep. When the nurse, a squarely built older woman with grey shot through her hair, walked in and saw him, she said, "You might as well go home. He's doing fine, and he'll be here tomorrow."

Wasn't that a sweet phrase? "He'll be here tomorrow," Jarrod repeated.

"Yes," the nurse said with a smile.

"Well, I haven't had time to check into a hotel yet," Jarrod said, "and I don't live here, and he's all I've got left, so would you mind if I stayed here a little while?"

"I'm really not supposed to, but..." The nurse looked over at his father. "Your Dad saved a lot of very young people from God knows what. If he doesn't deserve an exception to the rules, I don't know who does. If anyone gives you any trouble, just tell them to see Nurse Haver, all right?"

"Thank you, Nurse Haver," Jarrod said.

She nodded. "We've had all sorts of requests, *The New York Times, The Washington Post, Time, People*…"

"He'll love that," Jarrod said sarcastically.

"Your father doesn't like publicity?"

"He's a behind-the-scenes kind of guy."

"Not anymore," Nurse Haver said. "Whether he likes it or not."

"He won't," Jarrod sighed.

# CHAPTER TWENTY-FIVE

'The alleged shooter,' Diana read, 'Carl Edward Van Meter, was an Iraq War veteran dishonorably discharged after...'

"Why do you want to read about such a perfectly horrible individual?" her mother asked. "Anyway, didn't I tell you no news for a while? Hadn't we agreed on that? I swear, we might have a lot less of these...situations if they didn't give these sick people so much publicity."

How had her mother snuck up on her? It was like living with a five foot five cat, silent until she didn't want to be anymore.

Diana had been hoping to find out about Keyes; with McAuliffe opening back up tomorrow, maybe it was time to tell her mother about everything.

"Mom," Diana said.

Rita turned around. "Lunch is ready," she announced, walking down the stairs and motioning for Diana to follow. "Ready, that's a laugh. I just barely brown some hamburger, and I call it ready."

"Mom," Diana called louder.

"Come downstairs," Rita yelled.

* * *

"Mom," Diana said, "there's something I should tell you." But then the plate of very rare hamburger patties was in front of her, and Diana started wolfing them down.

Watching her daughter tip her head back so the meat could fall down her throat, Rita got a sudden image of that iconic dinosaur moving its head down to a felled carcass, ripping at the meat and tipping its head back to swallow the way her daughter just had. Or, perhaps using its tiny—and much joked about—arms to hold a smaller, struggling creature until its head could be bitten off and the rest of its body consumed in the same manner.

Nothing in nature was truly vestigial, Rita knew. T. Rex fossils suggested that the arms hadn't been evolving away. A recent study, in fact, suggested the arms could bench press over four hundred pounds each. That was, of course, provided you could get the creature on a bench big enough. So the arms, by human standards, were very powerful, and weren't even truly small. They were actually around three feet long, so they were small only in proportion to the rest of the Tyrannosaur's forty-foot body.

Rita, who had always used observation, logic, and the scientific method to see the world, watched her daughter tip her head back again, another swallow of meat traveling down her throat.

Rationality and lucidity had helped her deal with her father's alcoholism, her mother's staid reactions to it, and the loneliness of being an intellectually curious young woman growing up in a small coal town whose livelihood shrank even as its contempt for education grew. In trying to remain calm and observe, she had gained scholarships and knowledge, had even met a man with whom a marriage worked at least long enough to have a wonderful daughter. An ordered mind kept her sane when the world, always threatening to fly apart in a thousand different directions, got scary.

Accidental gene splicing was like anything else, she supposed, even it had happened to her own child.

Rita watched Diana go after another burger, thinking yes, Diana was her child, but she was also something else; something at once so old you could only find glimpses of it in the fossil record, and something so new only a terribly out-of-control technology could have created it.

And through it all, the one thought that wouldn't leave Rita as she watched Diana tilt her head back and swallow again: that it would all be incredibly fascinating if it wasn't so damn scary.

Finishing the latest burger, Diana paused. "That was so good," she said.

*That might be a compliment if it weren't coming from an indiscriminate eating machine*, Rita thought, but instead gave her daughter a wan smile and took the plate away. "I'm glad you liked it," Rita answered.

"I can take the plate back..."

"Don't worry about it," Rita said, turning away with the plate and using the chance to dab at a tear.

"Listen, Mom?"

Entering the kitchen, Rita rinsed off the plate.

"Mom?" her voice was closer now. Rita had a sense of her daughter leaning in the doorway.

"Yes?" Rita said, her back still to Diana. Rita stuck the plate in the dishwasher.

"Something I should tell you," Diana said.

Rita picked up a wet rag, wiping up around the sink. "What?"

"I know we've kind of been on a news blackout..."

"Mm-hmm."

"Well...Agent Keyes, he was..."

"I know he was."

"I...how did you know?"

Rita finally turned around. "I cheated," she said. "I got on the internet a few times."

Nodding, Diana crossed her arms. "It might not be anything, it might not have been about me. I mean, it might not have been me he was investigating." *Tell her about saving his life!* Diana wanted to say, but when her mother looked down and swallowed, trying not to cry, she knew she couldn't add anything else.

"No sense worrying until we've got something to worry about, right?" Rita said, at last meeting her daughter's gaze.

"Right," Diana said, trying to casually laugh.

Rita nodded. "Okay," she said.

"Everything's going to be all right, mom," Diana said. "You'll see."

"I know," Rita answered, turning away to hang the rag over the faucet.

Diana made a tentative step toward her mother and stopped. When Rita turned back around, Diana was a bit closer, but the new nearness was not commented upon.

* * *

Keyes' eyes were open when the day nurse walked in. She said, "Well, hello! And how are you this morning?"

Trying to say 'okay,' Keyes succeeded only in nodding, then motioning over to Jarrod, asleep in the chair next to the bed.

"Who is he?" the nurse asked. "Is he your son?"

Keyes nodded. The nurse grinned, then gently shook Jarrod's

shoulder. Waking, he looked at her uncomprehendingly for a moment. Then, as if suddenly remembering where he was, Jarrod stood up.

"Your father is awake," she said.

"Thank you," Jarrod answered, taking his father's hand in both of his own.

"Well, I'll let you two, uh...I'll leave you alone for a little while. Would you like some breakfast, Mr. Keyes?"

Keyes looked hopefully at Jarrod. "Can you get him two scrambled eggs? And a bagel?" Jarrod asked for his father, who nodded. "Maybe a little bit of fruit?"

"That shouldn't be any problem for the hero of McAuliffe High."

Jarrod, eyebrows raised, looked back to his dad while the nurse left. "The hero of McAuliffe High?" Jarrod asked.

Keyes rolled his eyes.

# CHAPTER TWENTY-SIX

"It looks like we won't be doing a special assembly," Mr. Bidderson said.

Regarding his class from left to right, he asked, "Any ideas on that?"

He was met with a sea of unraised hands.

"Anything?" he asked again.

But there was nothing.

Diana remembered the white-taped face turning toward her. She didn't know what the tape was supposed to do; obscure his face, of course, but was it like war paint? Meant to terrify?

He had looked at her smugly, confident in his ability to kill, knowing his bullet would tear right through her.

The smile she saw was the ugliest smile in the world. Like Rhonda's smile before she'd sent her back.

Diana had seen the steak-knife smile of the most fearsome land predator ever to walk the earth, but there was no guile in that grin, there wasn't even knowledge, not really; it was a dumb display of what nature had given the T. Rex.

The truth, she knew, was that it wasn't a smile; to think it was a smile was...what would her mother have called it? Anthropomorphism? There was no steak-knife smile, not really. If the Tyrannosaur was aware of its status—and she thought it was, on some level—it did not take pride in the fact.

It simply knew what it was. What nature had honed it to do, after millions of years. It was power, and aggression, and hunger, yes, but there was no acceptance, rejection, or celebration of those qualities. Nature had designed that terrible grin. There had been no choice in the matter for the huge, extinct creature.

The T. Rex had a nobility that Tape Face would always lack.

Diana found her hand inching upward, until, raising his eyebrows, Mr. Bidderson said, "Yes, Ms. Dunphy?"

"We don't want to call attention to him," Diana said. "We want the first day back to be a normal day as if he'd never come here."

Mr. Bidderson nodded and pointed to Diana. "And Ms. Dunphy gets a gold star for today," he said. Then he addressed the class. "Such people as came here three days ago want attention," he said, "they want *effect*. In a pluralistic, hopefully still small-d democratic society as this one, they are the equivalent of the aberrant cell. They must not be celebrated, only excised with as little disruption as possible. Now, please open your texts to chapter seventeen so we can talk about the Great Depression, and I mean the economic one, not the times our Mr. Falchuck..."

Mr. Bidderson snapped his fingers in front of Karl Falchuck, a big, lumbering kid wearing a *Star Wars* sweatshirt.

As Falchuck startled awake, Mr. Bidderson said, "Not the times our Mr. Falchuck might seem blue because of a bad history grade..."

As Mr. Bidderson turned back to the board, he briefly caught Diana's eye, smiled, and nodded.

* * *

Monica Waverly, Homeland Security's Public Information Officer for Ohio, sat in the chair next to Keyes' hospital bed, her phone aimed his way.

"Okay," she said, "I'm recording."

"As I stated previously," Keyes went on, "I was at the school as a routine follow-up on the recent explosion at Gotelle, just to see if anyone might have noticed anything unusual about Andrea Fain or Thomas Orton."

"And then you heard the shots..." Ms. Waverly prompted.

Keyes nodded. "And, as the only sworn officer in the building, I went out..."

"Bravely went out," she said.

"Please," Keyes said, "I wished I had worn adult diapers. I was wetting my pants the whole way."

"Can I say that?" she asked, turning to Keyes' regional boss Reginald Solti, a tall, thin man standing near the door.

Solti shook his head.

"But it's so funny!" Monica said. And it humanizes..."

Now Solti shook his head and moved his finger back and forth in a 'no, no' gesture.

Ms. Waverly sighed, disappointed. "All right. This should be enough for the press conference."

"Very good. That's in a couple hours, so you'd best get to it." Solti made a show of checking his watch.

Ms. Waverly stood up, looked to Keyes and said, "You're a hero whether you admit it or not."

"Please," he whispered.

"You're a hero to me. And to a lot of other people, too. Certainly to all those kids, so...don't sell yourself short."

"I just happened to be there. And believe me, I wish I'd been somewhere else."

"Don't put that statement in the press materials, either," Solti said, "especially because I know *that* one's not true."

Ms. Waverly stood there for a moment, then abruptly leaned forward and kissed Keyes' cheek. She quickly left the room.

Keyes and Solti exchanged a look. "Your fan club," Solti said. "You might as well get used to it."

"An awful lot of appreciation for an old ex-Marine almost got himself shot to smithereens." Keyes said.

"Except you didn't get yourself shot to smithereens. Instead you shot the bad guy to smithereens."

Keyes kept quiet.

"You know, I got offered a spot at CIA." Solti said.

"Really?" Keyes said. Congratulations. I think."

Solti grinned. "Which means my spot as regional coordinator opens up. And thanks to your heroics here..."

Keyes scoffed.

"Uh-uh," Solti said, pointing to Keyes. "Thanks to your heroics, there's only one person anybody's talking about to take my spot."

"Seriously?"

Solti nodded. He made a 'money' gesture, rubbing his thumb against his four fingers. "Plus," he said, "isn't regional closer to where your son goes to college?"

Keyes nodded.

"Then hopefully this isn't a matter up for much debate?"

Keyes laced his hands behind his head, looking up at his old friends the ceiling tiles. He allowed himself a deep breath.

* * *

Diana sat her desk, her laptop on. Rita was on Diana's bed, one leg over the other.

On the screen, Monica Waverly finished reading her prepared statement. "...in following up on some routine investigatory matters related to the recent explosion at Gotelle Memorial Institute, Agent Keyes responded to gunfire in the hallway at McAuliffe High and charged bravely forward, soon surprising the assailant..."

"He's a big hero now," Rita said.

"Mm-hmm," said Diana.

"Maybe he'll forget all about you."

"Maybe."

Rita stood up and stretched. "Could be we caught a lucky break, huh?"

"Yeah," Diana agreed.

Rita put her hands on her daughter's shoulders. She kissed the top of Diana's head. "Go to sleep now," she said, "school night."

"Yes, mommy," Diana said.

"Don't 'yes, mommy' me, do it!"

Diana stood up. "Yes, mommy," she said, and picked up her roll of floss. She headed into the bathroom.

* * *

Later, after she cracked open the door to her mother's room to find her quietly snoring, sleep mask in place, Diana pulled on bike shorts and hoodie.

She climbed down the tree and began to run, stopping only when the hospital was in sight.

It was easy to find intensive care, even easier to get past the nurse. When she saw Keyes in bed, his chest rising and falling, the beeps of the machine he was hooked up to keeping a regular time, Diana slipped into the room, quietly closed the door, and sat in the guest chair.

"Mm..." Keyes said, stirring. "Jarrod?"

"No," Diana said softly.

He raised his head, looking up at her, then settled back. "Okay," he said, "Super Girl."

"I wouldn't exactly say *that*," she answered.

"Stopped a bullet from an AR-10," Keyes said. "I don't know what else to call you."

"Diana."

"Right. Diana..." Keyes was quiet for a moment.

"Listen, I need to..." Diana said, and swallowed, unable to continue.

"Need to know what? What I'm going to do?"

"Yes."

"Why? You here to kill me?"

Killing Keyes was never a consideration, but now that he'd said it, she didn't know why she was surprised he brought it up. "No, of course not," she said.

"I'm the only witness. To your secret identity."

"I'd never do anything to hurt you, Mr. Keyes. Didn't I prove that four days ago?"

"I suppose you did."

"I just need to know if you're going to tell everybody. Because I would like to tell my mom first. Before she learns about it some *other* way."

"Ms. Dunphy," Keyes said, "before this, all I wanted to find out was what the hell happened to Harvack, Orton, and Fain. Now? Now I'm just grateful. Grateful I'll have more time with my son, maybe be a grandpa someday provided he can find a woman up to his exacting standards. Anyway, how could I tell anyone and not be put away somewhere?"

"You could have me tested or something."

"No."

"You promise?"

He nodded. "Far as I'm concerned, Harvack, Orton, and Fain double crossed somebody, or were double crossed, who knows? It's not as if it was some great injustice. Combined, they probably have more blood on their hands than Pol Pot."

"Paul who?"

Keyes sighed. "I wish you young people would read some history."

Diana stood up.

"Could you do me one favor?" Keyes asked.

"Of course," Diana said.

"What happened exactly? Why are you this way?"

Diana sat back down. She began to talk, and it was actually good to get it all out: the year of Rhonda and Artie, her father and mother, Operation Crock Pot and its aftermath, the Tyrannosaur....

When she was done, Keyes sighed again. "You're going to have to be very careful," he said.

"Careful of what?"

"Yourself, Ms. Dunphy. You're not just very young, you have unprecedented human abilities. It's going to be very hard not to use them. The tendency, if one has power, is..."

"...that if you have power, you'll use it," Diana said. If you don't, you'll go to church?"

"That's a rather cynical view."

"Is it?"

"I'd say."

Diana stood up again, heading for the door.

"Miss Dunphy," Keyes said. She turned to him. "Just watch yourself, will you? All kinds of dangers out there, even for the bullet-proof. Maybe especially for the bullet-proof."

"All right," she said.

"Don't you have school tomorrow?"

She nodded.

"Then why don't you get out of here? Get some rest. And let an old man get some sleep."

"You're not an old man."

"Tell that to my birth certificate."

"Good night, Mr. Keyes."

"One thing." Keyes said, sounding sleepy.

"What?"

"I don't expect to hear any more reports, *ever,* of people eaten or half-eaten out here, you get it? I hear anything like that, this relationship could change."

"Don't worry," Diana said, and went quickly back into the hallway.

She was home in twenty minutes. Getting into her pajamas, Diana felt something like relief.

'All kinds of dangers out there,' she remembered Keyes saying, 'even for the bullet-proof. Maybe especially for the bullet-proof.'

*Yes,* Diana thought, *he's right, and mom's right.* She was going to lay low—she had to. Had to go strictly low-profile from now on. Maybe things felt scary before, but not now. Now things were going to get back to normal. Or as close to normal as she could make them.

*You know that's not going to happen*, she heard herself say.

*Of course it will!* Diana answered.

*No. It won't. You want him too much.*

*Want who?*

*You know who.*

Diana paused for a moment, reaching under the bed for the thumb drive and the satellite phone.

Studying them, she lied back down on the bed.

*I've got to keep things quiet*, she said to herself.

*Right. Like he's going to let you? And anyway, he was the one who killed dad and made you into a freak. Rhonda and Artie were just the murder and freak-making weapons.*

Putting the phone and the thumb drive back under the bed, she pulled the covers up around herself and shut her eyes.

## CHAPTER TWENTY-SEVEN

Rita made thick patties out of the two pounds of organic, grain-fed beef she'd bought.

Even if her daughter was, for all intents and purposes, a human-dinosaur hybrid, a better diet never hurt anyone. Sure, there were no cows back when the T. Rex roamed the earth, but if there were, they would have eaten grass, right? Or some kind of foliage. They wouldn't be pumped up with all sorts of antibiotics and artificial growth hormones and God knew what else.

Lightly browning the burgers, Rita putting them on a paper towel covered plate to soak up some of the fat. Not that Diana couldn't have used a little more fat in her diet, but old habits.

When her phone rang, Rita recognized Craig Farkus' number and picked up. "Craig," she said.

"Yeah, listen, are you available later today?"

Flipping over a burger, Rita answered, "I suppose I can be, what's going on?"

"Some tests. On the oil we got that night."

"Something wrong?"

"Something unexpected. Can I come get you around nine-thirty or so?"

"All right."

"Great. Thanks."

Craig clicked off as Diana came downstairs. Rita already had ice in the small cooler. Diana grabbed one of the already finished burgers and quickly polished it off, throwing her head back to swallow.

Watching this, Rita said, "Please tell me that when you're in school, you eat in private?"

"Sure, I'll tell you that, if that's what you want."

Rita sighed. "Diana..."

"What?"

Rita turned off the burner. "Don't you get tired of all this beef?"

"Haven't yet."

Replacing the already fat-soaked paper towel with a new one, Rita lifted the last of the burgers on to the plate, waiting for them to cool. "I'm not kidding, Diana," Rita said, "if that's the way you have to eat..."

"It's not the way I have to eat, it's just a lot easier."

"Well, then maybe instead of going to the cafeteria, you should..."

"Mom, there are kids there who shove entire sandwiches into their mouths, then close their lips and chew. There are others who just order Jell-o cubes and swallow one after another until they can't swallow anymore like it's a contest. Another girl I know waits till plums are really rotten, I mean, *really* rotten, so you can just reach in and pull out the pit. And then..."

Holding up a hand, Rita said, "I think I get it."

Diana nodded, packing the burgers into the cooler. Snapping the lid closed, she said, "Thanks for the burgers!" She kissed her mother and walked out of the house.

* * * * * *

Diana had been walking for perhaps five minutes when she smelled something familiar. She stopped, closing her eyes and sticking out her tongue.

Chuck...

Soon she heard running feet behind her. "Hi, Chuck," she said, before she saw him.

"Hey," Chuck caught up to her, a little out of breath. "How'd you know it was me?"

*What am I supposed to say to that? I could smell you? Probably not the best idea.* "Who else would it be?" she finally answered,

"I don't know. LeBron James?"

Diana thought it over. "Footsteps were too heavy."

"C'mon, he outweighs me by probably a hundred pounds!" Chuck protested.

"Hello?" Diana answered. "And he also happens to be LeBron James."

"Why didn't you say Usain Bolt?"

"Because Usain Bolt would have arrived at school by now."

Chuck thought it over. "I could have been Prince Harry."

Weighing the option for a moment, Diana said, "Okay, Prince Harry. I figured it was either you or Prince Harry and I took my shot."

* * *

Frannie Lightfoot drove past in her Miata, watching Diana and

Chuck. Next to her, Sascha DeFries was chewing gum while texting. "Now that's an odd couple," Frannie said.

"Mm," Sascha replied, "who?"

"Double D and Chuck Leadingham," Frannie answered.

"Not with her new bod," said Sascha, still intent on her screen. She stopped chewing long enough to blow a bubble.

"You think that's it?" Frannie asked.

Sascha shrugged. "Leadingham's a bod guy, I think. You saw that Rhonda, or whatever her name turned out to be, chick, didn't you? As my dad would have said, she was loaded for bear."

"Double D sure isn't."

Sascha shrugged again. "You seen her legs?"

"She's not that hot."

Sascha stopped texting and looked at Frannie. "What is it with you and her? So she beat you in basketball one time, so what? She's going to graduate from OSU with an accounting degree and vanish." Sascha went back to her phone.

"I'd love to break them up."

"You and Leadingham?" Sasha let out a dismissive exhale of breath. "Right. Didn't you try that already? At Noreen's party? Hate to say this, honey, but he didn't even know you were there! Him and that Rhonda chick were all over each other, don't you remember? Noreen took all those pictures."

Frannie turned to Sascha. "What pictures?"

"You know, *those* pictures, I can't believe you didn't hear about 'em!"

"Of Leadingham and that Rhonda chick?"

"You don't know about that?"

Stopping so that Sascha had to look over, Frannie asked, "How *those* are those pictures?"

Sascha shrugged. "I'll text Noreen and you can see for yourself."

* * *

Rita pulled on her coat and walked outside. Craig leaned over, opening the passenger door, and Rita got in.

The car, a late-model Lexus, smelled vaguely of cigarettes. She had never known Craig to be a smoker, but there were people who did it only in private.

As he drove out onto the road, Craig said "Sorry to have to do this. I know it must be a really hard time."

"It's all right. Good to get out, actually. What's the problem with the oil?"

"The viscosity. It's just...strange."

"What kind of tests have been run?"

"So far, just hydrocarbon feedstock analysis and evaluation."

"What did that turn up?"

"It's in the glove compartment."

Rita opened it up. She started reading.

* * *

"So, Mr. Bidderson said, "what are we to make of the second amendment? What is its actual text?" He looked around the class. "Anyone?" he asked.

Andy Nurch, a big guy with a crewcut, raised his hand. "The right of people to keep and bear arms is not to be infringed."

"Ah," said Mr. Bidderson, "in the popular lexicon, Mr. Nurch might be considered correct, but actually what the amendment says is..."

Diana's stomach grumbled. Loudly.

Looking around, she hoped no one heard. And then...

...then she smelled something.

She stuck out her tongue, turning to the window.

Diana saw a woodchuck.

Staring at it like a cat who had just seen a mouse, Diana watched it race across McAuliffe High's front lawn, fat shaking all over its stout little body.

*No...no*...she told herself.

She had to calm down. What was she going to do, excuse herself, run outside, chase the thing down, and then, in full view of the entire school, break its neck and eat it?

*The monster is you*, she remembered Dr. Siddons saying, and it had to be true. "The Monster is you," she repeated ever so softly, forcing herself to turn away from the window.

"Ms. Dunphy?" Mr. Bidderson asked.

"Yes?" she replied feeling almost faint. *The monster is you*, she thought.

"Something to add?"

"Isn't there something about...bearing arms in a militia?" Diana asked.

"Ah," Mr. Bidderson said, "yes!" He went to the board and began to write. Diana kept her attention on him, trying to let the image of the woodchuck fade.

\* \* \*

Rita looked up from the papers. "This all seems relatively normal," she said, noticing only then how unfamiliar the surroundings were. It looked like they were out in the country somewhere, but where?

"Craig," Rita said, "where exactly is the sample?"

"See, Rita, that's the thing..."

Rita noticed a huge, black SUV passing them. After a moment, it turned into their path.

Craig slowed down, then stopped. Rita turned around.

Another black SUV pulled up behind them.

Craig looked at her, almost regretfully. "The sample we really need is, well...you," he said.

# SISTER

"Come not between the Dragon and his Wrath."

-Shakespeare-King Lear Act I Scene V

# CHAPTER TWENTY-EIGHT

Diana stood on the stairs outside, waiting for Chuck to arrive. How had it happened, their routine of walking home together?

*It was okay though,* she thought. *It was really all right, the walking to and from school. I hope he likes it, he must like it, right? Or he wouldn't do it, right?*

Was it actually possible that Chuck Leadingham liked her? Liked her in the way people meant it when they said a guy liked you?

She couldn't think about that now, though...could she?

No. There was the guy on the satellite phone to deal with, and there was mom, who would probably tell her it was too risky. What if Chuck found out about her? The more they were together, the greater the chance of him finding out, right?

Although mom seemed to like him. That night watching the movie, they seemed to get along...

*Don't blame mom, you're the one who's afraid,* Diana thought.

*You're the one who doesn't want him to know what a freak he's walking home with.*

Diana's phone dinged. She frowned, picking it up and hitting the home button. A message read: "Picture's Chuck L. doesn't want you to see."

Frowning, Diana's finger hovered over the button. If he didn't want her to see them, maybe she shouldn't see them...

But then someone else's phone dinged, and someone else's, and people started clicking on the message, and a couple of guys ran out of the school's double doors laughing. "What a stud!" one of them said. "What a babe," said the other.

Sickened now, Diana hit the button. She was able to scroll through one photo, then another, and then she found herself walking down the stairs on legs that had turned to rubber.

Moving quickly, Diana put the school behind her, wanting to run, to *really* run, to T.Rex run. *No*, she told herself, *you can't be outrunning a car, not now. Low profile, remember? Now you just have to get home.*

*Yes, get home. Just get home!*

* * *

Chuck was at his locker when the phones started to ding. He ignored them, wanting to get outside for the walk home with Diana.

In the hallway, he heard a girl scream, "Oh, my God!" and laugh.

Closing his locker door, he saw people looking at him. Some turned away, embarrassed. Others laughed.

One of his friends, a fullback on the team, walked past with two other players. The fullback laughed, then held out his phone. "That's your best shot," he said.

Grabbing the phone out of the fullback's hand, he looked at it in dumb shock. "What the hell? Where did you get this?"

"Same place everybody else got it," was the answer.

One of the other players held up his own phone with his own set of photos. "Right on our phones!"

"No," Chuck said, thinking *Noreen*

He ran off as his teammates whooped and laughed.

Turning a corner, Chuck saw one of the guys from his history class. The guy looked at him and started clapping, and as much as Chuck wanted to stop and brain him, he didn't.

Instead, he ran to Noreen who was just shrugging on her backpack. "Noreen!" he said, coming to a stop, "What the hell?"

She turned away. "Leave me alone, Chuck," she said.

"You took pictures?"

"It was a joke! It was just a joke!" Noreen said as she walked. "My parents had a security cam, and I saw you two all over each other, and I just..."

"You just what? Now she's dead, you thought you'd share pics?"

"It was just a joke! I only showed 'em to a few people, and then some other people..."

"Other people?"

"Girls."

"What girls?"

"...found out about it, and then..."

"What girls?"

Noreen stopped, looking down. When she looked back up, she said, "Frannie Lightfoot, okay?"

"Frannie Lightfoot?"

"She's pissed at Diana Dunphy for killin' it in some basketball game, and she knows the two of you are, you know, and..."

"And what?'

She jabbed her finger into his chest. "And you didn't hear it from me!"

Chuck grabbed the finger, turning it slightly up. "Ow!" Noreen screamed.

Calming, Chuck let Noreen's finger go. *This is a girl*, he thought, *and you can't tune up a girl, no matter what*. He stuck his own finger into Noreen's face. "You don't take pictures of people without their permission when they're..."

How was he supposed to finish that sentence?

"Well, don't get into it with some chick at somebody else's house!" Noreen fired back.

Waving her away, Chuck ran for the front door.

* * *

Diana passed the dog, who didn't bark at her anymore, but whimpered low in its throat and lowered its head. All Diana could think looking at it was, *Meat! Good, blood-red meat!*

But she didn't attack. She forced herself to go on.

Turning her key in the front door lock, she yelled, "Mom?" in a voice that was surprisingly weak. "Mom?" she called again, and when she saw her mother wasn't home, she quickly changed out of her school clothes and into her sweats.

Diana didn't pause to wonder why her mother's car was still in the garage.

*She probably took a walk. Or maybe a friend picked her up.*

She slid under the car and grabbed the front axel.

It came up easily, all two thousand-some pounds, and Diana pumped out the reps, trying to unsee the photos she had just seen, thinking that perhaps the more weight she lifted, the more she could forget the images.

Lifting the car, she pulled her legs beneath it, and started her leg press routine, exhaling as she went. She did one, two, three presses...

*Don't think about it*!

Then five, six, seven...

*Stop*!

Then nine, ten, eleven...

*No more*!

And the phone rang.

She lowered her legs, then got her arms up beneath the front axle and put the car back on the floor. Sliding out from under the Honda, Diana thought *What if it's him? What could I say to him? What should I say to him?*

Picking up, resigned, Diana said, "Hello?" in a voice that sounded far away and wounded.

"Is this the Dunphy girl?" came the man's familiar, oddly pleasant voice. Concerns about Chuck and his photos were automatically gone.

"How did you get this number?" Diana asked, immediately closing her eyes and wincing. *He knows where you live*, she thought. *He said he did...*

"I have someone here who would like to speak to you," the man said.

Diana heard her mother's voice next. "Diana," her mother sounded urgent, "whatever they tell you to do, don't do it! Call the..."

Her mother's voice ended.

"Mom?" Diana called.

The voice came back on. "Ms. Dunphy," he said, "across the street is a black car with tinted windows."

Walking to the front picture window, Diana saw the dark sedan. After a moment, the driver's side window came down. A dark-suited man wearing a chauffeur's cap waved jauntily at her.

Diana felt sick. As if the bottom of her stomach had dropped out.

"If you hurt her..." Diana said.

"Get into the back seat," he said, "immediately. With the thumb drive."

Hanging up, Diana stood there for a moment, knowing she should get the thumb drive, but the anger was so strong...

The T. Rex was waking up.

\* \* \*

She was halfway down the front lawn when Chuck intercepted her. "Diana!" he said, "Uh...hi!"

Diana answered without looking at him. "Sorry, Chuck, not a good time."

He followed her, "Look," he said, "I-I-uh, if you've seen those pictures, I didn't, it wasn't..."

She stopped walking and looked directly at him. "It's all right," she said.

"It's not all right," he answered.

Over Chuck's shoulder, Diana watched the driver get out of the black car. "Chuck, please," she said, "we can talk later!"

"No, I want to tell you this now!"

"No, you don't!"

Behind Chuck, the driver had arrived. "Is there some problem?" he asked.

"No, no problem," said Diana

Chuck turned to the driver, confused. "Who are you?" he asked. Then he turned to Diana, indicating the driver. "Who's this guy?"

"I'm with the Department of Homeland Security," the driver

said, taking Diana by the arm, "and little Ms. Dunphy needs to come with us."

"Hey! Do you mind?" Diana said, refusing to move.

Grabbing the driver's hand, Chuck broke the grip, shoving his face into the driver's. "You're gonna be in for one serious tune-up, you put a hand on her again!" Chuck yelled.

The driver opened his coat, revealing a gun in a shoulder holster. Keeping his voice low, he leaned in toward Chuck. "Are we going to have a problem here?" he asked.

# CHAPTER TWENTY-NINE

"No," Diana said. "No problem!" She got between Chuck and the driver.

"Diana, who is this ass pirate?" Chuck asked. "He's not Homeland Security, they don't threaten you with guns!"

Her eyes still on the driver, Diana backed away, not only keeping herself between him and Chuck, but forcing Chuck slowly up the driveway. "Go home, Chuck, please," Diana said.

Shaking his head, Chuck said, "No way am I leaving you with this..."

The driver reached into his coat pocket, producing a stun gun, which he pointed in Chuck's direction.

Diana grabbed the driver's wrist. Hanging onto it, she turned and pulled, flipping the driver over her shoulder.

Chuck watched the driver sail overhead. He slammed into the garage door.

It took a minute to register that the garage door was about ten feet away.

"Self-defense classes! Duh!" She hoped that would cover it.

"Right," Chuck said, his voice oddly calm, "You taking self-defense classes on Krypton?"

"They have my Mom!" she blurted out. Taking a deep breath, she said softer, "I can't go to the cops."

"Go to the cops?" Chuck exclaimed, looking at the driver crumpled against the garage door, "The cops should be going to you!"

The driver's phone started to ring. They stared at the unconscious body, and then at each other. Finally, Diana ran over and fished it out of his jacket pocket. Holding the phone out to Chuck, she said, "Talk to 'em!"

"About what?" Chuck asked.

"I don't know, anything!" Clicking the home button, Diana slid the screen and held it out again.

"What's the hold up?" said a voice Diana could recognize, even standing a few feet away.

Chuck looked at Diana, pleading.

'Say something,' she mouthed.

Chuck put the phone to his ear, eyes closed. "Nothin" he said, deepening his voice.

"All right, then, get over here!"

"Mm-hmm," Chuck replied.

Diana lifted the garage door and effortlessly dragged the driver inside. Looking back to Chuck, she said, "We've got to get to wherever he came from!"

Chuck began hitting buttons on the driver's smart phone. "Let me see if he's got GPS," Chuck said.

"Why?" Diana asked

"My brother, he showed me something once. I might be able to find where he came from."

Diana nodded, starting to take off the driver's jacket. She

took out the gun, and making sure Chuck couldn't see, crushed it, then slid the weapon away under her mother's car. She put the stun gun on the floor and stomped on it once, shattering it.

After a few key strokes, Chuck called, "I think I found it!" He looked over to the garage where Diana was using duct tape to bind the arms and legs of the driver, who she had stripped to his underwear.

"Diana," Chuck muttered, shocked.

"What?"

"Well, you took his..."

"His what?"

"Clothes? Off?"

Rolling her eyes, Diana said, "I didn't molest him, I promise."

"That's not what I...I didn't mean..." Chuck stammered.

"I don't care what you mean," she said. "Do you really want to help out?"

Chuck nodded. Diana slapped the driver's cap on Chuck's head, then handed him the jacket and pants.

* * *

In the back seat as Chuck drove out into the country, Diana had time to think: *Is mom okay? Why do they want us? It's got to have something to do with Crock Pot, but what?*

And inside, the T. Rex smiling, biding its time.

*Someone's going to end up being really sorry*, Diana thought, and she saw the steak-knife smile grow wider until another thought came to her: *Yes, and there's a good chance it's going to be you, so calm down!*

When they had gone past houses, farmland, even telephone poles, they saw it on the horizon, perched incongruously in the middle of nowhere: a mansion.

"You seeing this?" Chuck asked.

"Yes," she answered.

As they got closer, they could see that it was surrounded by a thick, wrought-iron fence. Some crows lit on the top of the fence began to caw in warning, as if to keep them away.

"Sure," Chuck said, "that's not creepy, not a bit, not at all."

Diana remembered the Poe story Mrs. Segal had them read, *The Fall of the House of Usher*, it was called. If some movie company ever decided to film a modern-day version of it, this mansion is where it would have to be shot, no other place would do.

Up the long driveway they drove, stopping next to a speaker box. Chuck rolled down the window. "Maddox?" a voice asked.

Pulling the cap low over his eyes, Chuck answered, "Mm-hmm."

A loud buzz sounded, and the gates opened up, swiveling like the huge jaws of some titanic beast. Chuck drove through and onto a winding road.

As they headed to the front door, Diana said, "Just drop me off and get out of here, all right?"

"I can't just leave you here at Dracula's Castle!" Chuck hissed.

"Yes, you can! Please, Chuck, I don't want you to get hurt!"

Chuck stopped the car at the bottom of the stairs at the main house. Opening the rear passenger door, Diana hesitated a moment, looking at Chuck. "Get out of here," she said, "I mean it! Wait a half hour, if you don't hear from me call the cops, okay?"

Chuck said nothing.

"Okay?" Diana repeated.

"Okay," Chuck said sullenly.

"Promise me."

"I promise!"

Putting a hand on the back of the front seat to steady herself, Diana started to get out of the car.

Chuck put his hand on top of hers. "Diana," he said.

Diana stopped, looking over at him.

"I wish I'd known you before...I mean, I wish you hadn't been her best friend...because you were her best friend! It's like I never saw you."

"Chuck..."

"But I see you now, okay? I see you now, and I'm so sorry about everything! Those pictures, they..."

"This isn't the time to worry about pictures. I have to go, and so do you."

"Don't get killed in there, huh?"

Nodding, Diana stood up out of the car.

"Maddox?" asked a voice she recognized, even if it wasn't crackling over a satellite phone.

At the top of the stairs, a good-looking older man in a suit stood surrounded by three huge men in dark clothing. "Maddox," said the man, "you seem awfully familiar with the young lady, did you bond that much on the drive over?" His head swiveled to Diana. "And you must be the Dunphy girl, here to see your mother, no doubt. I'm an old friend of your parents. Mainly your father, though. Did he ever mention Zachary Guillermin to you?"

Diana shook her head. Guillermin beckoned her forward with two fingers, the gesture of someone who was used to having his orders followed.

Diana started up the stairs.

"You too, Mr. Maddox," Guillermin said.

Resigned, Chuck got out of the car and stood up. He took off his chauffeur's cap and looked sullenly at Guillermin.

"Mr. Maddox!" Guillermin smirked, "What a rejuvenating drive! I wish I'd come along, perhaps I could have lost twenty years myself!"

"Let him go," Diana said.

"Really, Ms. Dunphy, a man doesn't get to my position in life without taking advantage of every opportunity." Using his two fingers, Guillermin beckoned Chuck forward.

Chuck slumped a bit at the shoulders. "I guess we're really screwed now," he mumbled, joining Diana on the stairs.

# CHAPTER THIRTY

Inside, Guillermin walked ahead. The dark-suited men surrounded Chuck and Diana.

They were walking down a hall toward what looked to be shiny aluminum elevator doors. The mansion was strangely devoid of furnishing, painting, and light fixtures. The lone nod to the idea that it might have been a place people could occupy was the carpet they walked on, but even that, she noticed, only covered the path from the front door to the elevator.

"Your father and I had a bit of a history," Guillermin said.

"What do you mean, history?" Diana asked.

Stopping at the elevator, Guillermin turned back and gave Diana a little smile. Then the elevator doors opened and they all got on. When the elevator doors slid closed, they began a smooth descent.

"Funny place, Gottelle," Guillermin said. "A non-profit corporation funding all that strange private and public sector research? Not hard to find out what's going on in a place like that. Particularly if you make the right contributions."

Diana looked at Guillermin, trying to keep the T. Rex at bay. Trying to keep the hate out of her eyes.

"I figured what your father didn't know wouldn't hurt him," Guillermin said.

Without thinking, Diana clamped her hand around Guillermin's throat.

The nearest dark-suited man drew a weapon, and Chuck body checked him. Two other bodyguards drew their weapons.

Guillermin held up his hand, stopping them.

"Except it did hurt him," Diana said. Bringing her face closer to Guillermin's, she growled, "It hurt a lot of people!"

"Ah!" Guillermin said, "She shows herself!"

Now even angrier, if that were possible, Diana began to lift Guillermin up by the neck.

Chuck blinked, sill not quite able to believe it. The bodyguards aimed their weapons, but Guillermin once more found the strength to hold up a hand.

It was harder for Guillermin to talk now, but he managed. "The...young...woman...who went after...three highly trained... covert operatives...and...killed them all...!" Letting a tiny laugh escape, Guillermin went on. "You...really want...to kill me... before you see...your mother?"

Enough rage drained out of Diana that she was able to put Guillermin down on the elevator's floor.

They slowed to a stop.

She took her hand away from his neck. Guillermin rubbed it as the elevator doors slid open.

Turning to the now open sub-basement, Diana saw Crock Pot, completely re-created.

As she stepped out of the elevator, Chuck, Guillermin, and the bodyguards behind her, Diana realized that, no, it hadn't just been re-created, it had been re-made. The chamber was longer, wider, and...meaner, she decided. It looked as if the nastiest person in the world had studied her father's designs and said, 'No, that's entirely too *nice*. Add fins and structures that can impale anyone trying to get too close.'

Mom said that if it were even possible, it would take billions of dollars, and yet...here it was.

Done rubbing his neck, Guillermin walked up beside her. Barely aware of his presence, Diana gasped, "My God...how did you do it?"

"The hardware designs were easy," he explained, before walking in front of her. "The software, that was the hard part. Gunter and your friends..."

"They were *not* my friends!"

Guillermin shrugged. "They very much weren't my friends either, if it makes you feel any better." He walked around in front of her. "Harvack, Orton, and Ms. Fain figured out, unfortunately for them, that the hardware was key. Which is why they decided to go rogue, try to squeeze me for more money." He looked back to the new Crock Pot where various technicians were busy patching wires and welding plates. Guillermin said, "I do so hate opportunists. But that's a situation you took care of for me. Thank you very much. I really owe you for it."

Diana didn't know how to respond. She tried to find her mother in the crowd of technicians, then turned to Guillermin again. "Where's my mom?" Diana asked.

"Soon," Guillermin said. "You know, your father was rather... conservative in what he wanted to do. I've made some adjustments to his designs."

She found herself moving toward Guillermin again. "What kind of adjustments?" she growled.

Guillermin returned a sly smile.

* * *

Rita, overseeing a titanium plate being welded onto the skin of the new Tachyon Chamber, noticed her daughter at the elevator doors. "Diana?" she called.

Seeing Rita, Diana yelled, "Mom!"

Running over, Rita saw some bodyguards moving in and hesitated.

Holding up a hand to make the bodyguards stop, Guillermin pointed to Rita, then signaled her over.

Hugging her daughter, Rita then broke the embrace, trying not to cry. Taking Diana's hands in both of hers, she secreted a note into Diana's hand as she said, "I'm so glad you're all right!"

"Mom," Diana said, "are you working with these people?"

"I'm trying to keep you alive. Trying to keep both of us alive!"

"Mom," Diana said, indicating Guillermin, "how much does he know?"

"I know you were sent back through time and came back... shall we say...improved? The thumb drive should tell us the rest." Guillermin held out his hand.

"Give it to him, Diana," Rita said.

"Mom, tell me you're kidding!"

"Do it!"

"This asshole killed dad!"

"Not something I meant to have happen," Guillermin said, "let me assure you of that. That was all a rather unfortunate—or is that fortunate, I'm not so sure—improvisation by the most definitely unfortunate Harvack, Orton, and Fain." Now he looked at Diana with the utmost seriousness. "But there was only going to be one working Tachyon Chamber, and it was going to be owned by me."

Diana took a menacing step toward Guillermin. She could hear guns being drawn all around her. She stopped moving.

Watching all those weapons, she weighed her chances.

"Yes," Guillermin said, "you're not all that afraid of guns anymore, are you? The remains of Harvack's pistol indicated it had been discharged twice prior to exploding, a fact I found quite fascinating." Leaning toward her, he said, "So fascinating I sent a man to your school with an AR-15."

"You...what?" Diana gasped.

"What he was supposed to do was get a shot at you and then report back. Which he could have done if not for..." He gestured vaguely in Diana's direction.

"You endangered all those people?" Diana asked, trying to keep the growl out of her voice. "Just so...?"

"Oh, 'endangered.' " Guillermin said, "no one was hurt. No one was remotely hurt, except for my rather unfortunate associate, and her knew the risks."

"Mr. Keyes is still in the hospital," Diana growled.

"Keyes," Guillermin laughed. "That was the best thing that ever happened to him. A middle manager in a government job, and how he's being promoted, I'd call that a win-win."

"They said that shooter was some disturbed veteran..." Rita said softly.

"And so he was!" Guillermin replied. "Just not *that* disturbed. We were prepared for the worst, of course, had a cover story on the off chance your daughter...well, actually did what she did."

Rita got closer to Guillermin. "You didn't know that she'd survive if she was shot with a rifle, you had no clue."

Guillermin raised his eyebrows, shaking his head. "No. I didn't."

Rita slapped him across the face as hard as she could. The noise was distinguishable over all of the racket made by the assembly of the new Tachyon Chamber. Rita raised her hand to slap him again, but he caught it. "You only get one for free," Guillermin said, shoving Rita back toward Diana, who caught her.

"Mom," Diana said, "please get out of the line of fire."

"I will not abandon my child to this..."

"Yes, Rita, please do get out of the line of fire. Everyone is quite confident that any bullets fired today will go completely through you, and we really need that chamber finished." Turning to one of his men, Guillermin was handed a huge, menacing rifle. "This is a military grade prototype, loaded with newly designed armor piercing rounds," he said. "Designed to pierce the latest body armor." Snapping off the safety, he faced Diana, keeping the rifle pointed at the ground. "Our Mr. Harvack didn't have one of these, did he?"

Putting her hands up, Diana took a step back.

"It would not be remiss to point out that it was your father's idea to throw the explosives into the Tachyon Chamber in a misguided attempt to send them away. He could have simply run out of the room with you and your mother, isn't that true?"

Now she could feel the T. Rex waking up. "He was trying to save us and everybody still in that building or anywhere near it..."

"Isn't that true?" Guillermin repeated deliberately.

"You got some balls saying that," Diana growled, "maybe it's time somebody ripped 'em out!"

"Diana!" Rita said admonishingly.

Ignoring her mother, Diana went on. "My dad was the only one trying to help anybody that night. What were you doing? Sending Rhonda and Artie to kill people and destroy my dad's life's work!"

"Yes, Ms. Dunphy, but if you can take a step back I think you might find it interesting." Guillermin said.

"Interesting?" she asked in a full-throated growl.

"Yes," Guillermin responded, handing the rifle to his nearest man and flicking his chin in the direction of the Tachyon Chamber. "I told you we could be friends, didn't I?"

"Keep dreaming."

"Interesting choice of words. My dream and yours may dovetail."

"The only thing that's gonna dovetail is my fist and your—"

"You still don't see it." Guillermin shook his head. "Doesn't our re-built chamber make all those deaths...rather fluid?"

Diana stared at him with a flat, reptilian hatred.

"Is 'preventable' a better word?" Guillermin asked.

She frowned, felt herself calming, the growl diminishing, the T. Rex retreating...

Regarding her for a moment, Guillermin said, "Don't make the same mistake your father did,"

"Too late," Diana grunted, "I've already met you."

Guillermin grinned. "What I mean to say is don't be so narrow minded about possibilities." He looked to the Tachyon Chamber. "I so wish my own children were more like you. Dedicated, passionate, able to handle the power they've been given. It's the flaw of a parent to want to give one's children everything. I realize now how very bad that was for them. Because they were given everything, they ended up appreciating precisely nothing. Drugs, drink, crashed cars, crashed lives..." He shook his head, lost in thought for a moment.

"You're not Father of the Year," Diana said, "there's a surprise."

Guillermin laughed. "You're a tough one, aren't you? Well, that's all right. I already hold myself far more accountable as a parent than anyone else could. But I often think, 'if I could just go back in time, fix this, adjust that.' You're probably too young to appreciate the sentiment, but get to be my age, it'll resonate a bit more. Did you know that Thomas Edison deemed the motion picture camera to be so unimportant that he didn't even bother to patent it? Think of the billions that cost him, and then think of your father. Sending trash back in time to create oil?" He blew air out of his lips, a dismissive noise. "Have you studied enough economics in that cesspool of a public school of yours to know what creates wealth?"

She said nothing, her eyes flicking from Guillermin to the man with the rifle and back again.

"Scarcity," Guillermin said. "You don't want enough oil for everybody! That's a completely ridiculous idea! Make the United States the new Middle East? Why do that when the old Middle East works just fine...provided you give the army of the Crusades modern weapons. Let them completely subjugate the area, ridding it of its native population, but doing it almost a thousand years in the past. If you want to change the shape of our world, that's the way to do it."

"Dude," Diana said, "you're nuts?"

"Am I?" Guillermin asked. "So it would also be nuts to say...go back through time to prevent your father's death?"

Now Diana turned to the new Tachyon Chamber.

"It's all just a matter of modification, isn't it?" Guillermin asked.

"You think...you can do that?" Diana asked haltingly.

Guillermin shrugged. Grinning, he held out his hand.

"Give him the thumb drive, Diana," her mother said. "I can't make you. The power is all yours. The power is in your hand."

Diana looked in her hand. The note her mother gave her read, 'I can blow it up.'

Looking back to Guillermin, Diana slowly reached into her pocket. She withdrew the thumb drive, handing it over.

"A wise choice," Guillermin said, holding the thumb drive in the palm of his hand. "Mr. Farkus?" Guillermin called.

When Craig walked out, Diana growled, "You?"

Guillermin handed the thumb drive to Craig. "Me," he said, then walked back to the Tachyon Chamber and stuck the thumb drive into a computer.

"It's all here," Craig said after a few minutes.

Frowning, Rita walked to the computer. She looked over Craig's shoulder.

"Including a precise tachyon map of her trip back," Craig said.

Putting a hand over her mouth, Rita turned away. With her back to Guillermin, she switched the in and out points of two wires.

"Excellent," Guillermin said, walking toward the Chamber's door. "Can you join me up here, Craig?"

Craig got to the door as Guillermin spun the dial and opened the Chamber.

Putting his hand on Craig's shoulder, Guillermin nodded as if considering. "You've done an excellent job here, Craig. But what we really need now, to test this out—"

Shoved violently into the chamber, Craig tripped, falling to its gleaming floor. The door was closed, the dial spun.

"As I was saying, to test this out, what we really need is a volunteer." Guillermin pronounced.

# CHAPTER THIRTY-ONE

Craig immediately began pounding on the door of the Tachyon Chamber.

Diana knew he was screaming, clawing to get out, the way she had been. In spite of everything, she backed up, trying to measure the distance for a jump. If she could get there, tear off the door...

Tear off the door? She could just *open* the door!

Guillermin pointed to another technician manning the Chamber's controls.

"For God's sake!" Rita said.

"Oh, please," Guillermin said, "he gave us all the necessary information to destroy you and your ex-husband's work, you can't honestly tell me you're going to shed any tears over him?"

"You don't know what it'll do to him!" Diana called.

Guillermin turned back to her, a matter-of-fact grin on his face and said, "Listen, everybody, the super-strong, bullet-proof girl is telling us what might happen to him."

The technician fired up the Tachyon Chamber. A low hum began.

Diana turned away, putting her hands over her ears, trying to shut out the awful memory.

The hum got louder, accelerating into a whine.

The Tachyon Chamber began to shake, although much less than the first one had.

A brief, shimmering bluish light lanced out of the window in the Chamber's door.

It wasn't the bright and harmful brilliance of the beam from her father's design, the light that necessitated the goggles. It was something else.

*Something improved? No, something worse*, Diana thought.

There was another bright, green-tinged flash, and then all was back to normal.

The sound died down, an engine noise fading away.

Unable to help herself, Diana jumped to the door of the tube, not caring that Guillermin and all of his people, that her mother...that Chuck...could see her do it. None of it mattered, not at the echo of her own death and re-birth.

Through the window, Diana could see the empty chamber. Looking back at Guillermin, he and Diana locked eyes for a moment.

Guillermin smiled and shrugged. "Initiate re-constitution." He said.

Noticing a movement in her peripheral vision, Diana glanced over to see her mother making frantic 'get away from there!' gestures.

Running to her mother, Diana once more heard the hum intensifying to a whine.

The bodyguards, their attention still on the Tachyon Chamber, let Chuck slip past. He joined Rita and Diana, whispering, "What is this?"

"This is us getting out of here!" Rita whispered, putting one hand on the inside of Diana's elbow and the other on the inside of Chuck's. Rita backed up, gently taking the two of them with her.

The sparks arcing out of the Tachyon Chamber increased in both intensity and size.

Backing right up into what she could tell was a small metal cylinder, Rita closed her eyes, resigned.

She turned around. One of the bodyguards was holding a gun to her back.

"Nuh-uh-uh," the bodyguard said. Chuck and Diana also turned to look his way.

Immediately jumping between the gun, her mother, and Chuck, Diana put her arms out, trying to shove the two of them behind her.

The Tachyon Chamber rocked violently back and forth.

All three of them turned around.

The rear of the Tachyon Chamber was blown off of its base, landing diagonally away from the spectators.

The chamber creaked back and forth as if the world's largest rocking chair were in motion.

When that stopped, everyone stood still for a moment.

"Mom," Diana whispered, "what the hell did you do?"

"I didn't think they were going to send somebody *through* the damn thing!" Rita whispered back.

"What did you think they were going to do?" Diana hissed.

"I don't know, send some trash back or something?"

There was still no noise from the chamber.

"See?" Rita said after a moment, "Maybe nothing happened."

There was a loud boom from inside the Tachyon Chamber.

"Mom?" Diana said, "I think maybe something happened."

The Chamber's door, now facing them, buckled out.

The technician who sent Craig back slowly approached the Chamber, his brow furrowed. Bending forward, he looked through the window.

The Chamber was clean. It looked completely empty.

Turning back to Guillermin, the technician said, "He's not in the..."

Careening suddenly and violently off of its hinges, the door of the Tachyon Chamber shot out, striking the Technician squarely in the chest. He and the door sailed off against the wall.

There was a sound like a huge piece of bread hitting the floor jelly-side down.

A noise came from the Tachyon Chamber, as if a lion's roar had been mixed with a jet engine and something else: the plaintive cry of a baby.

A huge, scaly, brownish-green, five-fingered claw curled itself around one side of the door. Its twin appeared a second later on the other side.

"Something's definitely happened!" Diana said.

# CHAPTER THIRTY-TWO

A malformed, lizard-like head emerged from the door. It didn't look like a T. Rex, or even a mini T. Rex. It was something else.

Beneath each dinosaur eye were two more eyes, eerily human. When the eyes blinked, all six did so in unison, but appeared to be able to look around independently.

Its torso looked to be that of a flabby, late forty-ish man, melded into that of the T. Rex. The famous dinosaur's arms, subject of so many jokes, were human at least in their length, but ended in five-fingered claws.

Its legs were powerful and all dinosaur. Its tail, long and whip-like, seemed shot through with exposed human vertebra.

The ten-foot tall *thing* that stood up out of the Tachyon Chamber clearly never should have existed, and yet there it was.

Rita and Chuck were shocked, instinctively backing away, but Diana could only stare in mute horror. *It's me*, Diana thought, *it's me turned inside-out!*

The creature's six eyes swiveled immediately to Guillermin.

A rattling sound came from its throat, and then it made its first move toward its old boss.

Guillermin indicated the man holding the rifle. "That will be enough of that," he said.

The Rifleman took a bead, then fired, the gunshot echoing off the walls even as the creature was knocked backward. Slamming against the Tachyon Chamber, it slid to the ground, forked dinosaur tongue lolling out of its mouth.

It lay motionless.

Guillermin looked disappointed. "Well, that will never do. We need someone to turn out...prettier. The way Ms. Dunphy did. Can we try this again? Do we have a volunteer?"

"Volunteer?" Rita exclaimed. You can't run it again! Not with the door off, you'll blow the whole area back to the stone age!"

"A little further than that, I think," said Guillermin, "and anyway, we'll have the door welded back on in no time." Guillermin put his hand to his chin, staring at Chuck.

"What?" Chuck asked.

"Speaking of volunteers," Guillermin mused.

Diana took a defensive stance, immediately getting in front of Chuck. Locking eyes with Guillermin, she said, "You'll have to go through me."

"Funny you should say that," Guillermin replied.

Behind Guillermin, the Rifleman advanced, holding the huge weapon with both hands. As he came forward, he stepped on something hard.

"Because we happen to have something here that will, in fact, go through you," Guillermin said.

The Rifleman frowned, moving his foot to the side. He bent to pick up what he had stepped on. He brought it up to his face.

"Right through you," Guillermin finished.

In the Rifleman's hand was the armor-piercing bullet he had

just fired at the Creature. It was flattened, as if it had struck something very hard and then bounced off.

The Rifleman whipped his head back toward the Tachyon Chamber.

The Creature was gone.

A huge, misshapen shadow fell over the Rifleman. He looked up, mouth agape.

The Craig Creature landed in front of the Rifleman but behind Guillermin. The Creature's lips curled past its steak-knife teeth.

Guillermin, all confidence as he faced the three captives, frowned as they backed away. "You needn't be that frightened of the gun. He's not going to use it unless you make him. Unless..."

Now it occurred to Guillermin that Diana, Chuck, and Rita were all looking at something behind him.

Turning around, Guillermin saw the Rifleman trying to take aim at the Creature.

Too late. It grabbed the rifle out of his hands.

"...you...make...us...?" Guillermin whispered.

The state-of-the-art, military grade rifle broke in two as if it were no more substantial than a dried twig. Its pieces were flung away, clattering into the darkness.

The Creature's six eyes fixed on the man who used to have the rifle. Quickly, far too quickly for a creature of its size, it grabbed the former rifleman, lifting him up.

The man screamed, putting his arms up defensively as the Creature's mouth opened, its jaw seeming to unhinge. The man's screaming grew muffled as the terrible mouth surrounded his head.

Chuck and Rita looked away.

Diana couldn't. Trying not to watch, she seemed to need to study...

A spray of arterial blood hit Guillermin in the face, splattering over his suit. He moved his hand down his face, trying to clear away the blood.

The creature took a few more bites then discarded what remained of the Rifleman's body.

It tilted back its terrible had, swallowing the way a T. Rex would.

The way she would.

The mass of blood, gristle, and bone that used to be Guillermin's employee moved down its throat in two gulps.

Quickly getting past the dumbstruck Diana, then past Rita and Chuck, Guillermin pointed to the man who had the gun trained on them and shouted, "Do not let them leave!" before he ran for the elevators.

The Craig Creature's reddish-blue tongue lapped the sides of its steak-knife smile. Then it began to look around.

It locked eyes with Diana.

She backed away, putting her arms behind her as if to protect Chuck and Rita.

*My God*, Diana thought as the Creature's lips curled up over its teeth, *is it smiling at me?*

Eyes still locked on Diana's, it settled back onto its haunches and then sprang forward.

Diana put her hands up instinctively, but the monster sailed effortlessly over her, Rita, Chuck, and the bodyguard.

A crowd had gathered around the elevator in a half circle. In the center of the circle was Guillermin, frantically punching the elevator's 'up' button.

Landing on two of the technicians of the group's outer ring, the creature picked up the screaming men and smashed repeatedly them into each other. The bloody masses that remained were barely contained in what was left of their clothes.

One of the bodyguards aimed his weapon at it, but the Craig Creature slapped the gun out of his hands. The gun smacked against the wall, then clattered to the floor as the Creature advanced on the bodyguard, mouth wide open.

The other bodyguards opened fire almost in unison. Closing its eyes, the Creature put its arms protectively across its face. The gunfire drove the Craig Creature away. It fell onto its back.

Jumping into the now open elevator, Guillermin pounded the 'close' button.

As the metal doors slid closed, the bodyguards clicked on empty chambers

All eyes narrowing, the Creature growled, then grabbed a huge piece of the Tachyon Chamber's ruined base and flung it at the elevator.

Metal smashed on metal. The elevator doors buckled in.

\* \* \*

Inside the elevator, Guillermin saw the doors bend toward him. As much as he punched the 'up' button, the compartment——his prison—refused to rise.

\* \* \*

Diana, managing to once more put herself between the gun and her people, tried talking to the bodyguard. "You think this guy cares about you?" she asked. "Look what he did to Craig!"

"Who's Craig?" the bodyguard asked.

Diana's shoulder slumped. "Seriously?" she asked.

\* \* \*

The Creature ripped out the doors of the elevator. It reached inside.

Guillermin felt its scaly claws circle his throat. "No!" Guillermin managed to choke out, "Craig, I'm here, and I'm not going anywhere, you've seen to that, the elevator is completely destroyed, I can't go anywhere, you've got me, but her..." He pointed to Diana, who was still talking to the bodyguard.

The Craig Creature turned around, studying the scene.

"She's getting away!" Guillermin gasped.

The creature turned back to Guillermin.

"I know you hate me," Guillermin said, "but isn't it her fault, too? They did something to the Chamber, you know they did, it's why you came back the way you came back!"

The monster swiveled its misshapen head back to Diana.

"You should have come back like her, normal, only stronger, better! Except you didn't, right?"

Exhaling, the Creature almost laughed. Its hands tightened around Guillermin's neck, and he gasped, barely able to breathe.

\* \* \*

"I'm not going to convince you, am I?" Diana asked.

"I don't know what you're..." the bodyguard said, and Diana grabbed his gun hand, shoving it up toward the ceiling. She squeezed until he screamed and the weapon fell.

Diana meant to shove him, but threw him into the air. Striking the wall a good twenty feet away, the bodyguard slid to the ground, unconscious.

"I gotta learn to control that better," Diana said. She turned to her mother. "How do we get out?"

"There's a door back here," Rita said, "I'm pretty sure it leads to the stairs!"

"Check it out."

Rita sped to the stairs, stepping over debris and puddles of who knew what.

Chuck hadn't moved. "You too, Chuck, go!" Diana cried.

"Not without you," Chuck responded.

Diana shook her head. "Go now!" she said, and then her tone softened. "Please!"

"But—"

"We don't have time to argue!"

"But—"

"You didn't want to leave me alone with Guillermin and that's what got you down here in the first place. Listen to me now, okay? I'm telling you to go!"

"But," Chuck said, pointing to something over Diana's shoulder.

*Oh*, Diana thought, right. *This has to be the part where...*

She finally turned, knowing full well what she was going to see.

The Craig Creature towered over her. Perhaps three feet away, it grinned, its mouth bloody.

"My, Grandma," Diana said, "what big teeth you—"

The Craig Monster swatted her away. *Crap*, Diana thought, as she flew through the air, *this is what it must feel like to be Superma—*

Diana impacted the wall, then fell to the floor, unmoving.

# CHAPTER THIRTY-THREE

"Diana!" Chuck called. "Diana?"

She was still just lying there.

All six of the Creature's eyes met Chuck's two eyes.

Not breaking the stare-down, Chuck knelt, picking up a section of thick pipe. He stood and, with everything he had, smacked the thing across the face.

The pipe connected once, twice, three times, the monster's head moving with the blows. When it looked like it might be getting a little wobbly on its feet, Chuck pressed the advantage, smashing the pipe once more across the top of its head.

Chuck drove it back with blow after blow until the monster just grabbed the pipe in one huge, scaly hand, stopping it in mid-arc.

It lifted the pipe—and Chuck—off the ground.

Chuck dangled there while the Monster brought its face closer, licking its lips.

"Heh," Chuck grunted, then let go, dropping to the floor and scurrying away.

Now running as quickly as he could, *faster than I did even for the final touchdown against Phinneas High*, he thought, Chuck watched everything suddenly skew to the side.

He landed chest first on the ground.

Turning over, he had time only to see what had happened; he had slipped on what looked like a huge puddle of oil, or coolant, or something.

The Creature landed on top of him, legs on either side of Chuck's body.

Trying to slide away, Chuck found himself caught by the lapels, caught and held, then lifted.

Struggling against the monster's sheer and steady strength, his own hands over the huge claws, Chuck tried to go anywhere except where he was going, which was toward the thing's huge, gaping mouth.

It opened, a black abyss lined with huge, sharp teeth. Its breath stank of a fresh kill.

Chuck got his hands just below its chin, trying to push back, but they were the struggles of a mere mortal against something straight out of Hell. *God*, Chuck thought, *what a stupid way to go: monster food!*

The mouth opened wider, the terrible breath misting his face. Saliva landed in his hair. Turning his head to the side, eyes closed, he felt what he thought might be the tip of a sharp tooth on his cheek...

Something slammed into the creature's side with such force that its arms gave way, forcing Chuck's head down, away from the mouth.

Chuck and the Creature were forced to the wall. Chuck

struggled up, sitting for a moment before Diana dragged him away.

She got him to his feet and walked him quickly toward Rita who waited near the door to the stairway.

"Go!" Diana said.

"But..." Chuck gasped, "you..."

"Chuck," Diana said, "in case you haven't figured it out yet, I'm better equipped to handle this than you are! I'm sorry, but I just am!"

A huge, scaly hand clamped onto Diana's shoulder. It spun her around, and she found herself face-to-face with the grinning nightmare.

"Take my Mom and get out of here, Chuck!"

Drawing its huge arm back, the Creature was about to swing. Diana ducked under the scaly mess of an arm, then drove the heels of both hands into the creature's chin.

Its great mouth snapped closed, and it screamed, a terrible mix of infant and ancient. Stunned, it staggered back, a trail of blood visible in the air for the barest moment. Then it collapsed.

Diana looked around for Chuck. When she saw him with her mother, she jumped, clearing the twenty feet between them.

Chuck stared at her, not quite believing it.

"What?" she asked.

"You," Chuck said, "that's like...how far is that?"

Diana rolled her eyes, pushing past him to her mother. "Mom," she said, "what happens if we started this thing up now?"

"I don't even know if you can, it—" Rita looked over what was left of the Tachyon Chamber. "Okay," she said, "it looks like most of the necessary connections are intact, but...you'd really have an explosion! Or more likely an implosion...or an explosion, then an implosion, or... !"

"Okay," Diana answered, "I get it. Now out of here, both of you!"

Rita grabbed her daughter by the elbow. "Diana, you can't, it's suicide!"

"Do I look like some emo girl to you?"

"What does that mean?"

"Chuck," Diana said, "will you explain emo to her?"

"It means..." said Chuck.

"No," Diana said, "I mean can you explain emo to her as you both run like hell out of here?"

"Diana, no!" Rita shouted.

"Mom, we can't let this thing out of here. And we can't leave Dad's ideas in any kind of working shape for this asshole—"

"Diana!"

"—to use to screw up the world! Now go!"

Turning back to the Craig Creature, Diana saw it was stirring. "Go!" she yelled. "I mean it!"

Diana jumped.

Landing on the monster, she knocked it to the ground again, then got behind it, putting her arms around its neck. Managing to turn back to Rita and Chuck, she yelled, even louder, "Get out of here, I'll be right behind you!"

Chuck and Rita launched themselves past the door and up the stairs.

The monster stood up, taking Diana with it, then ducked violently down, flipping her over and onto her back.

As she tried to stand up, the monster caught one of her feet it its huge claw. Diana watched in horror as her foot disappeared into the greenish-brown fist.

She was shoved violently away. Arms and legs out, trying to break her fall, Diana struggled for balance until she hit another huge piece of wreckage.

Grasping it, trying to steady herself, Diana took perhaps half a breath.

The piece of wreckage began to move.

Before Diana knew what was happening, she and the mass of twisted metal were lifted into the air. Beneath her, the Craig Creature grinned as it held her and the wreckage aloft.

"Uh oh," Diana said.

She was thrown, landing against the wall, pinned between the wall and the hunk of metal.

Diana got her arms under the huge shard of titanium, trying to push it off of herself. Then the Creature landed on top of it.

Looking up at the terrible face, so human and so *not*, Diana knew she couldn't allow herself the luxury of revulsion. Somewhere, the thought bubbled up: *He's not that different from you.*

It brought its head closer to hers, cocking it to the side. She could smell the carnivorous, blood-tinged breath, and thought, *Is that how my breath smells after I've eaten an uncooked pot roast?*

Its face came in closer, closer, almost as if it were going to kiss her.

*Figures*, Diana thought, still trying to lift the wreckage away, *I don't get to kiss guys like Chuck, instead I get Son of Godzilla.*

Ever closer, it finally hissed, "S-s-sister!"

And *that* pissed her off.

"I am *not*," Diana said, glaring into its eyes. She clenched her jaw, getting her hands under the metal. She strained, pushing the wreckage and the monster standing on it violently off herself.

The whole mess landed against the opposite wall with a muffled clang. The creature lay with the wreckage over itself, appearing dazed.

Bloody, clothing ripped, Diana stood to her full height. "Your sister!" she finished.

The Creature seemed to revive a bit, then looked at her with real hate in its eyes. It pushed the metal away, then said, "C-c-cousins then?"

It jumped, kicking Diana in the face before landing.

The blow snapped her head back before sending her against the wall again and then to the floor.

*Damn*, Diana thought, *thing can really hit—*

It kicked her in the face again. Diana shook her head, trying to clear it only to get hit once more. She tried to get up, and it punched her, sending her back down.

*Do I have enough strength to roll over?* she thought. *Roll over, at least do that...face the ugly—*

She rolled over, suddenly unable to breathe. The creature had encircled her neck in its huge, clawed hand.

Getting both of her hands around its scaly, wrist, she could only struggle, trying to break the grip, as it lifted her toward itself, its long, obscene tongue starting to curl out of its mouth.

It put its other hand around her neck.

Diana closed her eyes, concentrating on breaking the wrist that was already there.

She felt something wet against her face.

The Creature's tongue.

Diana opened her eyes. She watched the monster take its other hand from her neck. It instead caressed her face.

"I that's how you treat your sister," Diana said before letting go of the Creature's wrist, "I'd hate to see you with your mother!"

She shoved her thumbs into the monster's eyes.

It screamed, the noise of a jumbo jet arcing down for a crash. Its misshapen hand fell away from Diana's neck and she rolled away, coughing, then got to her feet.

\* \* \*

In the wreckage of the elevator, Guillermin, having witnessed the entire fight, tried to call to Diana, but was having trouble making a noise after the Creature's attack. *What the hell did that thing do to my neck?* Guillermin thought. If he could just speak loud enough, get her attention, he knew she would help him. She had to help him, in spite of what happened to her father! She was good at her core, monster or not. She'd do the right thing! She wasn't a murderer...not really! Most important, he couldn't die like this, not down here!

"H-h-help," Guillermin stammered, but the rasping words were lost in the wreckage of the elevator, lost in the cavernous sub-basement full of sparking debris.

* * *

Diana turned on the computer. She initiated the sequence.

The Craig Creature, blood running from its eyes, screamed again, then roared in anger, even now trying to find her.

Diana took the thumb drive out of the computer. She looked at it, just for a moment, her possible key to a normal life.

*Oh, hell*, Diana thought, *when did the terms 'normal' and 'life' ever go together?*

The first hum of the Tachyon Chamber began.

Crushing the drive between her thumb and forefinger, Diana threw it into what was left of her father's lost dream.

She was running for the exit when the Craig Creature, half blind, landed in front of her. Without thinking, she smashed two fists into the its gut.

It doubled over, but she pivoted, grabbing its torso.

Diana heaved, throwing the monster a good thirty feet back into the cavernous room. It landed with a dull thud, banging its huge head on a tank labeled "Liquid Nitrogen."

The hum was getting louder, and Diana knew she only had seconds before it accelerated into a whine.

Throwing open the door, she bypassed the stairs, instead jumping from landing to landing, wondering for the first time just how far below the ground Guillermin had built the damn place.

The Tachyon Chamber's hum grew louder as the Craig Creature sat up. It tried to clear blood out of its uppermost eyes, shaking its head.

Something was glowing white hot. What remained of the Tachyon Chamber was starting to pulse, a blue, then a green glow emanating from its ruined door.

In the elevator, Guillermin had to look away.

The Craig Creature hissed.

The new Tachyon Chamber exploded with a high-pitched roar.

# CHAPTER THIRTY-FOUR

Bursting through the stairway doors, Diana jumped to the mansion's exit.

In mid-air, she heard it—the dull roar of the explosion below her.

She felt the heat at her back as she landed on the outside front stairway, then jumped down to the landing.

Diana was running when the Tachyon Chamber's released energy shot up the stairwell in the blink of an eye, matter converted to energy, and the new energy was hungry for more matter.

The heat behind wanted to draw her back in, she could feel it.

Diana ran for all she was worth, but it was getting harder, like running in slow motion, in a dream.

*Was it time itself?* she thought. Was time slowing down so the huge, failed experiment could claim her once and for all?

She set her jaw and kept running.

*No way*, she thought, *you're not going to take me, not after all this*.

Legs and arms pumping, Diana saw the gate just ahead. The black sedan was ahead of her, the car she and Chuck had taken here.

*Mom and Chuck,* she thought. *They're in that car. They have to be in that car!*

Diana smacked her hands on to the back of the black car, pushing as she ran.

\* \* \*

Rita and Chuck had just swerved past the gate when something hit the car's trunk. Looking back, Chuck saw Diana, running and pushing.

"Get it in neutral!" Chuck exclaimed.

"Neutral? Are you—" Rita looked back and saw her daughter. Turning back around, she popped the transmission into "N"

A split second later, it was as if a volcano had gone off behind them, but instead of lava, a clear and deadly white light was shooting out of the earth.

Diana grimaced, pushing harder, running faster.

The pure white light, plasma light, shot out of the mansion's windows. The light turned blue, then green, and then the top of the mansion was blown off.

Just as quickly, the roof debris was sucked back in, and then the walls of the mansion were sucked in after it, and then the nearest trees bent back toward the implosion.

Leaves were sucked away, then bark. The denuded trees themselves, at first holding stubbornly onto the soil, were ripped away, roots and all.

The lawn flipped up in strips, then back into the maelstrom, but still the car continued. What was left of the wrought-iron front gate, already mangled, lay on the ground before them, and

304 • SHELDON GLEISSER

Diana pushed the car went roughly over it, bouncing both Rita and Chuck so that each hit their head on the car's roof.

"Ah!" Chuck said.

"Uhh..." Rita grunted.

Rita looked back only to see her daughter, still pushing and running.

The fallen gate stirred, then stood up like a huge, black snake. The implosion claimed it, too, first tearing the gate out as one piece, then, as it crumbled into separate sections, taking the entire metal mess.

Something was happening now, Rita could tell, some subtle shift in the implosion's pattern. The intense backward pressure on the car had lessened; it had gone down to a pre-thunderstorm high wind.

Rita watched the blue-green light float above the hole it had dug for itself. It went from blue to green and then back again before shrinking down, soon to the size of a small house, then to a car, then perhaps to a beach ball, and next to a pinpoint. It glowed brightly, so brightly she had to turn away, and then it was gone.

The wind stopped. The danger was over.

Diana stopped the car just in front of a small group of trees, then collapsed on to the car's trunk, barely able to stand.

She managed a look back at the smoking crater.

Chuck and Rita both got out of the car.

Rita whispered "Diana..."

Neither Rita nor Chuck knew what to say.

Rita started to cry. Chuck put his arms around Diana.

"It's okay," Diana said, standing up. "I'm—"

Rita made a small, ecstatic noise in her throat before throwing her arms around her daughter. "Diana!" she called, putting her arms around her daughter.

Chuck came in, enveloping both Rita and Diana in his arms.

Diana frowned. "Okay," she said, gently but firmly pushing the two of them away. "Yeah. Getting a little weird there."

"I so don't believe you got out there before we did!" Chuck said. "And pushed the damn car all the way here!"

Shrugging, Diana stepped out from between them, looking at the smoking hole where Guillermin's great plan used to be. "What can I tell you?" Diana asked. "T. Rex DNA. It's probably not for everybody, but—"

Diana looked at her tear-stained mother and then at Chuck. "I'll take it," she said.

# CHAPTER THIRTY-FIVE

A late-model Honda Accord drove ahead of a newer black BMW on the flat, nondescript surface roads between Columbus and Delaware, Ohio.

Rita drove the Honda, her daughter in the front passenger seat. Every now and then, Diana turned around to wave at Chuck, who was behind them, driving the black BMW they had taken from Guillermin's driver.

Sighing, Rita watched her daughter wave at Chuck. In the rearview mirror, she could see the young man grin and wave back. "Diana?" Rita asked. "Eyes on the road?"

Diana clicked her tongue. "I'm not *driving*," she said.

"Yes," Rita answered, "and that is *why* you're not driving."

"I could have. I've gotten my license."

"Sure," Rita said, hiking her thumb back toward Chuck. "But you have too many distractions."

Diana turned back toward Chuck, waving again. Rita saw him wave back again.

She shook her head. "Has it occurred to you that we're doing a borderline illegal thing?"

"Borderline?" Diana said before giving a loud, theatrical sigh. "That's one border we passed a long time ago."

"Well, help me look!"

"Okay," Diana said. "It's all the same, though, it's all pretty much the middle of nowhere."

"The whole idea is to minimize our visibility."

Diana frowned. When she saw a field surrounded on three sides by thick stands of trees, she spoke. "There!"

Rita signaled a left turn, pulling over onto the grass. When the BMW pulled in parallel, Diana grinned at Chuck and pointed to the trees. "You should probably back in," she said.

"Yes, ma'am," Chuck replied, pulling ahead, then backing in so the BMW's trunk was almost touching the trees.

Rita maneuvered her car just slightly ahead of the BMW, parking the Honda diagonally so that it hid most of the other car. "Okay. I'll go out there and watch while you..." Rita gestured vaguely with her hands.

"While we what?" Diana asked.

"You know, the..." Rita gestured again.

"Mom," Diana said, "when you do this," she repeated her mother's gesture, "what do you mean? Do you mean let the guy out of the trunk and give him the car keys?"

"Yes, yes!" Rita insisted. "Just go, get moving!"

Rita was up and out of the Honda, sprinting to the road. Seeing no traffic, she turned to Diana and gestured vaguely once again.

Diana got out the same time Chuck did. Walking around to the trunk, Chuck pointed the key at the lock and it chirped, popping open the hatch.

Guillermin's former driver, zip ties around his wrists and

ankles, blindfold on and gag tied around his mouth, sat up in his underwear. "Mmnph?" he said.

Chuck threw a pile of clothes into his lap, then got out a pocket knife to cut the zip tie around the driver's hands.

Diana put her hand on top of Chuck's. When he looked at her, she shook her head, then leaned over, grabbing the zip tie and pulling it apart. After freeing the driver's legs the same way, Diana made a 'come with me' gesture and ran for the Honda, Chuck in pursuit.

Landing in the driver's seat at the same time Chuck landed in the front passenger seat, Diana gunned the Honda to her mother. Chuck got out, leaning the seat forward so Rita could get in, and then the Honda's tires met asphalt with a great, grunting squeal.

"I wanted to drive!" Rita said from the back seat.

"I know you did," Diana intoned smugly. "Now buckle up!"

Risking only one look at Chuck, Diana grinned at him. He smiled back, nodding.

"Eyes on the road?" Rita asked.

"Only on the road," answered Diana.

"Damn right."

"Language, young lady!" Diana added.

Behind them in the field, Guillermin's former driver blinked and looked around. Then he stepped out of the BMW's trunk in his underwear.

\* \* \*

"Do you know where Lewis and Clark went?" Mr. Bidderson asked.

Looking out the window, Diana didn't know the question had been directed at her.

"Ms. Dunphy?" Bidderson asked.

"Huh?" Diana asked, finally turning back to her teacher.

"I said, do you know where Lewis and Clark went?"

"Somewhere in, uh...the Louisiana Purchase?" she asked.

"Correct," Bidderson sighed, "in a kind of a shallow way."

"Sorry. Shallow's the best I got right now."

The class laughed.

Bidderson regarded her for a moment. "Why should now be any different from any other time, Ms. Dunphy?"

The class laughed again.

Diana found her attention going to the window once more. "The new land," she said.

"What?" Mr. Bidderson asked.

Looking at the bland suburban landscape, Diana said, "They were exploring the new land. Where no one had ever been, right?"

"Well...no white settlers had ever been there," Bidderson replied, before pulling down a map of the United States. "Many were critical of the Louisiana Purchase, but Jefferson's insistence on..."

Her teacher's voice faded into the background.

Diana watched a crow land on a tree branch near the window. It cocked its head, looking quizzically her way, blinking its impassive black eyes.

*Hello, cousin*, Diana thought.

\* \* \*

Seated on the front stairs of McAuliffe High, Diana had the cooler between her knees, eating another barely cooked hamburger.

Chuck plopped down next to her, then leaned back, elbows on the upper step. "What are you thinking about?" he asked.

"Mmmm, nothing like a handful of ground beef that's barely had a match lit under it!" She popped more of it into her mouth.

"I mean what are you *really* thinking about?" Chuck asked.

"I don't know," Diana said, looking around to make sure they weren't being overheard, "how come we haven't heard anything?"

"You mean about..." He made a ball of his hands, then violently separated them, making an explosion sound.

"Yes, exactly!" Diana mocked the explosion sound.

Chuck laughed. "You're not doing it right."

"Not doing it right? Who died and made you king of the explosion noises?" She took another bite of burger while Chuck laughed. "I'm serious. Even if Guillermin's place was in the middle of nowhere—"

"—which it was—" Chuck said.

"You'd think an explosion—"

"Implosion."

"What?"

"Isn't that what your mom said it was? An implosion?"

"I don't know! Whatever it was, you'd think a...an...event that big would be picked up somewhere, there'd be some mention of it, but no! And my mom can't find anything either, and—"

Chuck placed a finger directly over her lips.

Diana quieted.

They were looking at each other, studying one another's faces, when Chuck said, "How about we don't do that gift horse in the mouth thing, huh?"

"You and my mom," Diana said as Chuck moved his face closer, "always with the gift horses."

Diana closed her eyes, waiting.

"Dunphy, Leadingham," came a familiar voice, "school property, you know the rules."

Opening her eyes, Diana saw Mrs. Mallard walk past.

Diana straightened, a little embarrassed, and called after the retreating girls' gym teacher. "Mrs. Mallard?"

Mrs. Mallard stopped, turning to her. "Yes?" she asked.

"Are there tryouts?"

Mrs. Mallard frowned. "For what?" she asked.

"What do you have to do to get on the basketball team? Are there tryouts?"

"What?" came a familiar, high-pitched voice. Frannie Lightfoot was standing behind them, hands on hips, a scowl on her face.

"Ms. Dunphy," Mrs. Mallard said, taking a few steps closer, "as far as I'm concerned, you've had your tryout. Be at practice tomorrow, four o'clock, okay?"

Diana grinned. "Okay," she said.

"I-I'm the team captain," Frannie interjected, "don't I get a—"

"A what?" Mrs. Mallard sighed, continuing the walk to her car.

"A say in who gets on the team or not!" Frannie insisted, catching up to her coach.

"No," Mrs. Mallard replied, "you don't."

"But—" Frannie sputtered.

"When I was your age, there were plenty of girls on the team I didn't get along with, but you know what? Pretty soon, we all..."

As their voices faded off, Chuck turned to Diana. "Is that really fair?" he asked.

"Is what really fair?" Diana countered.

"C'mon," he said, standing up, "dinosaur DNA, and all those other girls don't have it?"

Diana grunted, popping the last of the hamburger into her mouth. Standing up, she stretched and and said, "I won't tell if you won't."

## CHAPTER THIRTY-SIX

Keyes pulled his car into a group of other mud-spattered vehicles. They were clustered near a pit, but all Keyes knew about the area was that it was in western Pennsylvania.

Getting out of the car, Keyes pulled his coat tighter. A man in perhaps his early forties wearing a watch cap and a blue pea coat came running up to him, waving both hands in the air. "Mr. Keyes?" the man asked, "are you Mr. Keyes?"

"That's me," Keyes said as the man held out his hand.

"I'm Emerson, the guy who called." Keyes took the offered hand and began walking beside Emerson.

"How can the Department of Homeland Security help you, Mr. Emerson?" Keyes asked.

"Well, I...I don't know how to answer that, I think I needed you to see this for yourself before we did much more excavation, this is such an incredible find, but...okay, see—" Emerson came to a large pit dug in the countryside. A ladder stuck up from the ground, and he started to climb down. "I went to school with

Aaron Dunphy. I mean, he was a couple of years ahead of me, and really, one of the greatest TAs I ever had, and when I heard about what happened? I felt just awful, everybody who heard about it felt awful."

Seeing that Keyes wasn't following him, Emerson looked up.

Keyes sighed. "I had, uh, an injury recently," he said. "Climbing down the ladder, might be..."

"It's okay," Emerson replied. "Anyways, about what I was saying? I went to school with Aaron Dunphy, he was my TA, and..."

Keyes tried not to wince as he put his foot on one of the rungs and climbed down, gratified that it actually didn't hurt as much as he thought it would. He did feel creaky, though, in a lot of places he hadn't felt creaky before. Finally on the squishy ground of the pit's floor, Keyes faced the still talking Emerson.

"...physics, specifically time displacement, which was never my... what I mean to say is, great guy, but we're talking strictly, I don't know what you'd call it..."

Keyes frowned. Emerson was taking him toward what looked like a huge skeleton.

"...an intact brachiosaurus, all I could think was how lucky I was, but then we saw it..."

"Saw what, Dr. Emerson?"

"What you're about to see, there are signs of predation on the fossilized bones, something big, T. Rex most likely, but then there was something else, something so extraordinary! What Aaron Dunphy was working on, I mean, I liked the guy, but I thought he was crazy, everybody thought he was crazy, but..."

Keyes' eyes widened when they got to the huge hipbone of the brachiosaur.

"I know, right?" Emerson said. Keyes scrambled for his phone, almost dropping it into the mucky ground before catching it. Then he framed up and immediately began snapping photos.

"Before it all went south," Emerson asked, "was Aaron Dunphy trying to do something with time travel?"

* * *

Chuck sat with Patrice, watching Diana run Frannie Lightfoot all over the basketball court.

Patrice tried not to stare at Chuck—he was, after all, the boyfriend, or at least the *something* of her best friend, but he was a little too easy on the eyes for her not to steal a glimpse here and there.

Chuck laughed, then clapped his hands at Diana's latest crazy block of an attempt by Frannie to get a ball into the basket. Turning to Patrice, he pointed and said, "You see that?"

"Mm-hmm," Patrice said, still looking at Chuck.

* * *

Diana was washing her hair when Frannie stepped into the shower. "I thought we had an agreement." She said. "I leave you alone, you leave me alone?"

Washing the soap out of her hair, Diana replied, "Well, agreements like that usually come to an end when you make sure everybody in school sees nasty pictures of my friends."

"Oh," Frannie said, "so that's what he is? Your *friend?*"

"It's none of your business what he is," Diana said, grabbing her towel.

"How long is this going to go on?"

"I don't know," Diana replied, "how long does it take to become team captain?" She walked out of the shower.

* * *

"Isn't your mom gonna be mad?" Chuck asked as he and Diana got to her door. "I mean, you on the basketball team?"

"I kinda haven't told her yet," Diana muttered.

"Diana!" Chuck said, stopping, "All those fancy moves? People will think—"

"What?" Diana asked.

"That you're—"

"That I'm what? Part dinosaur?"

"I don't know about *that*, but...they'll think *something*'s up."

"People will think what they think," Diana stated. "I'm tired of worrying about it. And anyway, there's no law that says you can't beat Frannie Lightfoot."

"No, but I'm..." He looked away.

"What?"

"I'm worried, okay? I'm concerned."

Smiling wryly, Diana said, "Concerned? About?"

He looked down at the ground, then met her eyes. "You. About people finding out, dragging you away somewhere..."

She took his hand. "No one's going to find out and drag me away somewhere."

"People had their phones out. They post some of your moves on Youtube and..."

She took his other hand. "People will just think it was done in some program, like After Effects, or whatever, okay? Nobody believes anything they see on Youtube." She got on her tip toes, moving her lips closer to his face. "You shouldn't worry so much," she whispered.

Chuck brought his face down to hers...

...and Rita opened the door. Looking stricken, she said, "Diana—"

"Mom—!" Diana answered.

"Oh," her mother said, "hello Chuck."

"Mrs. Dunphy," Chuck cleared his throat.

Keyes leaned out from behind Rita. "Hello, Diana," he said.

"Mr. Keyes!" Diana exclaimed. "Hello! How are you feeling?"

"I'm fine—"

"And the new job?"

"Also fine, I—"

Looking at both of their faces, Diana thought, *Something's wrong, what is it?*

"Maybe you should come in," Rita said.

* * *

Seated on the couch with Rita, Keyes passed her some photos. "I took these at an archaeological dig in Pennsylvania," he said.

Frowning, Rita studied the pictures. First on the pile was a huge, partially unearthed dinosaur skeleton. "What are we looking at here?" she asked. "Brachiosaurus?"

"Yes," Keyes said, "specifically the hipbone of a brachiosaurus."

Edging in behind the couch, Diana pointed to the dinosaur's huge hipbone. "What are those scratches?" she asked.

Keyes turned to her. "Those scratches are why I'm here," he said. Turning back to the stack of photos, he put the first one on the bottom, revealing the next, closer shot. "This is where it gets, uh...interesting."

Diana and Rita both stared, mouths open. On the hipbone was written, "Aaron Dunphy, born Nov 12, 1978. Still here! Diana and Rita, I love you!"

Rita breathed in suddenly, putting the back of her fist to her mouth. "My God," she said, "is it real?"

"The archaeologist, a Dr. Emerson, he knew your husband, he confirms the markings are not fresh, they were put on those bones over sixty-five million years ago." Keyes said.

Diana walked to the picture window, feeling not just light-headed, but light-bodied.

"No..." Rita said, starting to cry, "Oh, no..."

"Mom..."

"He survived!" Rita cried. The explosion, or the implosion, whatever it was...must have taken him back!" She looked away from the pictures, now sobbing almost inconsolably.

"Mom," Diana said again.

"He died there, all alone, all those millions of years ago!"

"Not yet," Diana added.

"What?"

"He hasn't died yet," Diana said.

"Honey, what are you talking about? He's gone! He's as gone as it's possible to be!"

Shaking her head, Diana said, "No, he's alive. In the past."

"Diana, don't even think about it, it's impossible!"

"Put a quarter in the jar, mom," Diana said, the corners of her mouth turning up into a smile, "because nothing's impossible!"

# ACKNOWLEDGMENTS

This book greatly benefitted from the patient contributions of Larry Weaver who helped knock the story into place across multiple drafts in multiple mediums.

Mindy Zimmerman did likewise, and helped immensely in getting Diana to sound less like a fifty-ish neurotic Jewish man and more like a sixteen-year old girl.

I'd have been nowhere without Josef P. Matulich, who after more rejections than I can count, suggested I attend the Imaginarium Writer's Conference in Kentucky with him back in 2017. There I pitched the novel to Mr. Tony Acree of Hydra Publishing, who thankfully took it on. My favorite singer does a ballad where he sees a werewolf drinking a Pina Colada at Trader Vic's and "his hair was perfect." I never saw Josef drinking a Pina Colada at Trader Vic's, but his heart is perfect.

Stuart Thaman worked a minor miracle with his excellent line editing, helping this book's focus, simplicity, punctuation, and of course, spelling.

# ABOUT THE AUTHOR

Sheldon Gleisser was awarded the Individual Artist Grant from the Greater Columbus Arts Council in 2002 for his short play Version 2.0. written with Robert Flanagan. His short story Souvenir was runner-up in the 2006 Mary Shelley awards, sponsored by Rosebud magazine, for new stories of Horror, Fantasy and Science Fiction. Gleisser's short story Converts was runner-up for the same award in 2008. Another short story, Secrets of the Hive, was runner-up in 2010, with a fourth short story, Stillborn runner-up in 2012. Gleisser was part of the 2005 and 2012 Screenwriting seminars sponsored by the Squaw Valley Community of Writers. Another short play he wrote with Robert Flanagan, Mother of Presidents, was part of Evolution Theater's Columbus Bicentennial Playwriting festival in 2012. His screenplay Out of Print won the Best Northcoast Screenplay award (meaning best script written to take place in Ohio) at the Ohio Independent Film Festival in 2013. (614) Magazine published his short story And Son in December of 2015. And Son was republished in Rosebud magazine in their fall 2016 issue.